FALLEN CREST FAMILY

THE 2ND IN THE FALLEN CREST SERIES

NYT & USA Bestselling Author
TIJAN

Interior Formatting by Elaine York/Allusion Graphics, LLC/ Publishing & Book Formatting
www.allusiongraphics.com

DEDICATION

This story is dedicated to my readers! You guys inspire me.

CHAPTER ONE

When I arrived at the party, it was the largest I had ever seen. The mansion was filled with people. The doors had been left open and the overflow spilled out to the front lawn. The driveway went around a large fountain, which a few girls had gotten into. Their shirts were soaked to their skin and their hair was messily rumpled, giving them the wet sexy look. I knew the guys, who stood with their drinks at the side, enjoyed the view. More than a few had that dark promise in their eyes. They wanted sex and they wanted it now. One of the girls squealed as a guy swept her in the air.

I rolled my eyes and pushed past.

Public parties were always considered the best, but this was in a whole new league.

When I stepped onto the front steps, a blast of heat came at me from inside. There were people everywhere. I pushed through the crowd until I was on a back patio. The backyard stretched out with another pool, a basketball court, and a tennis court. There was too much to even look at with all the people, but I could tell the place was phenomenal.

Some girls dashed past me, giggling, while guys chased after them.

Then someone bumped into me from behind. I heard, "Oh, I'm sorry," before I turned around and saw who it was. I found myself staring in the crystal blue eyes of Adam Quinn, someone whom I had considered a friend until two months ago.

"Oh." His voice dropped, and he stood there without saying

anything else. After a moment passed, he glanced to the side and slid his hands into the front pockets of his jeans.

I smirked. He was dressed appropriately with custom-tailored jeans and a loose-flowing shirt that was left unbuttoned. A white tank was underneath. It fitted like a second skin to his abdominal muscles and chest. I saw that he had been working out more, but whatever. What did I care? He had dropped our friendship two months ago, and since Adam was the Golden Boy for our school, Fallen Crest Academy, everybody else had followed suit. No one talked to me anymore, even his neighbor, the one person I had come to consider as a real friend.

I asked, though maybe I shouldn't have, "How's Becky?"

He flinched.

A small sense of triumph flared through me, but it was so small, and it was gone instantly.

"Uh," he looked away before his jaw hardened, and he met my gaze again. This time he didn't blink. "She's good. I think she's dating someone from your school."

"My school?"

"FCP. You know what I mean. Their school, you're one of them now, so…your school."

"I still go to Fallen Crest Academy."

He clenched his jaw. "I heard something else."

All senses went on alert. I knew what he was talking about, but I hadn't known it was already on the gossip mill. This wasn't good. "What'd you hear?"

He shrugged and looked away. There it was. I knew it was only a matter of time. Adam could never be honest with me for too long.

"What'd you hear?"

"Come on, Sam."

"Come on, what?" I knew he was going to leave. I sensed it and grabbed his arm as he started to inch away. "What did you hear?"

"Let go of me." His eyes hardened as he looked over my shoulder. "I don't think I'm supposed to be talking to you."

"What are you talking about…" But the words left me as an arm snaked around my waist and pulled me back against a hard chest, a very hard chest.

Mason's chin came to rest on my shoulder and he breathed out. The air caressed my neck, and I felt the possession in his demeanor. A tingle raced through me, especially when his hand slid down my waist to rest on my hip. He pressed me back against him again. I felt every inch of him now and fought against closing my eyes when my desire started to overtake me.

"I should be going," Adam mumbled before he turned. But then he stopped. His face was twisted in an unnamed emotion. "Thanks for inviting everyone to the party."

"Not my party." Mason straightened against my back. His hands held me firmly in place, but I could feel the coldness from him now.

Adam didn't squirm; he straightened and never looked away. He had learned. Then his eyes caught mine for a second before he looked away again. A shiver went over me. I saw his anger in that second, but he only replied, "Your best friend's place. Your party."

"This is Nate's party?" I twisted around, but Mason didn't let go of me. His hands had a firm grasp on my hips. When he didn't look down, his gaze still fixed over my shoulder, I slid a hand around his neck and tilted him downwards. He met my gaze then and I tried to stop myself from melting. His green eyes softened and a small grin came over him. When he lifted a hand to rub against the top of my lip, I closed my eyes. A groan escaped me before I realized what I was doing. Then I grabbed his hand. "Stop."

"Stop what?" His amusement was evident.

"This is Nate's party?" That meant one thing. This was his place, but did that mean…"Is Nate moving back?"

And then someone threw his arms around us and we were pulled in for an even tighter hug. "Hello, my peeps!" Logan's breath smelled of booze and as he hugged us again. "I love you guys and you know what else I love?"

Mason grimaced, but I still caught the small grin at the corners of his lips. He deadpanned, "Nate's pussy?"

Logan threw his head back and let loose a hoot. Then, even as he died down, he couldn't wipe the silly grin off his face. And he wasn't trying, not even the slightest. "Yeah, maybe." His eyes turned to me and I was caught by the intensity in them. An abnormal look of earnestness was in them, albeit slightly blurred from booze, but it was there. It was the most sincere expression Logan had allowed me to see in a long while. He reminded me of a five-year-old little boy in that moment, one with shaggy brown curls and dark chocolate eyes that made so many girls' hearts melt. "Did Mason tell you? Nate's moving back for the last half of the year. How fucking fantastic is that?"

Very. Nate was the fourth member in our group, but it hurt. He hadn't said a word, but Mason couldn't stop from grinning at Logan so I forced myself to put it away. Nate was back. That was all that mattered, and then realization hit me as I looked around. This enormous place was his.

"This is Nate's place?"

Yet, even as I asked, I knew it was. Both of them didn't answer, silent as I looked around again. There were so many people at the party. I recognized a few from my school, obviously with Adam there, and I knew there were students from Fallen Crest Public as well. I saw a few of Mason and Logan's friends and figured more from their school were there as well, but two schools couldn't have been everyone? Who else was there?

"Dude, tell her."

Mason admitted with a smirk, "Nate's got some high placed friends."

Just then a well-known actor strolled past us with his arm around two girls.

My mouth dropped open. I couldn't believe it, but I should've. Nate's parents were movie directors. When he wasn't getting in trouble with Mason and Logan, they tried to keep him with them as often as possible. Of course he would've met more than a few from the Hollywood scene. But, still, I couldn't believe it.

I grasped Mason's hand and squeezed tight. "My mom has a huge crush on him."

He wrenched his hand away as he stepped back. Logan held up both arms. "Hey, whoa. Too much information, girly."

"What?"

Mason grimaced. "We don't want to know who your mom jerks off to."

"What?" Oh my word. They thought—I sputtered out, "No, I didn't mean, I mean, NO!"

Then both started to laugh. Soon their shoulders shook as more laughter slipped from their clasped lips.

A wave of embarrassment came over me. I was pissed and mortified. When I lifted a hand to slap Mason's arm, he caught it instead and twirled me so I was in his arms again. My back was to his chest and his arms came around in front of me. He turned so we faced Logan before his hands slid down to hold my hips still as he started to rub against me.

Logan cringed. "Oh please, guys. I live with you."

Mason bent forward so his lips were next to my ear. I felt them curve into a grin. His breath tickled my skin. "Feel free to go away now, brother."

"Correction." Logan flashed us a dark look. "I have to live with you. I need to rectify that soon." Then he saluted us both with two fingers in the air as he turned and walked away. He hadn't gone more than a few steps before his stroll turned into a saunter. His hands slid into his front pockets, his shoulders leaned forward a bit, and a different vibe came over him. It wasn't a surprise when a group of girls clambered over to him. With his shoulders hunched forward, it gave him a vulnerable appeal that was almost irresistible to girls when it was mixed with an already dangerous reputation.

Mason chuckled against my ear. Then he caught it with his teeth and bit down gently.

Tingles raced through me and I lifted to my toes as his teeth scraped against the bottom of my earlobe. He drew it out, gently and lovingly. Sensually. A burst of heat flared between my legs. The same throb started deep. As his hips moved forward, I felt him behind me and closed my eyes from the pleasure. The throbbing was almost too much now. The same desire I always felt for him started to take over. I felt my control slipping.

"Mason," I gasped as I arched my back against him. My arm lifted to behind his neck. When I held him in place, his lips started to nibble downwards and I was barely conscious of being turned in his arms. My breasts were pushed against his chest and he lifted one of my legs so he could fit further between them. I arched against him. I gasped for breath, but his mouth covered mine instantly.

He took control.

He commanded his entrance, and I was helpless against him. His tongue slipped inside my mouth. Mine brushed against his. A growl emanated from him. It sent a rush of power through me that was intoxicating. I wanted more and my tongue met his again, this time to brush slowly against his. Then I pulled away, but not before I flicked the tip of my tongue against his top lip. As my eyelids lifted, heavy and saturated from lust, I saw the answering yearning in his. Then his eyes flashed in determination, and I knew it wouldn't be long before Mason would be in me, deep and hard.

An elated shiver ran through me. I wanted nothing more than that.

"I know the two of you are horny rabbits and in love and all that, but I don't think you want to make an amateur sex tape right here."

We broke apart, panting, and took in the grinning sight of Nate's face. He gestured to where a group had congregated. I saw more than a few cameras in the air with fingers to the record buttons.

"Hi, Nate," I croaked out. A heated rush of embarrassment flooded me. I couldn't believe I had almost lost control or that

Mason had as well. He set the tone most of the times. I trusted him, but a tingle of addictive power went through me as I remembered the sound of his own groan. I held him as captivated as he held me.

Mason cursed under his breath but swept us around so his back was to the group and I was shielded from the audience.

"Hi, Sam."

I flinched at how cheery Nate sounded. Mason's hand swept down before he held my face to his shoulder. I felt his tension as his voice reverberated through his chest. "Thanks, man."

"Any time." His tone was amused. Then I felt Nate's lips on my forehead. He whispered before he darted off, "It's good to see you too, Sam. Take care of my boy."

Mason groaned as he brushed my hair from my face and looked down into my eyes. I tilted backwards and saw the warmth in his gaze. My heart skipped a beat. I couldn't believe it. We'd been official for two months, but it never got old. He never got old. He never tired of me. I wasn't sure what I would do if that happened, if any of those nightmares occurred.

All I knew, as Mason continued to hold me to his chest, was that I couldn't lose him. Who the hell was I trying to kid? I couldn't lose any of them, Mason, Logan, or even Nate. They were the only friends I had in my life now.

I felt panic start to rise, but I forced it down. I had to. I couldn't lose it, not in his arms. Never in his arms.

CHAPTER TWO

The rest of the night had been free of drama, and I was relieved. Mason stuck close to me as he always did when I would attend parties, but I knew there were a ton of his friends who wanted his attention. For the most part, the friends from their school stuck close to each other. I wasn't part of that group. Even though I was dating Mason, they still considered me as an Academite, their term for the snotty rich kids. That was fine. I was far from the normal economic status of my classmates, but I knew that wasn't the real reason I hadn't been welcomed into the group. Mason and Logan's father was one of the wealthiest men in town, but they were accepted into any circle.

I wasn't stupid.

The girls didn't like me because I got Mason, who had been deemed unavailable except for the few times he chose someone for sex. Now he has a girlfriend, and they're pissed. The girls in their tight circle cursed at me, insulted me, even pushed me against a wall a few times, but it was always done when Mason or Logan weren't around. As for the guys, a few of them would glare at me while the others stayed away. Nate told me during one of his visits that some of the guys worried if I would change Mason.

I made a point not to.

I never argued when Mason said he was going to a party. After the third time of getting tripped or elbowed by the girls, I stopped going with him. He'd been confused, but I shrugged when he questioned me about it. I told him that I'd rather go for a long run and he dropped the conversation. It hadn't even been a lie. I loved running, and I had never enjoyed parties. I had gone before because my two best friends and boyfriend wanted me to go. But they weren't my friends anymore. I had no friends at my own school; no one would invite me to the parties, even the ones that weren't Public Parties, the name coined for those thrown by anyone who went to Fallen Crest Public School. They were the best ones.

And Nate's party exceeded everyone's expectations.

When I had stood in line for the bathroom, a girl said she saw people from four different schools. I hadn't been surprised. Mason and Logan ruled their school. Those at Fallen Crest Academy clamored for their attention as well, and with Nate's contribution, I was surprised more schools hadn't shown up. Even after Nate had been forced to move away after getting into too much trouble with Mason, he came back for visits often enough to feel as if he lived there. He came back for his and Mason's last semester in high school. They would end it together, and then they would start again. Mason didn't talk about college much, but I knew that he had already committed to a university where he would play football for them. Nate was going as well. They were going to be roommates, and if anyone were to ask my opinion, I had a feeling that Logan felt out of the loop. He and I had one more year in high school, but this was the point in my thoughts when I stopped thinking.

I didn't like to think of that time when Mason would go away. Hell, I didn't even like to think of my dilemma for next semester.

"You're thinking," Mason mumbled next to me as he rolled over and wrapped his arms around me. He reached over my waist and tugged me back against him. One of his legs shifted over mine, and I was securely enveloped by him.

I grinned when the tingle started. It didn't take much anymore, just a touch and the memory of what was to come rushed through me. When I turned to face him, his eyes were sparkling down at me. A small grin curved up and his green eyes searched mine. They darkened with lust when I lifted a hand to cup the side of his cheek. I licked my lips as my throat went dry and moved even closer to him.

I couldn't get enough of him.

"Sam," he murmured.

"Hmmm?" I started to explore his chest. My hand slipped down and rounded his slender waist. I rubbed over his muscles—they were structured and photo-shopped to perfection. When one of my fingers slipped underneath his boxer's waistband, he sucked in his breath. I grinned from the anticipation and addiction I had to him. I loved touching him. I loved making him groan in pleasure, and, as I pushed him to his back and settled over him, I loved looking down and seeing him helpless to my touch. It made two of us.

"Fuck, woman," he growled in a husky voice. His hands settled on my thighs as I straddled him. His fingers dug in when I dipped down and licked his neck. Then I moved farther down, and his hands dug in even farther. He had a cement hold on me when I teased the edge of his boxers, but then his phone went off and we both froze.

It rang again.

Our eyes met because we both knew who that was. We had discussed it the night before when I made the decision to turn my phone off. Since the party was at Nate's home, or his parent's home as Mason explained, he wanted to stay the night. It was an easy decision. The Kade mansion, where my mother had started to boycott any nights Mason slept in my bed, or his best friend's place? There'd been no need for a discussion. We did, however, have to discuss what we were going to do when my mother would start calling. I wasn't a fan of turning off my phone. Not many called or texted, but there'd been times when Mason or Logan had been hurt. I missed a phone call one time after Mason had been in a bad fight. I vowed never to experience that panic again. However, Mason promised that if I turned my phone off, he would deal with my mother and his father in the morning.

The phone rang for the third time.

He growled and cursed at the same time as he rolled out from underneath me. He picked his phone up in one swift movement as he stood from the bed and went into the bathroom. "What?"

The shower turned on, and when I crossed to the doorway, he had put the phone on the counter and was ignoring it as he stepped underneath the spray. When he shut the water off, his father's voice was still going strong over the phone. He sounded furious, but I knew it was more from my mother. Analise was like a starving dog going after a bone when she got something in her head. And she had decided that I would not be fornicating with my stepbrother.

That didn't go over well with Mason, who told them both to fuck off. More fights ensued, raised voices, threats, even blackmail had been mentioned once. None of it fazed Mason. He withstood all of it and I started running longer and longer each day. Then one day, after I returned from a five hour run, my mother surprised us both as she told me that we could see each other, but we were not to sleep together. Ever.

That rule wasn't followed, but she was still trying to enforce it. God bless her determination.

"...and you will tell Samantha to return her mother's phone call. Analise is beside herself. We had to go to the hospital for her to calm down. She couldn't sleep last night."

Mason rolled his eyes after he finished drying himself off with a towel. He stepped close, pressed a kiss to my forehead, and shooed me into the shower. With a quick wink and a slap on my ass, he strolled back to the room with his phone in hand.

When I was done showering, the bedroom was empty so I dressed and headed for the kitchen. Our room was in a small hallway, but I stepped out onto the second level that was in a circle. There were more bedrooms on the side as I passed them towards the stairs at the end of the circle. The entire house was set up in a large circle, with the fountain centered below. As I went down the stairs, the water was flowing freely, but I heard noises from a back corner so I veered to the left. I went through a living room and cut across the top corner to the kitchen.

A large group had congregated around the counters and the island in the middle. Nate was at the stove. One of their female friends was plastered against his side. She wore a skimpy piece of white cloth that barely covered her breasts, sans bra, and ripped jean shorts that hardly covered her cheeks. As she gazed up at Nate, seduction written all over her face, I couldn't stop the gag from my mouth.

The sound echoed over the room, and all conversation stopped.

I didn't see Mason or Logan. It was the group of friends who barely held back their loathing. One of the guys straightened from the counter, beer in hand, and glared at me. "You got a problem?"

Nate was in front of him within seconds. "Ethan, man, don't start this."

"Start what? Did you hear her?"

"Yeah." Nate's seductress positioned her hand to her hip. She struck a defiant pose. "Did you hear her? It was rude, Nate. It was directed at me. She thinks I'm a joke."

"And you haven't been rude to her?"

A shiver went down my back as I remembered the look in Nate's eyes when I first approached. He'd been easygoing, laid-back. Then he went to a neutral stance, but now his eyes glittered with rage. An aura of authority emanated from him. The girl stepped back and everyone fell silent. It was my first glimpse of this side of Mason's best friend. If I had ever doubted their bond before, I didn't anymore. Change the body, the looks, and he could've been Mason. They held the same authority. Nate was just showing his in front of me for the first time.

His lip curved up in an ugly sneer as he stepped closer to Ethan, who had straightened from the counter. The beer spilled as his hand jerked around it, squashing the can in a crinkled ball of metal.

Nate's voice was cold, eerily cold. "You've all been rude to her, and they don't know a thing." He waited a beat as his gaze swept the group. "Why don't you ponder on that, huh? You think they'd stand for your attitude towards her?" Then he whipped his gaze back to Ethan, whose jaw clenched from the scrutiny. "You want your ass kicked? Keep being a bitch to her." He stopped abruptly. His chest heaved up and down before he bit out, "She hasn't said a word. Ponder that too, you asswipes."

"Baby," the girl whimpered. She held a hand out.

Nate ignored her and brushed past me. His jaw was still clenching and before he disappeared around a corner, his hand turned into a fist. But then he was gone, and I was left alone with a group that hated me.

All of them turned their hostile gazes to me.

I gulped. Oh my.

I held my breath, waiting. Did I attack? Hell no. But should I wait to be attacked? I knew they would and then heard a whispered snarl, "You bitch!"

There it was.

It was Nate's seductress. She stood in front of me, brazen with nearly nothing on, and tossed her long brown hair over her shoulder. Something shifted in me. I had come to remember a few of their names. Kate was the ring leader. I was pretty certain she had a 'benefits' relationship with Mason before he went steady with me, and this girl was her best friend forever...Parker, if I remembered correctly?

I opened my mouth, ready for some retort. I wasn't sure what I was about to say, but it was coming. I only hoped it made sense, or that it didn't get me in more trouble. I'd grown tired of the female catty showdowns, and this was certainly one of them.

But then Ethan flung his beer can into the sink and grunted. "Leave her alone, Parks."

Her mouth fell open on a gasp and she rounded to him. Her boobs flopped side to side from the motion. "Are you kidding me?!"

He sighed as he ran a hand over his tired face. "Come on. Nate's right, man. Leave her alone. Kade likes her, leave her be. She ain't going anywhere, and I'm getting tired of this. I don't want to get my ass handed to me by them, and you know it's gonna happen. You're going to say something in front of them and everything will go to hell for us."

"But—"

He stepped away from the counter as he crossed his arms over his chest. The sleeveless, ripped shirt exposed the biceps that now bulged from the motion. His chest grew in size as well. "It ain't happening, not on my watch. Get going. Go tell all the little girlies. I know they'll have a hay day with this one."

Her mouth hung open, no sound came from it. Then one of the guys let loose a snicker and she exploded, "Shut the hell up, Strauss! This ain't got a goddamn thing to do with you."

His snicker doubled in volume. A slap to his thigh was heard as he chuckled, "It sure fun to watch you getting your rear end handed to you."

If she could've killed me, she would've in that moment. The blood drained from her face, and she crossed her arms over her chest. Her lips were stiff as she promised, "I will make you pay for this. The guys might be okay with you, but the girls won't be and we're no picnic, honey. You better watch out from now on."

As she stormed away, I knew her shoulder was going to slam into mine. With gritted teeth, I reacted before I thought about the consequences and I shoulder-checked her instead. She bounced back into a counter, and gasped again. The loathing had always been there, but now white-hot hatred came at me. A low growl emitted from her throat before she rushed from the room.

Again, there was silence in the room.

My heart dropped to my gut as I waited for the next showdown. There were a handful of girls spread out among the other guys.

I wasn't stupid. I had learned that Mason and Logan's friends from Fallen Crest Public were the rough and tumble sort of kids.

They weren't from money. They didn't give a damn about whose daddy paid for their trip overseas or the secret trysts of which daddy was with which mommy, or even who was cheating with whose secretary. These were the kids that partied hard, played harder, and turned into a single unit against an outsider. They were tight-knit. They were closed-mouthed. And they weren't stupid, even though I knew those from my school would mislabel them as that. They were far from stupid and I knew something pivotal had just happened.

Ethan, the fourth in command after Mason, Logan, and Nate, had turned against one of the girls. I also knew that meant there would be a divide. The girls would hate me, while the guys were now okay. And judging by the relieved shoulders and carefree laughter in the room, the guys might've been hoping for this for awhile. Then again, who would willingly want to go against Mason and Logan?

But I still had a fight on my hands. The girls were going to be the toughest, and since they had divorced from the guys' support, I figured they would be worse than normal. This was going to be hell.

Kate was the leader. Parker was her sidekick, but there was another twosome that made up the core group of their four. Natalie and Jasmine. They weren't in the kitchen that morning, but I knew they were somewhere. They were going to be coming for me, somehow, someplace.

Ethan went to the refrigerator and grabbed another beer. As he leaned against a counter, crossed one faded jean-clad leg over the other, and folded his arms across his chest again, he smirked at me. "You need to learn how to kick some ass because you're going to need it. Those girls don't care two hoots if Mason and Logan don't like it. Those girls are vicious. They stick together like a pack of jacked-up wolves. You best get some bite to you."

Oh great. I didn't think running long distances was going to help me with that, but I couldn't be surprised. I had known this would come. This was a group that you had to fight your way in to prove you deserved your spot amongst them.

There was a reason why Mason and Logan were friends with them.

CHAPTER THREE

Mason wasn't in our room when I went back, so I went in search for him. As I was going past some stairs that led to the basement, or one of the basement areas, a whistle stopped me.

"Sam, what's going on?"

Logan came up with no shirt and his jeans unbuttoned. His hair was messily rumpled, as if he'd just woken up or just had sex. With him, I never knew. And then I got my answer.

My eyes went wide. Jessica was behind him. Her shirt was twisted to the side and she was zipping up her own jeans when she saw me. A thick bunch of her hair slipped over her face and covered her eyes, but she brushed it back before she stopped behind Logan.

A smug smirk came over her as she leaned against the wall. "Hiya, Sam. How's it going?"

I rounded on Logan. "Are you kidding me?"

Regret flashed over his face, but then he reached for my hand. "You okay? You seem upset."

"You screwed her?"

"You seemed upset before you saw us. What's going on?"

"Oh." I bit my lip. He didn't want to talk about Jessica, I got the message. I hated it. I hated the idea of him and her together. It was one of my worst nightmares. "If you date her, I'm gone."

His eyes widened a fraction, but that was the only reaction I got from him. A cocky glimmer came over him and he rolled his shoulders back. "Oh, come on, Sam. It's not like that. I promise."

"Jerk," Jessica hissed.

"But something else is going on. What is it?"

"Logan." I pressed my hands against my forehead. A headache was coming on. I already knew that I couldn't stop it. It'd be full blown within an hour and I'd be on the bathroom floor very soon. "I can't deal with this right now. Do you know where Mason is?"

A snort came from the sideline.

I whirled on her. "Do not make one more sound. This morning hasn't been the greatest, and I'd love to take it out on you. I really would."

Her haughty eyes met mine, but there was no retort. I was shocked. Jessica wasn't one to not have a hateful comment ready on the tip of her tongue. That was who she was, spiteful and mean. But then I realized she was keeping quiet because of Logan. I wanted to throw my hands in the air and pull my hair out. She was back to him. I couldn't believe it. I didn't know what she had said to him or done to him to do whatever they did together, but I knew it was sneaky. Then I remembered something else.

"Aren't you dating Jeff?"

She shrugged. "Yeah, but it's not like we're based on good relationship morals. You should know that more than anyone." A smug look came over her.

I wanted that look gone, and I reacted before I thought about it. I raised my hand and slapped her.

She gasped. When her face snapped back to mine, the old Jessica was back in place. The hatred I always saw from her was there. She sucked in her breath. Her chest rose up and down in dramatic breaths, and I knew she was trying to keep herself under control.

I said, heated, "You were my best friend for years. I dated Jeff for three years. If you think I was more hurt because you screwed my boyfriend for two years, then you really are a shallow person. I lost a friend, you idiot. I lost *both* of my best friends at the same time."

A different look came to her then. Her hand fell from her cheek slowly.

"Hey. Okay." Logan stepped between us. His hand touched my elbow, and he urged me up the stairs. "What's going on? What happened this morning?"

I let him lead me down a hallway and away from her. When I glanced back, Jessica slipped further down the hallway. I hoped she was leaving. I couldn't handle her being there, not in my world. I wouldn't let her destroy my life again.

"Hey."

I snapped back to him. I was still shaking from the anger inside of me. "Did you sleep with her?"

He grimaced again and ran a hand through his hair. As he rubbed at his jaw, he let loose a deep breath. "Man, I wasn't thinking that through last night."

"So you did."

It stung, it stung a lot.

"Yeah," he whispered. "I am sorry, Sam. I didn't think about you. That seemed so long ago, and I was drunk. I was alone. I was on the couch downstairs, and she was there. She was whispering all these great promises to me. Her hands were all over me. I liked her touch last night. I liked it a lot. That girl is good in bed, but damn, I should've thought more clearly. I really am sorry."

"She took my friends away." It hurt to admit that, but it was the truth. Jeff hadn't been a stand-up guy, but I was certain that she had seduced him. And she had gotten Lydia to cover for them. She took them both away. When it had come out, she tried to turn more against me. Whatever I had done to her, it must've been horrible, but I had no idea. That was the worst part of it. I had no idea why someone who I had loved since we were kids hated me so much. Had we ever really been friends?

A strong arm wrapped around my shoulders, and I was pulled against Logan's hard chest. He dipped his head and pressed a kiss to my forehead. "I'm really sorry, Sam. But I promise last night was the one and only time. I won't have anything to do with her again. I'm sorry."

I nodded. It took some of the pain away, but until Jessica had sprung up in my life again, I had no idea how much I'd been hurt by her. The door was open now, and more pain came through. Then I blocked it. I repressed it all back down again, and tuned into what Logan was saying, "…pool house maybe."

"Huh?"

"If you're looking for Mason, he's probably in the pool house. It's where he and Nate hang out. They think no one knows about it, but we all do. It's their alone time together." He winked at me as he squeezed me close for one more hug. "You okay?"

I nodded. "Yeah, I'll be fine. She brings bad memories. That's all."

"Okay." Then he yawned and ran a hand over his face again. "I've got to wake up. Man. You eat yet?"

"I was in there, yeah."

"Okay, go check the pool house. I'm sure he's in there. I'm going to get some grub." He pressed one more kiss to my forehead before he let me go. As he left, I watched him saunter away. I rolled my eyes. I didn't think Logan knew how to walk without a cocky strut.

When I slipped out through one of the patio doors, there were more people in the pool. A group had congregated at some of the tables near it. I didn't recognize any of them so I continued to the pool house. When I stepped inside, Mason was at the bar. He sat on a stool with a cup of coffee in front of him. It looked like it hadn't been touched, but the steam still rose in the air. He was hunched over with his phone stuck to his ear.

"Hey."

I jumped and whirled around. Nate sat on a couch with a grin from ear to ear. His shoulders shook in amusement, but he gestured towards Mason. "He's been on the phone the whole time."

"He was talking to his dad." I glanced over, but he hadn't looked up or acknowledged me. Then I heard his next words, "Fuck off, dad. I mean it!" The hostility in them blasted me. I jumped in reaction but was dumbfounded when I heard Nate's soft laughter. I whirled back around. "You think that's funny?"

"Yeah." The laughter died away, but a small grin was still in place. He lounged back on the couch and threw one arm to rest on the top. "When Mason gets pissed, it's never good for the other person. And since it's his dad, I'm excited for what we're going to be doing."

"If that's what you want, fine." Mason's loud exclamation was followed with a curse as he dropped his phone on the bar. He shoved back from the stool but stopped when he saw me. All the rage drained from him, and he sighed before his head slowly hung down. "I'm sorry, Sam. I am."

"What are you talking about?" My throat was suddenly so dry. It was painful for me to speak. "What did your dad say?"

"Your mom's being a bitch. We're supposed to head home right now."

"What else did he say?" I knew there was more. I could see it on his face, but he shook his head. "Mason."

"We should go home."

This wasn't good. Mason didn't stand down to anyone and that was what he was doing. Dread turned to a sick feeling. I didn't want to go into that house. I didn't want to deal with my mother, not when she had affected him like this.

Nate stood with us. He had a small grin on his face, like he was anticipating some fireworks. But Mason held a hand out. "No, man. Just me and Sam."

The grin vanished. Nate straightened to his fullest height of six feet and one inch. His shoulders squared back. "You sure?"

"Yeah."

"Logan?"

"Don't tell him what's going on." Mason touched the small of my back and urged me ahead of him. He paused at the door. "Keep him here. Keep him happy. He can't rush into this, he'd make it worse."

Nate nodded. Mission received and accepted.

As I watched the exchange, a different perverse feeling came over me. This was the dynamic between the two that I didn't like, where they cut everyone else out. If they did it with Logan, I knew they could do it with me. That didn't sit well with me. I didn't like the idea of Mason having someone 'handle' me as he had Nate handle Logan at times.

But I didn't say anything. I was too scared to, not because of how Mason would react, but because I couldn't handle any more deep stuff. The hurt that I was blasted with when I saw Jessica still felt raw. It made me realize how much I had suppressed at the beginning of the year, and that was just the tip of the iceberg. There was so much more pain where that came from, and right now, as Mason and I slipped around the side of the house and went to his car, I knew we weren't headed to an afternoon of kissing and cuddling. We were headed to meet with my mom and his dad. Not good.

Once we had left the driveway and headed back towards town, I reached over and turned the radio off. Then I leaned back and took a breath. I readied myself. "Okay, so what did your dad say?"

Mason kept driving. He didn't visibly react, but I knew he tensed. I felt it from him. Then he clipped out, "Your mom wants one of us out of the house."

"What?"

He jerked his head in a nod. "And I don't want to go. I don't want you sleeping somewhere else or me somewhere else. I don't want to have to sneak in to see my girlfriend or even having your mom breathing down our backs when one of us is in the house. I've dealt with so much more than her. It's pissing me off. And you, where was she when she dumped you in our house with no friends and no father? She took off with my dad. Now she suddenly wants to come and act like your mother?" He cursed again and shook his head. The anger in his eyes made them glimmer. "I can't believe her and I can't believe my dad. He's always known the deal. We raised ourselves. I raised Logan. He was never around. He was either cheating on our mom or away on business trips. I raised Logan. He didn't. I swear to god, he wants to start laying the law down as my father? I'm eighteen. I'm gone the end of the summer and he's doing this now?"

I'm gone the end of the summer. Those words hit me hard. I fell back against my seat. I knew Mason would be leaving, but I hadn't really thought about it. He was going. He was really going.

He would be gone.

I didn't want to go back to the mansion. "Stop the car."

"What?"

"Stop the car." Something fierce came over me. "Stop the car now."

"Why?" But he slowed it down and turned into a parking lot. "What's going on?"

I shook my head and rasped out, "I'm not doing this with them. You're right. I know my mom wants us to stop sleeping together, but we can't." I wouldn't stop. I couldn't.

"Hey, hey." His voice was low and smooth. He cupped the end of my elbow and turned me towards him. "We won't. I promise. I just don't know what to do with your mom. My dad said that she's going nuts. She's making all these threats—" He stopped abruptly.

Oh god.

I asked, with my heart pounding, "What is she saying?"

"She's threatening to leave him if I won't stop seeing you."

"Are you kidding me?"

He shook his head. There was a deep pain in his eyes. It stabbed me in the chest. "What else?" I knew there was more. I needed to know all of it now.

"She said that if he can't control his kid, then she'll control hers. She's saying that she'll leave him and take you away."

I waited a beat.

I let his words sink in. And then I went with my gut. "She's lying."

She had to be lying. That was all there was to it.

Mason didn't say a word.

I knew my mother, and I knew she wouldn't leave James Kade. There was no way. He was her bread and butter. He was her soulmate, or so she thought, and he loved her. I knew David loved her, but he didn't love her as much as James Kade did.

I squeezed Mason's hand. I squeezed until I feared it might come off, but I couldn't stop. "She's lying. Analise knows that James won't want to lose her. He loves her that much, so she's bluffing. She won't leave him. She knows he'll step in and stop her before she does."

He fell back against his seat and said quietly, "I know, but it's going to work. He's going to kick me out to keep her."

My eyes closed. My mom really was a bastard. So much other emotions came up within me, but I pushed them back down. I rasped out, "What do we do?"

"We can't call her bluff. Then he'll really do it."

And that was the crux of it. My mother was sending an ultimatum. Her or his son. James had to choose and we knew who that would be.

CHAPTER FOUR

We didn't go back to the Kade mansion. We had another two weeks of break before we had to make any decisions so we went to Los Angeles. Just him and me. It was needed.

He called Nate after we turned the car around. He told him that we were going to be staying at one of his mother's places. Then he called Logan and told him the same, except he said that it was because we wanted some alone time. Neither had been happy, particularly when he said it might be for awhile, but neither argued.

I knew both wanted their partner in crime for whatever adventures they thought would happen, but the truth was that I wanted to get away. The tension had become unbearable at home between Analise and Mason. Neither would back down, and I was scared of what could happen. Logan stayed out of it, mostly, but there were times he would stir the pot. A smartass comment would come out or he would insinuate how the sex must've been good between Mason and me. And he loved to share his own sexual stories. Analise looked ready to explode when she was reminded how sexually experienced they were.

My stomach twisted in knots again as I remembered a few of those times. James and I were the quiet ones, but I could tell he was affected as well. I didn't understand the dynamic between him and his sons, but I knew it was a strange one.

"Here we are." Mason slowed his Escalade and turned into a cobblestone driveway that led to a large door. A doorman was in front of the sliding glass doors. As a black limousine paused in front of us, a woman in a nude-colored dress stepped out. She wore sunglasses and her blonde hair was swept up in a fancy bun. As we watched, she waited for the driver to pull a piece of luggage out of the back for her. Instead of handing it to her, it was handed to the doorman, who swept his hand out so the doors slid open. Then he followed her inside. It wasn't long before the driver returned to his seat and the limousine pulled away from the doors.

"Your mom has a place in this building?"

"Yep, she's got one of the top floors."

My mouth dropped.

He flashed a grin. "I told you my mom was wealthy. My dad's money can't touch hers. This is only *one* of her places, and trust me, this is the one she rarely uses. You saw that lady just now?"

I nodded.

"My mom hates her." He shrugged. "No idea why."

"That's why your mom doesn't come here that often?"

He nodded as the doorman appeared again. Then he pulled his Escalade up to the door. When we both got out, the doorman broke out into a friendly grin. He wore a navy blue suit with a yellow tie. He looked older, possibly in his fifties, with graying hair. His smile lit up his face. The blue in his eyes turned warm, and the affection he felt for Mason was evident. He drew him in for a hug and clasped him on the shoulder with his black leather gloves. "It's good to see you, Master Kade! It's been so long."

Mason's own smile was ear to ear when he stepped back. "It has been."

The man still held onto his arms. He didn't drop them when his smile slipped a little bit. "And your mother? Is she here with you?"

"Nah, Stuart. I hope she won't find out that I'm here." Then he extended a hand towards me. "This is my girlfriend, Sam. We're on break from school so we're hiding out."

The warm eyes turned towards me, and they sparkled as he took me in. "I see." His hands fell away from Mason's arms. "She is a beauty, Mason. You have done well."

"I think so."

With both of their attention on me, I flushed and looked away. Beauty? What was he smoking?

"And Logan?"

"Nope. It's just me and Sam."

"Ah, I see. One of those vacations."

"Yeah and mum's the word, Stu."

"Of course, Master Kade."

A curse slipped out. "Come on, Stu. Mason. You're supposed to call me Mason."

"Of course, Master Kade." Then I looked back and he held out a hand to me. "And what shall I call this exquisite beautiful creature? I cannot call you by your personal name, Sam. Samantha? Mistress, hmmm? What is your last name?"

"You can call her Samantha."

I took his hand, and my eyes went wide when he lifted it for a kiss. His cool lips pressed a chaste kiss to the back of my hand, but the friendliness in his eyes overwhelmed me. He wasn't inappropriately friendly. I knew it was from the respect he held for Mason. It took my breath away for a moment.

"I cannot," he murmured as he let go of my hand. "I have not earned the right to use her first name. What is your last name?"

"Strattan."

"Mistress Strattan it is." His smile deepened an inch.

I wanted to groan as I realized that I would be called that from now on. Awkward. And if any of my friends heard him—no. I didn't have any friends. It didn't matter.

The front lobby wasn't big. There was a front desk, an elevator, and a small sitting area. As we went to the elevator and reached the 24th floor, I found myself staring at something I would've seen on a television show. The floor was modern and chic with white couches in front of a fireplace and a red table beside the kitchen. When Mason took my hand and led me to our bedroom, there was a plush white comforter on the bed with gold trim. The far wall was a floor to ceiling window, with a view that overlooked Los Angeles. It was spectacular.

"As promised," Mason drew my attention towards the closet. He toed it open for me. "You won't need clothes. My mom keeps clothes here for everyone. We have a few cousins your size and she loves to dote on them. When they come here, they know they don't have to pack."

"And you?"

He grinned and gestured towards the dresser that was painted white. It matched the comforter. "I keep clothes here, so does Logan. This is the place we use when we come to see her."

"You have cousins?" He'd never told me about them before.

"Yeah." A fond grin appeared. "They're crazy and spoiled, but I think you'd like them."

"From your mother's side?" Obviously.

"She has two brothers and a little sister. They all have kids. Logan and I stay with dad, but we try to see them every now and then. It's been awhile."

"How long?"

"Since the summer. We went on a cruise with our cousins. My mom was in heaven. She loved having us with her side of the family."

"Mason." My chest hurt. The question I was about to ask was one that I'd had for awhile. "Why do you live with your dad? Why is it so important for you to stay?"

He seemed taken aback as he sat on the bed. Then, with a somber expression, he lifted his hand for me. My heart pounded with each step I took until I touched his hand with mine. His fingers were cool at first. He wrapped his hand around mine and warmth from him enveloped me soon after. Then he tugged me between his legs. As he fell down, he lifted me with him to straddle his waist. Then he gazed at me. The somber expression darkened to something else, something that stirred my heart.

He spoke in a soft voice, "Before this year, it was because of football. We stayed with our mom after they got divorced, but the school we were going to didn't have a good football team. Then dad told us about *your* dad. He wanted us to go to Fallen Crest Academy, but when we actually moved there and toured the school, I knew the team wasn't going to be good enough to get recruits. So we went to Public. They got a new coach, someone I had heard about. It seemed more promising. The team was better. The guys were bigger, tougher. They were more serious about football, so we went there. It was the right move for me. I don't know about Logan. He's not as serious about football as me. I think he just played because I did."

"And now?"

His grin softened as he reached up and traced the side of my face with his finger. He brought it down before he cupped the side of my face. His lips touched my cheek, softly and tenderly. My eyes closed as he moved to my lips. Heat started low within me but rose at a rapid pace. My heart picked up, and I was panting before his lips touched mine fully. Then he opened them, demanding more, commanding more from me, and I answered. My mouth opened. As his tongue swept inside, mine rubbed against his. It was one of my favorite things to do. We were connected, inside and out. Then I wanted more. It was always the same. I'd always want more with him.

As he pulled away, I groaned, but grinned as I heard his soft chuckle. I rested my forehead on his when he panted out, "What do you think?"

I grinned, feeling silly from how happy I was. "Because of me?"

His hand cupped under my head and tilted me back. My eyes opened and widened when I saw the fierceness in his. "I won't get run off from you. I love you, Sam. I said it before and I mean it. I won't let your mom control my life."

When a thread of hostility slipped into his tone, my heart raced. I knew he didn't like my mother, but I was starting to wonder if he hated her.

He continued, "I was okay with her moving in. I had one year left. I didn't figure she could do much damage in that one year."

"What about Logan?" My hands lifted to his shoulders. I took hold there.

He shrugged as he bent and placed a soft kiss on my shoulder. Then he sat further up and slid a hand underneath me. He lifted me even closer so I wrapped my legs around his back. We were fully aligned together. Remove his jeans, mine and he could've slipped inside of me. I felt him harden against me. The feeling of him was intoxicating.

"Before you, I think he would've moved back with our mom. He liked our old school. He liked going to school with our cousins. Two of them, James and Will, are just like Logan. They're the three musketeers."

I shuddered at that thought. "Three Logans?"

"Yeah." Mason chuckled again as he gazed up at me. "But that was awhile ago. Why are you asking?"

"You think he'll stay another year?"

"He will since you'll be there. You know both of us want you to transfer to Public. We have a better track team. I've talked to you about that before."

I sighed as I remembered those conversations. Mason brought it up once when we had been in bed. Then it was raised again at the kitchen table. Logan brought up the topic, Mason jumped in, and I was double-teamed. I never told them what I had decided, but the truth was that I wasn't sure.

Fallen Crest Academy was a better school, but they were right. Fallen Crest Public had a better track team. Mason went to their track coach. He agreed to meet with me and he watched me run every day over the last week. He timed how long I would go on their inside track, but he hadn't said anything during our last session. I wanted to wait until I knew that it would be worth the transfer.

"I don't get it, Sam. Why do you want to stay there? Douchebag turned everyone against you."

I grinned down at him, at the frustration in his voice. "You look cute when you're pissed with me."

"Then I must be cute whenever we talk about this. I'm always pissed with you about this. Why won't you transfer? It makes no sense to me. You could get a scholarship, Sam. Let's be real here. Do you really want to depend on your mom's help to go to college? Or your dads'? Neither of them has contacted you recently. Have they? And what's up with that?"

A different headache was coming on. It was low and probing. I shook my head. I didn't want to discuss either of them. "I understand why you want me to transfer. I get it. I do. But I don't know if it'll be worth it. I haven't even heard back from Coach Grath. I might not make the team, so why would I transfer schools?"

"Besides not going to school with Douchebag and all his little followers?" He grumbled, "You have no friends over there. They're weak as hell."

"Maybe." They were. "But it's a good school. I've always gone there and my dad—"

I looked away, but his fingers were quick as lightning. He grabbed my chin and kept me from turning away. I started to struggle, but his hold tightened. It was useless. He'd already heard.

His eyes narrowed to slits. "That's why you don't want to transfer, isn't it? Because of your dad. You think it's one way to still see him, don't you?"

I fell quiet. It wasn't because I didn't want to talk about that. It was because I couldn't. My throat swelled and it felt like an elephant was on my chest. It hurt to push past both of those emotions, or ignore how my heart rate skyrocketed.

"Sam."

I shook my head. I tried to look away, but a tear slipped out.

He cursed under his breath and then bundled me in his arms once more. I curled up in his lap as he folded me against his chest so we were both settled against the bed's headboard. Then he brushed some of my hair away from my forehead. His fingers slid down and brushed away more of my tears. I couldn't stop them. I never could when I really thought about my dad. So instead, I tried to never think about him.

Another soft curse slipped past his lips. He pressed a kiss to my forehead. "I'm sorry. I am."

My hands curled into his shirt. I held on with a desperation I never would've shown four months ago. Now I couldn't help myself with him. I needed him. Hell, I starved for him at times.

He continued to brush more of my hair from my eyes. "How long has it been?"

I shook my head. It still hurt to talk.

"If they won't reach out to you, you should reach out to them."

I looked up now. Panic coursed through me. He couldn't be suggesting…

He nodded. "You heard me. You go to them and find out what the hell is going on."

A ragged chuckle ripped from me. It was so easy for him. If people stood in his way, Mason went through them. It wasn't a question if they would stop him. It was a question of how he would go through them, if he would stomp them down, barrel through them, or just throw them out of his way.

Things were different with me.

"Why are you laughing?" He tilted my head back again.

I shook my head. God, it hurt sometimes.

"Talk to me, Sam," he groaned.

I closed my eyes. "It's not why we're here."

"What?"

"We're here to get away from all that stuff. I don't want to talk about them right now. We're here to spend time together, just you and me."

His hand fell away from my hip. "Are you serious?"

I lifted a shoulder, but I looked away. Then I bit my lip. My heart started to pound again. And I waited…

There was a heavy silence between us.

I continued to wait.

"Fine."

Relief flared through me. My shoulders relaxed as the sudden tension lifted from them. I didn't realize how important it was for him not to press the point. I would handle my fathers, the biological one and the one that raised me, one day. I just couldn't handle them this day, but one day... I would have to one day.

CHAPTER FIVE

It was early when his phone lit up. Logan was the first to call at six in the morning. When Mason checked the time, he cursed and sat upright as he took the call. I listened from beside him, even though I turned my own phone on and saw twelve voice messages from my mother.

"Wait, slow down."

I could hear Logan's excited voice still going strong on the other side. After another minute, a savage curse came from Mason. His shoulders tightened and his jaw clenched.

My heart sank. It wasn't good.

Then I sighed and got up from the bed. It was time for me to handle my mother. Mason and Logan were great buffers, but I was the only one who had the voice to quiet her. As I dressed, I felt his eyes on me. After I emerged from the bathroom, showered and fully dressed, he stood and held his hand over the phone. "What are you doing?"

"We're going back."

His eyebrows went high. "We just got here."

"I know." My heart was in the pit of my stomach. I was tired of feeling it there. I needed to stop hiding from my mother and from the situation. I'd been hiding since our parents found out about us. This had to stop.

"You're sure?"

I nodded. I knew I had the resolved face on and Mason removed his hand from the phone. "Hang on, Logan. We're coming back."

It didn't take long to pack our stuff. We hadn't packed anything to begin with. As for the break from reality, this one had been a short one. A part of me was pissed that we had even come. Enough was enough. I wasn't going to be harassed through phone calls by my mother. And I wasn't going to hear her threats through other people anymore.

Stuart held the door for us as we left. The Escalade had been pulled up, waiting for us. The smile on Stuart's face slipped a bit when he caught my eye, but he gave Mason a hug before he drove off. After a quick stop for breakfast and coffee, we were on our way back. The ride was passed in silence, tense silence for me. I glanced at Mason, but he seemed relaxed. Then again, this was his lifestyle. He didn't relish confrontations, but he didn't fear them either.

I wished I had that same quality. Sparring off against a catty girl was different from going against my mother, a mother that I knew I should've respected. I should've followed her rules from day one, but to be truthful, if my relationship with her had been better than my relationship with Mason, things might've been different. I bit my lip as I admitted to myself that I might not have slept with him. I loved him. I needed him, but I had been alone. I had been hurting. And I had been wasting away. He came at the perfect time, but things changed because of him. I was stronger now.

I had to be.

It was a few hours later when Mason took my hand in his. "You ready for this?"

The words couldn't come. I watched as he turned into the driveway. My mom's car was there. Logan's Escalade was beside hers and there was an SUV that I didn't recognize.

"I can turn around again. You don't have to go in there."

"I do." The words ripped from me and came out a hoarse whisper. I was terrified of my mother in that moment. This wasn't going to go well.

"Sam."

His voice stopped me when I was going to reach for the door. I looked back and melted. A soft plea was in his eyes.

His hand took mine again. He held on tight. "Don't let her ruin this."

I nodded, but there was a ball in my throat. The tears were about to spill.

"I can't promise what I'll do if your mom fucks with our relationship anymore. If she ruins this…" Raw desperation slipped from him, but it was mixed with a deadly warning as well.

I rushed across the car and pressed against him. My lips found his, and I tried to give him everything in that kiss. I wanted to give him my soul so I didn't let the kiss end. When he was about to pull away, I held on tighter.

"I won't let her change anything." I couldn't.

As we headed inside, the raised voices carried over us. I was sure the neighbors could hear when my mother shrieked before something shattered in the next room. My feet froze in place. My heart lurched into a stampede and a wave of dizziness swept over me. Good god. I was transported back to another time when my mother threw a fit. She screamed bloody murder that night, so long ago, as she tore pictures to pieces. She threw plates across the room. A bat was taken to the China cabinet. All the dishes had been destroyed. At the end of her fit, four hours later, there had been nothing left intact.

"*You did this!*" she raged as she pointed her finger at me.

But that'd been six years ago. I was a month away from turning into an adult. I swallowed those emotions and pushed them down. I hadn't been haunted by them for so long; I wasn't going to start now. She wouldn't have that power over me.

"You okay?" Mason tugged on my hand with a frown.

Sweat broke out on my forehead. Heat flared inside of me. He couldn't see me like this. I had kept it together for so long; I didn't want him to see how that night had left me broken. So I swallowed all of it and nodded.

I tried to remember that I was seventeen. We were in a different home. We had a different life now.

"Sam."

"Yes?" The word ripped from my throat. I winced as I heard how hoarse my voice was. But then I was taken aback when he lifted his hand and brushed away some tears. His hand was cool against my skin. I breathed his touch in. It was soft, tender. I needed it at that moment. Hell. I needed his strength. My mother had taken all of mine in that one second.

"Hey, hey." He stepped close to me and framed my face in his hands. He peered down with concern. "What's wrong?"

I shook my head and pulled away.

"Stop."

I brushed his hands away.

"She did this to me!"

I jumped back from the ferocity in her scream. There was a rage there that I thought she had lost so long ago, but I was wrong. I wondered if she'd kept it hidden from James? Had it been there the whole time?

I swallowed a breath. My shoulders lifted up and rolled back. I knew what I would face in the next room, and then I stepped forward. I was ready for it.

Logan laughed before he ended it with a snort. "Are you fucking with me? No wonder she ran away from you."

"Logan!"

Analise screamed again before something shattered once more.

Logan cheered, "Do it again! Do it again, Psycho Woman!"

"Logan, shut up!"

"Oh, come on, dad. Look at her. She's crazy—"

I stepped around the corner, with Mason right behind me. The amusement fled from Logan as he took in the sight of us, or me. I couldn't have looked normal as my heart was pounding. My gut was telling me to run away from her. But I didn't. Mason brushed his hand against mine as he stepped around to shield me.

James swallowed when he looked up, but I couldn't take my eyes from my mother.

Analise was in her bathrobe with her hair done up. She looked like they had gone to a formal event the night before and she had gone to bed with her hair and make-up still done up. But there were black splotches on her face from where her mascara bled and her eyes were wild. Some of her hair stuck up, and she never calmed the strands. A plate was in her hand, but she lowered it as she raked me over with her eyes. They were cold, so cold. A chill went down my back.

This was the mother I feared from so long ago. She was back.

"You," she seethed.

I scrambled back a step before I realized what I was doing, but it was too late. Triumph flared in her depths. She still had that power over me, and her chest swelled up. As I watched her, I could see the power swelter inside of her. She thrived on it, but then Logan jumped to his feet. He had been sitting on a chair in the back. He cursed now.

She sucked in her breath and turned. I knew she was ready to blast him.

"And you want to know why we took off?" Mason's icy tone stopped everything. He gestured towards his dad and then swept a hand towards Analise. "Look at her. She's off her rails, dad. I don't want Sam near her."

Analise's eyes widened. Her hand clenched around the plate again.

I was frozen in place. Mason's hand reached behind him, and he pulled me close so I was pressed against his back. Then I closed my eyes. I was supposed to be the one fighting. I knew it had to be me, but I rested my forehead against his back. She had taken all the strength from me that I had accumulated over the last five months. She sucked me dry, and I was left trembling like I had when I was eleven years old.

"Samantha," she said in a sharp tone. "Look at me."

I trembled.

Mason laughed at her. "Fuck that."

"Screw you." This time it was Logan. His voice rose, as did his anger. "Who are you to talk to her like that?"

Analise sucked in her breath. "She is my daughter. I am her mother. That's who I am."

"Then act like it," Mason's tone was savage. He had stiffened to stone before me. "I don't know who raised you, but my mom and dad would never talk to me like that."

"Maybe they should've," she proclaimed.

My eyes clasped tighter, but I could see her in my mind. I knew her chin was in the air, her eyes were brazen, and she was open to a fight. My mother was a beautiful woman with dark black hair that was straight and sleek. She had a slim build and when she was dressed in form-fitting dresses, she looked elegant. A classic sophisticated look clung to her and made her seem angelic to men. I always knew when she wanted something because she would put on her soft-pink dress and cozy up to David with an endearing smile. She would use caresses over dinner to get what she wanted, and it always worked. He folded every time and from what I had witnessed, James Kade wasn't any different. She could've beaten me up and she would only need a trembling lip, a few tears, and remorseful eyes to pull him back in.

Analise might've been crazy, but she had power over the opposite sex. She used it as a weapon.

"Analise!" James scolded her this time.

I sucked in my breath. My hands were now fisted into the back of Mason's shirt.

"What—James?"

Gone was the rage. Her voice softened. She had stepped wrong. I started the countdown in my head. 3…

"You can't say things like that, not about my own children."

2…

Logan snickered.

1…

"Oh, honey," her voice melted. "I didn't mean it like that. I'm so sorry. I am. It's just—I've been worried about my baby. He took her away from me, and I'm losing her, James. I can't lose my daughter."

Cue the sniffles.

She whimpered, "I just love her so much, James. You can understand that, can't you?"

"Oh my god." Logan's disgust was evident.

"Logan," his dad barked, but he had already softened. "It might be best if you leave the room. All of you."

"Are you kidding me?" Mason gutted out. His hands rose in the air, in fists. "She's working you, dad. You're falling for this?"

James sucked in his breath. Then he delivered with cold disdain, "Your mother called today. She would like for you and Logan to spend your break with her at the Malibu Estate. I think it would be best for everyone to leave as soon as possible."

He cursed. "I'm not leaving Sam here. If I go, she goes."

"What—"Analise started.

"Honey." James' sharp rebuke quieted her. Then he turned again. "Mason, I think it's best if there was some distance between you and Samantha. You have proven that neither of you can act responsibly. I had hoped you would've when we first learned of your relationship, but your disappearing trick did not help your credibility at all." He sounded tired all of the sudden. "I have asked you on many occasions to cease from being intimate, at least under this roof, but you have discarded my wishes on every matter. You have given me no other choice. I will not allow you to disappear with Samantha one more time. Her mother was beside herself and you put both of us through hell as we worried where you might've gone or even if you were going to come back."

When he finished, the room was silent for a moment. And then

Logan threw his hands in the air, cursing as Mason bit out, "Are you fucking with me now?"

"No way." Logan shook his head. "We're not going. We go, she goes."

"I'm sorry, boys. I am. But neither of you are welcome in this home for the duration of your winter break." James seemed beaten down as he gestured to the side.

A large man came forward. He was dressed in a three-piece suit that stretched over his muscular shoulders and trim waist. His eyes lacked emotion as he nodded to Mason and then Logan. "Gentlemen."

"Are you serious, dad?" More curses came from Logan. "I can't believe this. What have *I* done?"

"Logan, we all know you support their relationship and have a soft spot for Samantha as well."

"She's like my sister."

"Regardless, you both protect her, which I find admirable, but you have become destructive to her relationship with her mother. You both need to go. You remember Howard?"

"And what if I refuse to go?" Mason stepped forward. His tone was hard.

"Mr. Mason." Howard stepped forward. "Your bags have already been packed and your mother is waiting for our arrival—"

"I'm not going," Mason cut him off. "Sorry, Howard, but I'm not twelve this time. You can't force me to go anywhere. I'm eighteen, dad. You can't bus me off anymore, and I won't play along this time."

"Fine, but you will not be allowed to see Samantha while she lives under this house."

"And what if she doesn't?" Mason folded his arms over his chest.

Everyone stood still at the stand-off between father and son.

I held my breath as my feet were still rooted where I clung to Mason's back. I yearned for his warmth, but my head hung down.

I couldn't bear the idea of making eye contact with my mother. I knew she would've won then. She would've known that she had reduced me to that eleven-year-old so long ago again. I cringed as I remembered that time. I couldn't go back to that pain, not anymore.

"Howard," James spoke. "You will accompany Logan to the car. If Mason refuses to go with you, you are instructed to leave within ten minutes."

"But—"

"Yes, sir." Howard turned. "Mr. Logan? The car, please."

"What—no way." Logan's mouth hung open. He was speechless, but then he rebooted. "Dad, come on. This is insane. You're kicking me out? Are you kidding me?"

James turned to him. He was so stiff. "I have been forced to play my hand and this is it, Logan. If you wish to remain in my household and spend the rest of your high school years here, with Samantha, you will do as I have told. You will vacation with your mother for the break. When you return, you will respect my rules. If you do not, you will have two choices. You can live with your mother or I will have you arrested as a runaway. You are not eighteen, Logan." Then he turned on his heel and addressed his oldest son. "And Mason, those rules pertain to you as well. I cannot make you go to your mother's, but what we *can* do is enforce those rules to Samantha. She is still a minor. If she leaves her mother's household, she will be arrested as a runaway."

My eyes closed again as I heard my worst nightmare come true. She had trapped me. New panic came over me and I gulped for breath, but then I heard Mason's shrewd laughter. His voice was soft, so soft it sent chills down my spine. "You've forgotten one fact, dad."

"And what's that?"

"You've got one month. She turns eighteen in one month."

Analise sucked in her breath and James seemed visibly shaken, but he sighed. "Fine, then. I have one month to undo the damage you've unleashed on their relationship."

"What?" Logan cried out again. "You seriously think—"

"Logan, LEAVE!" his father roared.

Logan's mouth snapped shut as Howard cleared his throat. Then his shoulders dropped in surrender. "Yeah, yeah. Whatever. I'm going."

When he shuffled past me, he folded me in his arms and whispered, "Don't worry, Sammy. The game's just begun. Take care." He pressed a kiss to my forehead before he headed outside. The big stiff followed behind, and then the door closed behind both of them.

Mason shook his head. "This is ridiculous. She's brainwashed you, dad. You don't see that?"

James closed his eyes before he rubbed a weary hand over his jaw. His hair seemed to have grayed over the last ten minutes. His voice was exhausted as he spoke, "I'm sorry that you feel that way, Mason. I truly am, but I have to stand with my future wife. Things have been run by you and your brother for too long. It's time I made things right again."

I glanced up at Mason. The dark promises in his depths made my stomach fall to the ground. I knew without asking that this was only the beginning. And for a second, I worried what he was going to do.

CHAPTER SIX

An hour later and I still couldn't wrap my head around how things had changed. Logan was gone, like gone gone. I wouldn't see him for two more weeks, when school would start again. And Mason was at Nate's.

I drew in a shuddering breath as I sat at my desk. My computer was on, but my hands hadn't touched the keyboard.

Mason was gone.

Mason couldn't see me.

Analise forbade me to see him and if I did, then what? I gulped. She made it clear that she would follow through with James' threat. The first moment that I would go to him, she would call the cops and have me arrested as a runaway. Could she even do that? I had no idea. Could she really force all of this? But Mason was right. I had one more month before I was legally on my own.

As I sat there, I saw a blinking light on my phone and pressed to hear the message.

A deep voice came over the phone, "This is Edward Grath, Coach Grath. I apologize for not getting back to you after last Friday, but I wanted to run your times by a few other coaches in the area." He drew in an excited breath. "Not only can I guarantee you a spot on our track team, but I will guarantee that you will get a scholarship after this year. I've already put feelers out for recruiters and one called me. They're very interested in you. If you keep running at these times, you will have no problem receiving a full scholarship to a college. Congratulations, Samantha. Give me a call this week. I'd like to start a training regime with you as soon as possible."

I sat there. I'd gotten on the team? He guaranteed a scholarship? I blinked as his words registered with me, then I scrambled for the phone again. This time I hit the button for Mason, but the line went flat. The operator informed me the line had been disconnected.

What the hell?

I pulled the phone away and stared at it. Had I hit the right button? He was on my speed dial. It should've been right, but after I did it again and then located his number in my contacts I was left speechless. Mason's phone was no more. I tried Logan, but it was the same results. They both disconnected their lines? Was it something against their dad? Why hadn't they given me their new numbers? I knew they would've.

Holy. I sat there, even more dejected than before. I had this great news and I couldn't tell the two people who cared about me.

Nate.

Even as the idea popped in my head, I knew I didn't have his number so I pushed away from my desk and grabbed my purse. I stepped into the hallway, but stopped short. Analise was there in a silk robe and a frown. She crossed her arms. "Where are you going?"

"I'm going to see Mason."

"No, you're not."

"Yes, I am."

Her eyes narrowed and my old fear flickered in me again. Since I had remembered that night so long ago, I couldn't undo the effects. I thought I had been rid of that power over me, but she had me in the grip of her hand. If she squeezed, I didn't know how I would react.

"No," she said slowly and softly. It was menacing. "You're not."

I swallowed a ball of emotion and rubbed my hands against my pants. Then I rasped out, "What are you going to do, Analise? What are you going to do if I don't listen to you?"

"Analise," she hissed. "You call me by my first name now?"

"I'm seventeen. I'll be an adult in one month. Your attempt to control me is pathetic." My words were so brave, but I struggled to keep my knees from knocking against each other. She'd hear and she couldn't know.

To my surprise, when I expected the old rage to return, she shook her head and stepped back. Her head bent down, and she swallowed back a tear. I heard the hitch in her voice, and I sucked in my own breath. I couldn't believe what I had just heard. But she spoke so softly, I strained to hear her. "Do you realize that having sexual intercourse with a minor is against the law?"

Silence. Complete silence.

Her words hit me like a ton of bricks. I felt blown over and kicked while I was still down. She wouldn't—she couldn't—but, wait…she could. "You wouldn't."

She lifted her head. A challenge was there. "Not yet, I haven't."

"No way." I shook my head. She wouldn't do that. She could ruin his life…

Then she cleared her throat and sighed. "I don't want to, Samantha, but I have been losing you since we moved in. I won't stand for it anymore. No one is going to come in here and take my daughter away from me. No one. Not your father, not your boyfriend, not your friends, no one." Her chest rose with each statement. She was bristling with anger again. "I won't even let you get in the way of our relationship."

She started down the hallway, but stopped and twisted back around. "And we're monitoring your internet if you decide to reach out to them. I don't want you anywhere near Mason *or* Logan."

"You can't keep me caged up like an animal. I'm an adult in one month."

"Then I have one month to get my daughter back. And I will do it." Her eyes narrowed. "If you go anywhere near Mason, I will have him arrested for statutory rape. I believe there are enough people who can testify that you've had intercourse with him."

No one would. People suspected. I wasn't a fool. Mason was a Kade, of course he was having sex with his girlfriend, but there was no proof. However, did I call her bluff? Then my heart sank. I couldn't risk it. It was Mason's life on the line now, and it was one month.

I took a deep breath. One month. I couldn't see him for one month.

Oh god.

I went back to my room, but it wasn't long before it hit me, really hit me. I couldn't see Mason. I couldn't see Logan. Panic settled over me and I went to the shower. With my clothes on, I turned the spray on full blast and sunk to the floor. When the water warmed, I hugged my knees to my chest and rested my forehead between them. Then I took in one gulping breath after another.

I could do this. I knew I could do this.

Hell.

I've done it before, when I had two best friends who weren't friends at all. That was when the names of Mason and Logan had seemed surreal. I considered them assholes then. I took care of myself then. I could do it again.

The hallway was dark and narrow. The walls stretched higher than I could see and as I walked to the bathroom, I couldn't catch my breath. There was something thundering in my ear. It wouldn't stop. I frowned against the pain, but I had to go to the bathroom. I knew my mom wouldn't be happy if I disturbed anything so I trekked down the hallway as silent as I could. My bare feet were so cold. The carpet didn't warm them up. I should've worn the socks my mom insisted I wear to bed, but I always pulled them off when she left my room. I hated sleeping in them. They would get caught on my blankets, and I would wake up with my blankets tangled all around me. As I stubbed my toe against something, I whimpered and fell to the ground. I opened and closed my mouth as I tried not to let any sound out. If my mom was sleeping, I dared not wake her. She would get so mad.

When the pain subsided and I knew I wouldn't cry out, I stood back up and limped forward. I really had to pee now, but I went slower. I didn't want to hurt my toes again so I felt along the wall as I went. When I got to the corner, I turned and paused. The light was on in the bathroom. The crack underneath was lit.

Oh no.

I pressed my hands between my legs. I had to pee so bad. I couldn't go there. My mom would be really mad then.

I started to shake back and forth. It was too dark out to use the bathroom downstairs. And too cold. I was shivering already as I waited for what I should do, but then I wondered if anyone was really in there. Maybe my mom had left it on by accident—no, not possible. She double-checked everything before she went to bed. Every light was turned off. Every door was locked. All the windows were checked three times.

If anyone left it on, then it was dad. Relief went through me. If he had done it, then I could use it. Or if he was in there, he wouldn't be mad at me. He never was.

Oh my god. I had to pee!

I inched closer to the door, but I didn't hear anything. Then I knelt and tried to see underneath the door. I couldn't see anyone either. Then, with a deep breath (I was so nervous) I started to turn the doorknob.

When it wasn't locked, a big smile came over me. It would've been locked if someone had been in there so I pushed it open.

Then I froze.

My eyes went wide as I saw the blood first.

"AHHHHH!" I jerked awake and bolted upright in bed. My scream stopped abruptly and my chest heaved up and down. I couldn't get enough breath. I pounded on my chest. My heart was racing.

I tumbled out of bed. My legs weren't steady so I fell to the ground. The sheets were tangled around my legs and I sat there shivering. I wasn't cold. I was hot. I felt my forehead and wondered if the burning was in my mind or not? But no, I wiped my hand over my forehead and felt the sweat from it.

Oh my god.

I took more breaths. I needed to calm down.

It was awhile before I could move. The sheer terror was still there. I felt it in my chest and I wanted to pound on it so it would go away, but it didn't. It lingered. Oh god. I wanted Mason. He should've been beside me. He would've caught me and I would've been in his arms by now, but I remembered what happened the day before.

I closed my eyes. Everything would be fine. It was only a month, but as I said that to myself, it didn't matter. I needed him then. So I did the next best thing I could think of—I grabbed my blanket and went to his room.

I stood in the middle of his room, and I breathed it in. It smelled of him, of men's cologne and his aftershave. I calmed a little bit because of that, but then I crawled underneath his covers. I had used his body to warm me up before, but I wouldn't have that now. I spread my blanket on top and curled underneath. I hugged his pillow to me and tried to go back to sleep again.

Two hours later, I was still awake. I rolled over and glanced at his clock. It was now three in the morning.

Screw it.

I hurried from his bed and flipped on his bathroom light. I pulled on a pair of his black warm-up pants with one of his school sweatshirts. Then I went to my room, slipped on my shoes, and grabbed my purse. On the way downstairs, I grabbed my keys and went out the door. When it locked behind me, I got into my car and headed to Nate's house.

It was a risk. A big one, but I needed to see Mason. It was 3:23 in the morning when I pulled into his driveway. All the lights were off and I didn't have a phone number to wake him up so I had one option. I pounded on his door and rang the doorbell until someone woke up. When some lights were turned on inside and I heard cursing, I stepped back and waited.

Nate threw the door open. His face was in a scowl, but he took one look at me and turned back. "Mason!" Then he threw the door open and I swept inside.

"Where is he?"

He gestured upstairs. "The room you guys used before."

I ran upstairs and met him halfway. Mason's eyes went wide as he saw me, but he didn't say a word. He caught me on the stairs, lifted me in the air, and turned right around. I couldn't take my eyes off of him. I drank in the sight of him.

My hand touched the side of his face, where it was rough with stubble, and I breathed out, "You look so damn good."

He groaned and looked down with a soft smile. "You too." Then we were inside the room. He kicked the door shut behind him and sank onto the bed with me. His lips fused onto mine, and I gasped. I arched up against him as I clung to him, and my legs wrapped around his waist.

I was starving for him. I was ready to explode before he even touched me, but when he did, I shoved him back and scrambled on top of him. It wasn't long after that when he flipped me back over and we both groaned as he slid inside of me.

When he moved to thrust in and out, my head fell back on the pillow. I was intoxicated with the feel of him. I would never get enough of him, but for now, for the next two hours, I would try.

CHAPTER SEVEN

After we made love a second time, I got up from the bed and started to pick up my clothes.

Mason shifted on the bed. "What are you doing?"

"I have to go back."

"Come on. They're not going to arrest you for running away. I called someone I know in law school. He doesn't even think they can do that."

"No, but they can have you arrested for statutory rape," I snapped at him but stopped and gulped as I saw his eyes widen. He jumped out of the bed and came towards me. I shook my head as I held up my hands. "Don't. I have to go back. I shouldn't have even come over."

"Hey, hey."

"Stop, Mason." I shrugged off his hand. But then my head jerked back up. "Did you get a new phone number?"

"What?"

"Your number's been disconnected."

"Are you serious?" He crossed to his jeans and pulled out his phone, and then he scrolled through and tried to call me. Nothing.

"Logan's too."

He tried calling a few others and cursed. "What the hell? My phone's dead." Then he groaned. "I can't believe this. He killed our phones. Shit." But there was another emotion there. Mason chuckled a second later as he shook his head. "That was a good move."

My mouth dropped. "Good move?" I took two steps, grabbed his phone and threw it against the wall. My chest was heaving as the fury churned deep in me. "This isn't chess, Mason. I couldn't call you. I freaked out tonight—I had a nightmare and I—" I couldn't talk about it. I didn't want to.

"Hey." His voice dropped to a soothing note. Then his hands were next. They touched my shoulders gently.

I stiffened and twisted away from him. He didn't get it. He didn't get it at all. "This isn't a vacation, Mason. My mom's not normal anymore—"

He snorted. "Was she ever?"

He didn't understand. He wouldn't. He hadn't lived with her when she—I closed my eyes. No. I wouldn't think of it. But the nightmare came back to me. All that blood. I shivered as I felt transported back to that time, in that hallway, as I pushed the door open and saw her.

"Sam!"

"What?" I was jerked back as Mason shook my shoulders. When I clicked back to our reality, I had to blink a few times to clear my eyes. He'd gone pale and he looked shaken. "What?" I missed something. I could tell.

He cursed. "Don't ever do that again."

"Do what?"

"You checked out, like you went somewhere else. You scared the crap out of me." His hand shook as he pulled me close to him and cradled my head to his chest. His head tucked down against mine as he tried to soothe me, or maybe himself.

I pulled away to collect my purse. "I have to go. I have to be back before she finds me gone."

He snorted again, but followed me downstairs and to my car. When I slipped inside, he knelt beside the window.

"Mason, I *have* to go."

Panic was starting to seep in. He just didn't get it.

"I know." Irritation flashed over his face. "Look, how do I see you? I'm not following these stupid rules. Forget it."

"She'll have you arrested—"

He rolled his eyes. "No, she won't. I know my dad. He won't allow that."

I shook my head. "Mason, you didn't hear my mom. She really meant it. She'll do it without his approval. He might not even know about it, but I know she'll do it. Something's happened to my mom. She's not the same anymore. She's how she used to be—" I bit off my words. Again. It was best if no one knew how she had been. They wouldn't know how to handle her. They didn't know how to handle her now.

Then I felt his eyes on me. They were seeing through me like they always had. Everything was going to be ruined. I felt it in my bones. She was going to ruin everything.

"Look, I love you. I won't let her do anything, okay? How do I see you?"

I shrugged, but I needed to go. It was five in the morning. James would be up soon. He was the early riser in the family. I had thirty minutes and it took me over twenty to drive there. "I have to go!"

"Okay, okay."

He jerked away from the car and I pushed down the accelerator. My car shot out of there. On the drive there, I gripped onto the steering wheel with white knuckles. I could barely breathe. Every light seemed to turn red when I got there. Curses slipped from me as I fought myself from tearing through the lights. It wasn't the worry of safety since traffic wasn't too bad, but I couldn't risk the chance of getting a ticket. Then they'd know. My mom would know.

As soon as I pulled into the driveway, I sprinted to the basement area and slid in through the bottom door. Then I let loose a huge breath. My hands were trembling, but I tried to be as silent as I could as I made my way up the back steps to my room.

When I got to my room, I couldn't calm down. Panic rose within me. My arms still shook. I tried crawling into Mason's bed. That didn't help either. There was a ball at the bottom of my stomach. It was twisting and churning, rolling over and over. The unease in me was burning up and all my emotions were fuel to its fire. It was lit and as I tried to ignore it, the flame built and built. Finally, I threw back the covers and went to my room for my running clothes. As soon as my sneakers were on and my earbuds were in, I bolted from the house. Everything inside of me was ablaze so I pushed hard in my run.

After an hour, the panic was still in me. It was slick and slimy. It crawled all over my body and I couldn't get rid of it. So I pushed harder. Another hour went by, but I was still feverish. My heart was pounding as the fear acted as a poison. It sent everything into hyperdrive. I was soaked in a cold sweat an hour after that. Then my hands started to tingle, but I continued to go faster. I felt something at my heels. I could hear Analise's voice. She chased me as I was now sprinting down the street. No matter how far I went, how fast I went, I couldn't outrun her. And then I collapsed.

I fell to the ground on someone's front lawn. My arms and legs were spread out and my chest heaved up and down. My pulse pounded throughout my body. It was one solid *thumpthumpthump*. I felt it all the way through my toes.

I couldn't move so I remained there and stared at the sky. The sun had risen a few hours ago, but the sounds of the morning were just starting. I should've moved. I looked like a crazy woman, but I couldn't. My limbs had turned off and refused to listen to my brain. I knew to get up, but my heart said to stay still.

I kept breathing. My chest rose up and down. The sick panic in my gut never went away, but I gulped breath after breath and I tried to numb it down.

"Sam?"

Oh god.

My eyes closed as I recognized that voice. I couldn't face him, not like this.

The sound of his car hit me like a cold wave. His tires moved slowly over the gravel on the road as he pulled to the side. Then his engine turned off and I gulped. I knew what was happening. When his door opened and closed, I needed to face facts. He was coming over. He was going to see the near-hysteria on me and he was going to ask questions.

Everything clenched inside of me. Then, as my body lifted up by its own accord, I looked at him with grave eyes. At the sight of him, freshly showered, with a pair of jeans and a tight tee shirt, everything went dead inside of me.

He was everything I was not.

He was the golden boy of a rich private school. He was gorgeous. He had talent. He was the football quarterback, most popular and most wanted guy in our school. He had it all. I had none of it.

I took a gaping breath and tried to remember who I had become, but it didn't matter. In that moment there was no Mason, there was no Logan. Not even Nate. They'd been stripped from me, and I was the same as I always wanted to deny before. I was the unwanted child to a hustler. My mother. I never wanted to admit it, but it was the truth. She had loved someone else, became pregnant with me, and hustled a stand-up guy to marry her. Enter David Strattan. He raised me, loved me—or so I thought—and loved my mother. Then came the time when she found another con, another one that fell in love with her, a better one—wealthier one—than David Strattan.

It was hard to swallow.

Adam crossed the street now, but I couldn't stop the thoughts racing in my head.

I was nothing. I had always been nothing. My mother tolerated me because I came from her. I felt like her. I felt like I had conned Mason into loving me. I had conned Logan into protecting me, but it was all a lie. If they saw inside of me—how I was the dirty spawn from my mother—would they still stand by me?

Adam's foot stepped onto the lawn where I sat.

I swallowed everything down. All the gravity, all the deadness, all the truth. Down it went, and I blinked at him, back to the shell I projected to everyone.

"It is you." He blinked in confusion. "Are you okay?"

I pushed it down so fast that I could almost pretend it was never there. I grinned up at him and grimaced at the same time. "I'm a mess, but yeah. I'm fine."

He shared my grin. The corner of his lip curved up to his cheek and a dimple showed. "I'm not going to disagree with you. One of those mornings, huh?"

My stomach dropped. My smile stayed the same. "Where are you headed?"

"Uh." He scanned up and down the street, but then shrugged before he dropped down to sit next to me. He drew up his knees in the same way I sat. His arms hung from them as he looked casual and relaxed. "To tell you the truth, I was going on a date."

"A date?" On a Tuesday morning?

"Yeah." His head ducked down in a sheepish manner. "It's my mom's idea to help fix her marriage."

I blinked at him. "Come again?"

He grimaced and rolled his eyes. "I know. It's stupid." Then he groaned as his head fell between his knees. "I can't believe I'm even doing this."

"How is your date going to fix her marriage?"

"Gawd, I have no idea. I really have no idea, but it's my mom's latest project. She likes to focus on everybody else's life rather than her own."

His head shot up and bitterness flashed over him. I expected it to go away the next second, but it stayed. Then I sat farther up. This wasn't the Adam who was angry at me because I was dating Mason. This was the friend I once thought I had.

He added, "He didn't come home last night so, of course, when I got up for basketball practice this morning she had already called a friend of hers whose daughter just moved here. I'm supposed to meet this Felicia girl at the Country Club." A hollow laugh escaped him. "And she timed it as the perfect excuse so I could 'teach' the girl how to play tennis at the exact same time my dad always has a match. I bet we're even on the next court from him." He shook his head, raking a hand through his hair. "I'm supposed to spy for her."

"She said that?"

"No, but she'll want to know everything about the 'date' and by date, I mean my dad's match." He glanced over and quirked an eyebrow up. "Did I tell you that my dad's been playing one of his executive assistants at matches? And she's got the boobs, the ass, the tan—everything for her to be a younger version of my mom?"

"You think he's trying to replace her?"

His arms dropped off his knees and he stood. His jaw clenched as he looked away from me. "I have no idea, but that's what my mom thinks. From the screaming she was doing on the phone earlier, I don't think she even cares who hears her anymore. Hell. She might already be playing the custody card. I wouldn't put it past her."

"What do you mean?" But I knew. This was something my mother would've done as well, but I had to admit that my mom was better. She would've been two steps ahead of Adam's dad.

"Playing the sympathy card so my little sis will take her side. I know my little brother already thinks my dad's an asshole."

"Isn't he?"

His shoulders slumped suddenly. A defeated breath left him. "Yeah, but I keep hoping he'll prove me wrong." He glanced down. "I'll never be like him, Sam."

"Why are you telling me this?"

"Because I have to say it out loud. I have to say it to someone so that it's real to me. My dad won't ever change. I know he's having an affair, but it isn't with his tennis partner."

"Who then?"

He looked away. His mouth flattened. "Does it matter? He's going to leave her and she knows it. Do you know what that does to our family? What it's like to live in that? It's like living in a war zone, but no one wants to admit that they could get shot any second.

I hate it." The same bitterness came out again. "I hate him. I hate her. Who would put up with that?"

I shot to my feet. Unnerved at the honesty from him and how exposed he revealed himself to me, I burst out, "Why are you telling me this? You dropped our friendship two months ago."

His mouth curved into a frown. His voice grew soft. "Because I was the asshole to you that I see my dad being to my mom every day. I'm sorry. I know you wanted my friendship. Hell, you needed my friendship. I knew that and I hurt you because you hurt me."

"You knew about Mason—"

He shot back, "That didn't mean I wanted to. I waited so long for you, Sam, and then you got scooped up by him." An ugly laugh wrung out from him. "That was a hard thing to swallow. I hate that guy." I opened my mouth, but his hand shot up. "Let me finish."

I closed it.

"I always thought the Kades were assholes. I still do, but I can't deny what I've seen with my own two eyes. They're good to you. They care about you, and he loves you. I see it in his eyes. He watches you when you have no idea he's even in the room. It's sickening to watch at times, but it's there and I have to deal with it. I hurt you, and I'm sorry for that."

I closed my eyes. Mason watched me when I didn't know it? That same familiar flutter came back in my stomach but tripled. I tried to hold back the smile that wanted to come out. Mason did love me, despite who my mother was.

"And I'm sorry about Becky. I lied to her so she wouldn't be your friend again. I already told her the truth and she's pissed with me, but she's scared of reaching out to you. She's embarrassed."

"What did you lie about?"

"I told her that you were using her because you had no other friends. I told her that you laughed at her behind her back a few times and that you looked down on her."

I gaped at him. Outrage was starting to boil inside of me.

He held up a hand in surrender. "I know. I know. I'm sorry. I really am and I'm going to make everything right. I will." His eyes held his promise. "I saw a counselor two weeks ago, and she said a few things that resonated. For me not to become like my dad, I actually have to *not* do the same things that he does. So I'm done lying. I won't lie to you anymore. I promise."

Why was he saying all these things? Not now, not when Mason had been taken from me and I was alone. But Becky—my heart sank at the lies he told her. If I was in her place, I might've done the same thing and gone away. Who wanted a friend who thought they were better than them?

"Can we be friends again, Sam?"

I expelled a ragged breath. A sense of doom started to settle, but I found myself nodding.

"You won't regret this."

I already did.

Adam visited with me a little bit more, but I had a hard time hearing his words. My mind was reeling as so much had changed in the last twenty-four hours. Mason and Logan had been ripped away. Adam and maybe Becky had come back in. And where was I?

When he left for his date, he was late but had a bright grin on his face. I finished my run back home. I felt raw. I felt exposed and vulnerable to anyone at that moment, but then I stopped in my tracks when I came to the house.

A security van was parked in our driveway. A man was kneeling at the door as I walked past him to the kitchen. There were two more focused on something on the wall. Analise stood with another who must've been their boss. He held the clipboard and was nodding as she gestured around the room.

Then she saw me. A dark smile came to her face. "Good morning, honey. I saw your sneakers were gone so I guessed you had gone on a run."

I gulped against the gloating in her eye. "What are they doing?"

She lifted a shoulder. "Oh, nothing much, honey. Nothing for you to worry about." Then her smile turned into a triumphant smirk. "They're installing a new security system."

My heart dropped. The cold sweat was back.

"We'll have security cameras in the house now."

CHAPTER EIGHT

I couldn't email Mason.

I couldn't call Mason.

I definitely couldn't see Mason.

By the afternoon, I was a caged animal: prowling my room, pacing back and forth, walking in circles, and snarling to myself.

So I did what I always did, I went running for the second time that day. Except this time my body was sluggish, my legs felt like lead, and I had a hard time pushing my demons at bay. After an hour of forcing myself to move faster than a crawl, I gave up and walked. And then I walked some more. After the second hour of walking, I realized that I was in a part of Fallen Crest that I was not familiar. It wasn't the 'bad' section, but it was definitely further than any of the hangouts I frequented.

"Screw you, Brandon! If you sleep with one more girl, there won't be anyone left to help out." A screen door banged shut and a rail-thin girl stood in front of it. She flung her arms back, one with a cigarette, and screamed inside, "I can't do it all alone, you know!"

Her response was a low curse, but she threw her head back in disgust before extending him the middle finger. Then she threw herself onto a metal chair behind the door. Another sat beside it with a bowl of cigarette butts between them. When the girl lit up, she exhaled dramatically and leaned back in the chair. A long pale leg braced on the wire rim that looked like a mini-bonfire container, and she pushed up so her chair rested on the back legs. As she sent out another puff, her eyes opened and then locked on me.

Shit.

I'd been staring the whole time, but I couldn't look away. That would be ridiculous now, like she'd caught me doing a bad thing.

Her hair was a dirty blonde mess. It was greasy, but for some reason it worked on her. It gave her a just-had-the-best-sex look. Her eyes were heavily made up to give her a smoky image, and her lips pursed together as she blew out some more smoke. "Hey, you."

"Yeah?"

"Come here." She waved her little fingers to me, beckoning me over. As I did, she gestured to the chair beside her. "Pop a squat." Then she leaned back again and studied me. After another drag, she narrowed her eyes. "Do I know you? You look familiar."

Everything was tense inside of me. I should've been exhausted. I ran for four hours earlier, followed by a two hour walk. Albeit that it was a slow as molasses walk, but it was still walking. It was movement, anything to keep me from doing something I couldn't do. When I had started out, I almost took my car, but I didn't trust myself in any vehicle. I would turn it around and go to Mason, I'd do it without a thought, and it wouldn't be until after both of us climaxed that I would realize the consequences. He didn't take my mother seriously, but I did. I had to for him or I would lose him.

A stabbing sensation seared through me. No one knew the lengths my mother would go to if she was pushed into a corner. Something had happened to make her feel boxed in. I had no idea what it was, but her true craziness was about to be unleashed.

"Hey!" The girl snapped her fingers in front of my face.

"Oh." I blinked rapidly. "Sorry."

She leaned back again on her chair after she flicked the butt onto the bowl between us. A second one was lit immediately, and she took another drag. "I know I know you. How do I know you?"

I swallowed a knot in my throat. "Do you go to Fallen Crest Academy?"

She snorted before a full-hearted laugh came from her throat. It was a low and raspy laugh. "God no. Thank god. Why? Do you?"

I nodded. "My dad's the football coach."

"No way." Her eyes snapped to attention. "My brother used to play football against them, that was three years ago. He ain't done nothing since—"

"I own this bar, Heather!" A roar came from inside. "I do *too* do crap."

She rolled her eyes. "Like I said, he hasn't done anything except screw my friends and run off ALL MY HELP." Her voice rose so he would hear inside.

She was awarded with another curse, but she chuckled softly as she took another drag from her cigarette. "Anyways, what's your name? Mine's Heather Jax. Idiot inside is Brandon, and my pops owns the diner side of our humble abode inside."

"Humble abode?" It was a run-down dive, and the customers gave me the feeling most had come straight from being incarcerated. The sign out front had the name Manny's scrawled over it in big white lettering on a black background with a green arrow pointed downwards. I'd never seen the place before, but what caught my attention had been Heather's screaming. The longer I sat there, the more a possible scenario played in my head.

She blew out the rest of her second cigarette. As she ground it into the bowl, I expected her to light up a third, but she merely folded back in her chair. Then she frowned and shot forward. "Hold on. Be right back." She was inside in the blink of an eye but back just as quickly with two Coronas. As she sat down and handed one over, she laughed. It was such a deep-throated sound that I knew Logan would've been all about her within seconds of meeting.

"Yeah, I guess you could call this place our humble abode." She shook her head as a wry grin curved a corner of her lip upwards. She tilted the bottle back and took a long drag. "It's ours and ours alone, no goddamn corporation owns it. We run it. Hell, we breathe this place. My mom bought it when I was three, but she took off when I was six. My dad raised us, the three of us, and we help out as much as we can. Brad's off playing football now. He got scouted to play for some big college across the country, but Brandon stayed. He does school online and runs the bar side of things. Dad does the books and I run the diner."

I had yet to take a sip from my beer.

She eyed me, half done with her own. "You sure I don't know you?"

Of course, she knew me. It didn't take a genius for me to realize this girl went to Fallen Crest Public. If she went there, she knew Mason and Logan, and chances were high that she had seen me at a party with them. Everyone went to those parties.

But a sixth sense nagged me. This girl didn't seem to give two cents about who Mason and Logan were. I wondered, no—I worried that she would hold it against me, and I didn't want that. I really didn't want that because as soon as I heard her yelling at her brother I already knew I wanted a job there. I wanted a place to hide from my mother as I tried to stay away from Mason for the month and this would be perfect.

"Are your customers dangerous?" The question slipped out before I realized how stupid that sounded, and offensive. God, what was my problem? "I'm sorry—"

Another deep-throated laugh sounded from her as she threw her head back. Then she finished the rest of her beer and tossed it into the bonfire. "Nah. No, they'd like you to think that, but they're all harmless. The most dangerous is Gus, but it's only because his farts are lethal. He lets them rip all the time."

"Really?"

"Yeah." Fondness lit up her eyes, but they grew serious after a moment. She focused back on me. "Come on, tell me straight. How do I know you?"

I hesitated. But then I went with my gut. She would be more pissed when she found out later, and I knew she would. It was inevitable. "I'm dating Mason Kade." Then I waited. The reaction would vary. She might want to use me, she might kick me out, or…I wasn't sure.

"Well damn then." She shot inside for another beer and clinked it against mine. "You got balls dating that one."

My mouth almost fell down. There was nothing, just…nothing. "I had a feeling you'd for sure send me off after I told you that."

Heather grinned and chuckled as she shook her head. She brushed back a bunch of her hair and yawned a full body yawn as she stretched. Her arms went wide, her chest went out, and her back arched against the metal chair. That's when I knew for sure Logan would've been salivating for the girl. She wore a tight red shirt, ripped at her waist to show off her midriff with a tight pair of washed-out jeans, torn at her knees and the ends. The girl looked like sex on a stick, or that's what Logan would've said.

"Nah." She gave me lopsided grin. "Something tells me you're a smart one and you picked me for a reason, just like I called you over. You want a job here, don't you?"

I did. I really did, but I bit my lip. I didn't know if Mason would approve, but it didn't matter. I needed something, anything to keep me from running to him. And this was the perfect hideout. It would make my mother furious.

"Yes." My confession left me in a rush.

"I saw that right away. It's why I called you over, plus, I've got a feeling that you've got spine if you know what I mean."

I snorted and, for the first time, relaxed into my chair. My hands folded into my lap as I settled more comfortably. "So do I have the job?"

"You ever waitressed before?"

No. "Yes."

"Liar." But she didn't hide the grin on her face. "You're hired. You start tonight?"

So much tension left me in that moment. I couldn't believe it. And I nodded, suddenly choked up for some reason. "Yeah. What time?"

She chewed on her lip as she scanned me up and down again. "The night shift starts in an hour. If you're dating Mason Kade, then that makes you their future stepsister. It's all that some of those wishy-washies talk about so I know that you live at the big fancy mansion of theirs and if you came walking all this way, there's no way you can make it there and back, can you?"

I shook my head and bit my own lip. Would I lose the job?

She jerked a thumb over her shoulder. "That crappy looking house is ours. If you want, you can shower in there. I could spot you some clothes for the shift, and then your fancy boyfriend can give you a ride home tonight? How's that sound?"

Wonderful, but I grimaced. I had no idea how I'd get home. I couldn't call Mason—even if I could reach him, I would end up in his bed tonight. Then it didn't matter. I'd figure something out so I jerked my head in a nod. "Sounds good."

She grunted in an approving sound as she stood. Then she hollered inside, "She's got a boyfriend, Brandon. Hands off."

"Yeah, yeah!" he grumbled back before he shouted a curse to follow.

She flipped him her middle finger, but it was only met with a smattering of laughter from inside. As we headed to their two-story home, she stuffed her hands into her back pocket. Her legs stretched out in a walk that I knew would've had Logan groaning from behind her. Sex on a stick. I tried to hold back my anticipation of introducing the two.

But then I was distracted as she showed me through the front door. The screen door banged open, and she strutted past a living room with two worn-out couches and a television positioned on a stand in the corner. The kitchen was small and sparse. A bare table sat in the dining room with boxes of liquor placed all over. When she noticed my gaze, she shrugged. "Sometimes my dad uses this place for storage. He thinks it's safer than in the bar where a few of our old employees weren't so trustworthy, if you know what I mean."

When I met her gaze, she nodded towards the rickety stairs. "Shower's upstairs. I won't scare you off by making you use Brandon and dad's shower. That whole area of the house is disgusting. Come on. I'll grab you some clothes too."

After she showed me the shower, which was in a bathroom that was clean and decorated in lace and pink, I relaxed a bit. It'd been awhile since I had been at a place that wasn't the lap of luxury. For some reason, this grounded me. I felt more settled, like no one was going to swipe me off my feet and run away laughing. Then I stepped inside the shower and breathed in the smell of lilies. When I used some of her body wash, I held back a grin at the image of Mason's hands on my body. He would've loved the smell on me. He would've loved to lather me with it before he would pull my body back against his. Then his hands would slide to my waist and slip down—

"We don't really have a uniform policy."

My elbow jerked up as Heather tore me from my thoughts. As it banged against the shower, a stabbing pain flooded me, but I bit back a curse.

She fell silent for a second before she cleared her throat. "You okay?" Her voice grew as she must've opened the door and stepped inside. Then she snorted at herself. "I don't even know your name. What is it?"

"Samantha," I called over the water. I hurried to finish rinsing my hair and everything else.

"Oh. Hello again. Mine's Heather. Again." She chuckled again. "I sound like a virgin on her first date with the Hulk. Stupid as shit." But she laughed again. "Anyways, what I was saying before is that we don't really have a uniform policy, but the girls all started wearing jeans and a tee shirt. They liked to show the girls and usually tore off the bottom to show off their stomachs, more tips. We have a lot of regulars, but on the weekends we'll get some rich pricks too. They're usually trying to hide from the wives or girlfriends, but they come around enough. The tips are good."

Rich pricks. I frowned as I wondered if Mason knew of the place.

Heather interrupted my thoughts again. "I put some jeans and shirts on the bed. Take your time washing up; just come down whenever you're done. You were sweating a bunch so I'll make some food too. You're going to need some good sustenance in you to get through the night. There are a few of the other servers that'll be bitches to you, especially if you tell 'em who you're dating." She paused a beat. "Not that I'll say a word. I won't. That's for you to share if you want. Something tells me that you're a bit on the secret side, but to each her own. My brother will go crazy. He loves the Kade boys. He reminisces about when Mason first showed up on their team all the time. You woulda thought that the Lord himself came to save their team from damnation from the way Brandon puts it. Okay, I'll be downstairs. See you in a few."

Brandon knew Mason? The other girls knew them? Then I cursed at myself. Of course they knew them. What the hell had I been thinking? But as I got out of the shower and finished dressing, I headed downstairs to find out because I wasn't going anywhere. This wasn't about Mason and me; this was about my mother and me. My chin locked with determination as I turned the corner and saw Heather in the kitchen. She handed me a plate with a sandwich on it.

Analise might not know it yet, but I was going to make her regret forcing Mason away from me. And getting a job at Manny's was the perfect start to enact some revenge.

CHAPTER NINE

Training that night was easy. The most difficult thing was staying friendly when a few of the customers got *too* friendly, but Heather stepped in and handled those situations. I figured out how to take orders, how to write it down on the pad, and to time when the food would be done for customers. Filling drink orders was easier, but I got frustrated a few times I would get one drink only to have the other customer at the same table decide on something else. Heather chuckled as she watched me get flustered, but she linked elbows at one point and gave the table a polite smile as she took their orders. I would've headed straight to the bar to fill 'em, but she completed another task on her way to the bar.

Multi-tasking was going to be a skill I'd need to learn, but by the end of the night I felt more confident. It helped that Brandon was nice every time I came to him with a question. He took the time to explain the different drinks and always told me not to worry; I would catch on soon enough. By the fourth time he issued that same support, I caught a frown from Heather across the diner. Something told me he hadn't really heard her warning that I was dating someone, but it didn't matter. I wasn't going to date him.

There were two other servers that showed up, both of them were nice, so nice that I wondered about Heather's warning from before. That was until the nine o'clock girl showed up. Her name was Gia and she would've been elated to reign with the Elite at my school. She had platinum blonde hair, manufactured boobs, and an outfit that barely covered her. A swimsuit might've covered more, but she was the shot girl as Heather explained. It was to be expected.

By the end of the night, I felt ready to do an entire shift on my own. Heather had cut me down to handling a few tables on my own. My feet killed, but I hoped it had more to do with my four hour run and the two of walking. And with that thought, I should've called Coach Grath back that day, but when I saw Heather earlier, I put it off. I would call him the next day and my training would start in the mornings since Heather told me that she needed me every night during break. I would get every other Thursday off, along with the opposite Tuesdays when school would start again. When I asked about the weekends, she assured me that I would want them.

After cleaning up, when everyone left, I was faced with a dilemma.

I had no way home.

I had my phone, but no number to call Mason even if I wanted to. I never got Nate's number and Logan's line had been disconnected as well. They would have no clue to come get me so I was left with one choice.

I called Adam.

He pulled into the parking lot within ten minutes, dressed in a green polo and khaki cargo pants. As I got a whiff of his pine cologne, I asked if he'd been on a date. Even his hair looked styled to perfection. He gave me an odd look, but shook his head. He had been at a party.

No surprise there.

When he asked if I wanted to go, I declined. Then he said the magic words. "It's at Nate Monson's house."

Oh god.

My stomach flipped over and my eyes closed. A girl could only have so much self-discipline. I already knew my decision when I braced myself. "Would you do me a favor?"

"Sure."

Then I asked for the impossible. "Come to my house with me and tell my mom that I'm hanging out with you and your friends only."

He flashed me a grin. "Your mom's not handling your relationship very well?"

"Try not at all." I held my tongue on the threats, the ultimatums, and what was actually at stake. I shouldn't be going, but I couldn't stop myself. One day. Only one day and I was already folding under the need to see him.

But, as it turned out, my mother was ecstatic to see Adam. She gushed about his father, and then asked how his mother was. The two had lunch plans the next day at the country club. When I expressed my concern that his mom might tell Analise where he'd actually been the night before, Adam assured me not to worry.

He rolled his eyes at me. "My mom has no idea what I do. We're not close, remember?"

I relaxed. I did remember, and I noticed how his hands tightened around the steering wheel. His knuckles were white by the time he pulled into Nate's massive driveway. But then I stopped paying attention to Adam when I saw how many cars were lined up and down the driveway. I couldn't count them, they covered his entire yard and they had still parked down the street. This party was massive. Hell, forget massive—this party was gigantic. My eyes were just as huge as I gazed over the crowd. They were everywhere, by the cars, roaming the driveway, on the road even. Adam had to slow down as he waited for a group to get out of the way. When they didn't, he touched his horn lightly and they moved to the side.

"I thought the last party was huge, but this one…" Oh my god.

"Yeah, Peter texted me that he saw people from seven different schools here." Adam shrugged. "Its winter break and it's the Kades, with Monson." He glanced over. "But you'd know all about that."

Yeah, I would. A small tingle sparked from the anticipation. Then I frowned. Peter—I cringed. That mean the Elite would be there, but of course they'd be there. Everyone was there. "Peter's here?"

He nodded.

That meant that Miranda was too. She had been dating Peter before she fell hook, line, and sinker for Logan. I tensed as I remembered the past few months. The Elite crowd at my school tried to use me to pull Mason and Logan into their group. More than a few times Logan had laughed in their faces. Miranda had referred to him as a manwhore and any girl who fell for him was a slut. So she looked like the fool when he turned his charms on her. It took one party, only one party, and she was walking around with his shirt on the next morning.

Logan dated her for a month. He had been persuaded to date her to protect me since she was the Queen Bee at my school and she made a few threats of making my life hell. If she was connected to Logan, she'd be happy and she wouldn't continue to go after me. But that hadn't been the real reason. That had only been the spin put on it so he would follow through with Mason's plan.

The real reason that Mason wanted Logan to date Miranda was to humiliate her. He knew if she started dating Logan, she would look like a hypocritical bitch. And she had. The rest of the Elite group revoked her role as their leader. She had condemned all the other girls for sleeping with Logan, only to dump her boyfriend of three years for him in one night?

The whole situation left me feeling uneasy. Logan had been used and he still didn't know it.

Mason wanted to hurt Miranda, but only Nate and I knew the real motivation behind it. Miranda pushed a button that Mason knew could've threatened his relationship with his brother. Me. There'd been another girl Logan had loved, really loved, who used him to get closer to Mason. Then I came into their lives. I fell in love with Mason, but he worried that Logan had feelings for me as well. When Miranda taunted him that he got the girl Logan really wanted, Mason nipped that threat in the bud. That was the real reason he had Nate convince Logan to screw her for a month.

Everything went off without a hitch.

Miranda's friends lost respect for her. Logan thought he was protecting me and Mason knew he wouldn't have to worry about Miranda anymore.

It left a sour taste in my mouth.

And then Adam dropped the last bomb. "Yeah, and I guess some of the Kades' cousins are here too. They brought half of the party with them when they showed with Logan."

"Logan's here?" I jerked forward in my seat. My heart started racing. Logan was here. Mason was here. This party was too big for any parent not to know about. I had to get out of there. "Stop. Stop the car."

"What—wait!"

It was too late.

He slowed for another group of people that crossed the driveway and I shot out of there. I had no idea what I was doing or where I was going, but I started to run towards the road. My heart was pounding; it was a solid thump in my ears. The same panic started again, it threatened to choke me, but I kept going.

I was distantly aware of Adam calling my name, but I kept going.

"Hey, whoa!" A husky chuckle sounded next to me as I tore through a group. An arm snaked in front of my chest. As I ran into it, I started to fall, but a strong arm curled into my waist and I was lifted before I fell to the ground. I was held against a massive chest, but I gulped as I saw Heather through a haze in my eyes.

She'd been laughing before. I saw the small lines still around the corners of her lips, but she grew serious as she saw my fear. My chest kept heaving up and down and I clawed at the arm that held me in place. He grunted behind me. "Damn, Heather. She's going to make me bleed."

"Hold her still, Norm!" Heather snapped at him. She softened her voice and brushed some of my hair out of my eyes. "Hey, hey. What's going on? What's wrong? What happened between here and Manny's?"

"You know this chick, Heather?" A different voice chimed in.

She gave him a dirty look over her shoulder. "Yeah, so shut your pie-hole. She's my friend."

"She's Kade's bitch. Drop her, Norm."

"Shut up, Channing!" She gave Norm a look over my shoulder. "You drop her and I will rip your balls off tonight after you've passed out. She's my friend."

The arm tightened around me. A deep voice rumbled through the chest that held me. "I don't know, Heather. I don't want to mess with the Kades. They might be rich pricks, but they don't mess around."

"They're not preps, Heather." That same voice argued from the side. It was low and full of warning. "You might like the girl, but she's theirs. We shouldn't even be here. I knew it was a stupid idea to come."

Heather's eyes snapped in irritation before she twisted back around. "There are no other parties. This one is it. Besides, we're not doing anything wrong. I know this girl and she's scared. I want to know what happened—"

"And if it's because the Kades did something to her? What then?" the guy mused. He didn't sound threatened, just reasonable. "She's not our problem. You're not sticking your neck out for her."

Her mouth dropped, ready to fight back—

He spoke over her, "I don't care. You're not pulling us into a fight against them and I won't let them hurt you. If it comes to it, we're walking away. All of us. You too."

"Channing," she seethed.

As she turned back, the haze had dissipated enough so I could think a bit clearer. I could also see clearer, and the guy who had been speaking was tall and lean. He had a model's face, but his body was covered in tattoos. The simple black tee shirt that he wore didn't hide the muscular build he had despite his lean physique. And I'd been right. There was no fear in his dark eyes, but he was wary. As he gazed down at Heather in front of him, there was also concern.

The plan I had to introduce her to Logan was gone now. I didn't know the story between those two, but she wasn't single. As I thought about it, I never asked if she had a boyfriend or not. I'd been so focused on keeping my own love life to myself.

"Norm." The guy sent him a pointed look. "Drop her."

"Don't—" Heather gasped.

But the arm abruptly released me and down I went. I caught myself before I fell all the way and choked from the sudden oxygen I could now breathe. When I looked up, with tears in my eyes, I saw that the guy who'd been holding me could've been a bodybuilder. He was a giant, but he gave me a timid smile. "Sorry about that. He said drop so I dropped."

I nodded as I still coughed from all the air. "No problem."

Heather glared at him before she touched my arm. "Hey, you okay, hon? What had you so spooked before?"

I shook my head. I couldn't tell anyone about it.

"Sam?"

It didn't matter now.

I turned and stared at Mason, who stood a few feet from the group. His hands were clenched in fists. There was no one behind him. He had come alone. His eyes never left mine, but I felt the sudden question in his depths.

I didn't think. I couldn't.

I ran toward him and he caught me as I threw myself at him. His arms felt like home as he held me against his chest and I breathed him in. My legs wrapped around his waist. When his hand brushed my hair back and he kissed my forehead, I burrowed into him. I couldn't have been anywhere else.

We were both going to hell.

CHAPTER TEN

Still enveloped in Mason's arms, I felt him look over his shoulder. "It's fine. I'll take care of her."

"You sure? She freaked." Adam's voice sounded far away.

I sucked in my breath as his hand ran down my face and arm. I didn't want the moment to end. I wanted to make it last as long as it could because when the real world came back, I knew there would be consequences, serious consequences, and I couldn't think about them now. The damage was done. I was already in his arms. My mom said not to see him and I had already broken that rule once.

"Yeah, she's fine." Mason's voice had a rough edge to it.

"Who's she scared of?"

I held my breath again as Heather joined the conversation.

Mason stiffened beneath me. He hated explaining himself. I lifted my head this time and looked at her. Slowly, but too fast for my liking, I moved so I could slide back to my feet. Mason kept his arms around me. He anchored me against his chest.

I met Heather's gaze and saw the concern in them. Something flickered in my gut. "My mom."

"Sam—"

I ignored him. "She's made threats if—"

Mason's arms swung me back up. He started walking back to the house immediately.

"Hey! Wait!"

He threw over his shoulder, "It's none of your damn business, Jax. Leave her alone."

"It is my business! She's my friend."

"Since when?"

I looked over his shoulder and shook my head. I didn't want her to tell him about my job. That was for me to do. As she saw the plea on my face, the words died in her throat. Mason kept going. When he went a few more steps, I saw the other guy grab Heather's arm. He pulled her back to their group, but then Mason carried me past Adam and as he fell into step behind us, he blocked her from me.

When we went into the mansion, the music tripled in volume. I felt the bass through the floors, through Mason as he swept up the stairs and towards our room. Our room. An excited shudder left me as I thought about the sanctuary of that room. It'd just be me and him...and Adam as he followed us inside.

Mason turned back, still holding me. "Dude."

"I just want to know that she's alright. I picked her up outside some bar tonight."

"You what?" He whipped his head to me and lowered me to the ground. "You were at a bar?"

Adam added, "Alone."

"You were *alone* at a bar tonight?"

I opened my mouth, ready to explain everything when the door was thrown open. Logan strolled in with a charming smile on his face and his arms spread wide. He snapped his fingers on both hands and bowed to us. "I've got it all fixed, Sam. You don't have to do anything your mother says."

I closed my mouth.

Mason groaned.

Adam spoke up, "Huh?"

Logan twisted around, frowning. "Dude, what the hell are you doing here?"

Adam had drawn to his fullest height, but his frown turned into a glower. His eyes took on a mean glint as he clipped his head towards me in a nod. "I'm the one who brought her here. I'm the one who lied to her mother for you. So I'm thinking I have some goddamn right to hear what the hell is going on."

Logan's brows furrowed together as his lips puckered. "You what?" He twisted around to me. "He what?"

I sighed, moving away from Mason's shelter, and crossed my arms over my chest. My stomach was in knots, but maybe Adam had a point? I had a feeling I would need more of him before this month was over. "Maybe he should hear all of this?"

"No—" Logan started.

Mason finished, "NO!"

I drew in a deep breath. Both of them already looked infuriated, but then the door opened again. Nate strolled in with a case of beer. He started to shut the door, but a hand shot through and slapped it back. Two heads popped in, grinning with red cheeks and glazed eyes. They had the same hair, brown and wavy like Logan's, and each of them had similar dimples in both cheeks. Wait—they were mirror images of each other.

Mason groaned, "Not now, you guys."

One of them ignored him and strode inside. His hand was stretched out as he marched towards me. His mouth was set in place with determination and he stopped before me. "Will Leighton." He slapped a hand on his brother's shoulder, who had followed close behind. Both had wide smiles on their faces. "This here's my brother James."

"James?"

He giggled as Will's smile became blinding. "It's a family name. Don't hold it against him."

"The ladies call me Jamison. Works better on their panties. Gets 'em a lot wetter, don't know why. Only the cousins call me James still." The other brother stuck his hand out as well.

I looked at both of their hands, held steady and waiting.

"Well?" the first prompted. "Mason's being grouchy and I know he's two seconds away from punching me, but I'd rather shake your hand first. We've heard a lot about you—"

Jamison giggled again. "Not anything good. Our moms are sisters."

Will nudged him in the chest with his shoulder. He moved him back a step. "Don't mind, James. He takes up for our mom. Not me. I've got Logan's back. And he's got yours so if you need anything from me or idiot here, you don't hesitate a second."

"Okay." Mason started to step forward, but Jamison shot a hand out to stop him.

"No, no, cousin dear. We're going. We know this is family meeting time, though you know Logan will spill it all to us later."

Will barked out a laugh, following his brother to the door. "Yeah, over a case of Guinness and soggy trousers by the pool."

Logan frowned. "That was one time. You assholes pushed me in. I couldn't take both of you."

Jamison threw an arm around his brother's shoulders. They turned so they were facing us and backed out of the room. "You were sniveling like a brokenhearted girl. And we have to take advantage every time Mase isn't with you."

Will shot his fist in the air. "And we'd do it again!"

"Out!" Mason strode to them, pushing them through the doorway before he slammed it shut.

There was a moment of silence before they knocked on the door and shouted, "Sniveling like a girl, Logan." The other howled in laughter. "Soggy trousers! Can't forget the soggy trousers."

Mason pounded on the door. "Leave!" Then he waited until the giggling faded.

Adam shook his head, perplexed. "Who the hell were those guys?"

"Idiots," Mason and Logan said at the same time.

Nate tossed a beer to both of them and popped open his own as he studied Adam with narrowed eyes. "They're cousins. What are you doing here?"

Adam drew in a deep breath. His shoulders lifted, his chest rose, and the tendons in his neck stretched. He was ready to explode, but I stepped forward. I held my hand out to stop any more interrogation. "He helped me out, okay? That's why he's here."

"Sam." Mason stepped closer to me. "Remember what he did to you."

Reality sunk in.

Adam snarled, "You're such a jerk. I'm trying to be her friend. I'm trying to—"

Mason had him against the wall in the next second. He growled at him, "I already told you what I'd do to you if you wouldn't stay away from her. Now you're trying this angle? Friendship?"

He struggled against his hold, but it didn't matter. With a cold mask over him, Mason looked lethal. He clipped out, "You turned her friends against her. I don't know what you've done to get her to forgive you, but it's not going to work. I won't let you screw her over again."

Nate and Logan wore similar expressions and as Adam looked around the room, the fight left him. He swallowed before his shoulders slumped down in defeat. Then he turned to me, but the damage was done.

I remembered. He had lied and pushed a friend away. He wanted to punish me because I wouldn't date him, and now after one afternoon where he apologized, I was ready to take him back into my world of friendship? I was nuts.

But he lied to my mom for me. He had the power to take back his words and my night would be blown. I swallowed painfully. He had the power to send Mason to jail. He couldn't do that. I couldn't let him do that. When I looked up and caught Mason's gaze, I knew he saw the fear on my face. I couldn't mask it. My hands started to tremble. I couldn't lose him.

Mason made the decision for all of us. "You're going to leave, Quinn. You're not going to say a word about any of this to anyone. If you want to try the friendship angle, fine. Help out. Be a pal to her. But if I get wind that you're working a different angle, I *will* follow through. Now, this is family only. We appreciate that you brought her here, but you're not welcome any further."

Logan grunted in agreement.

Adam gazed around the room with a soft plea. "Look, I care about her too. I won't do anything to hurt her."

Nate decided to speak up, "Yeah, well, you've hurt her enough. We all know it."

Shocked, I whipped my gaze to him. He had a serious look in his eye, threatening even as he stared Adam down. Then Adam stuffed his hands in his front pockets. His demeanor was submissive, but his next words lashed out in a snarl. "Family only? You got a screwed up family."

I sucked in my breath. Closing my eyes, I wanted to bang my head against a wall. Why had he gone there?

Logan flared up, but Mason grabbed Adam's arm and yanked it behind him. As he fell to the ground with a panicked scream, Mason twisted his arm and started to clench his fist around one of Adam's. His screams grew and he began to tremble on the ground.

"I told you what I would do," Mason warned, looking calm and cold.

Adam's screams cut off and a sob started deep from his throat. He began weeping instead as he pounded the floor with his free hand. He cried out, "I'll sue you. I'll sue all of you—"

Nate stepped forward. He was the closest to me and drew me behind him. Then he spoke in a quiet voice, "You already took her friend from her."

His sobs grew and an inhumane shriek came next. I could hear him struggling underneath Mason's hold.

Logan pulled me into his chest. He wrapped his arms around me and blanketed my head into his chest. He held his other hand over my ear.

Nate continued and I could still hear him. The softness of his voice sent chills down my back. "You keep saying that you want to be her friend, but you're hurting her. You're not hurting us. We don't care if you like us or if you sue us, but she does. Be the man you keep thinking you are." He stopped as he let his words settle for a second. "Taking her friend from her, that's what a coward does. It makes you look pitiful."

I didn't know how they knew about Becky, but I wasn't surprised they did. And Nate was right. I never would have done that to him.

There was silence for awhile. Everyone was eerily still. The room was already thick with tension, but now a different danger filled it. I closed my eyes. They could hurt him. If they really wanted to, they could do it. I didn't want them to hurt him. Adam could hurt Mason back. And then I heard Adam choke out, "Sam. Please. I'm sorry. I am. I—"

Relief flooded me.

"That's enough," Mason remarked, so calm while the anger simmered within him. It gave him a brutal edge that would've terrified me if I didn't know him from the inside out. I closed my eyes as I heard him saying something in a softer tone to Adam. I couldn't make out the words, but a sudden need to be in his arms surged over me. I needed his shelter.

"Leave."

My head jerked up. Logan's eyes glimmered in fury as his hand had dropped from my ear. It was curled into a fist now. His jaw was clenched tight. "Leave, man. Forget whatever the hell my brother's saying to you. Leave her alone. I mean it. If you don't, I'll pound your ass and send you to the hospital."

"Logan." Mason stepped away from Adam, but he kept a hand to one of his shoulders to hold him in place.

"What?" Logan jerked his gaze to his brother's. "You're going to let him go with that? Are you kidding me? He hurt Samantha, we all know it. Whatever the hell he said to that girl did the deed. We all know she stopped being friends with her. She doesn't have any friends anymore and it's because of this piece of crap. We pissed him off so he hurt Sam instead. You're damn straight that I want to beat the shit out of him. Let me at him. If he tries to sue us, he's gonna have to sue all of us. Four against one. If he's smart, he'll take the beating and keep his mouth shut."

Mason was torn. His one hand jerked in reaction and I knew he wanted to do what Logan was threatening, but then he caught my gaze. We both remembered the other bomb my mom could drop on us and Adam held a part of his life in his hands. If my mom knew I was here, she'd go to the police. She would file for statutory rape and Mason would be found guilty. Everyone knew he had sex, everyone knew that he had sex with me. If Mason was found guilty, who knew how long the damages could last for him, for us.

I jerked away from Logan. Adam had apologized. Why couldn't he have let it alone?

Then Logan continued to add to my nightmare.

He turned to me, his eyes pleading. "I talked to some people, Sam. Nothing will happen to you. So what if you get arrested as a runaway? Nothing happens the first time and the second time," he rolled his eyes. "You might get house arrest. That'd be drawn out in court, longer than a month. You can do whatever you want and your mom can't do a thing to you. You don't need to be indebted to this trash."

But the statutory rape charges would hold.

I drew in a shuddering breath. I hadn't talked to a lawyer, but I had a good feeling those charges could hold for a long time, longer than the month before I was an adult.

"Runaway?" Adam asked.

Mason turned to him. "Shut up."

Then Nate moved forward. A look of disgust twisted his features as he grabbed Adam and dragged him to the door. When he opened it, he clipped out, "You say a goddamn thing, and you'll regret it. By the time we're done with you, you'd be getting off easy with a pounding. Trust me. We've done worse to people for less."

Adam opened his mouth, but Nate shoved him out and slammed the door in his face. When he surveyed the room again, he slumped against the door. His head leaned back and he heaved a deep sigh.

I looked at Mason and found his eyes on mine. A look of vulnerability flashed over him. I shot forward and pulled him against me. His head dropped to my shoulder. Swallowing a knot, this was my fault. If he went to jail, it would be because of me. I couldn't let that happen. No matter what, no matter what I had to do, I was going to make this right. My eyes closed and despair swept over me. I'd have to go to my mom. I'd have to do what she wanted, anything, but she couldn't hurt Mason that way. No way.

"Why do I get the feeling something else is going on?" Logan pulled me back to the room. He raked a hand over his face and shook his head. "What the hell is going on?"

Nate and I both looked at Mason. It was his decision. He was the leader and it was his life, but when his head fell down my gut flared. He was going to lie. I knew it and I held my breath as I heard him mutter, "Nothing's going on, but it'll go on her record, Logan."

"What? Come on—"

Mason's head snapped back up and his eyes were inflamed. "Leave. It. I mean it. She could get arrested and that'll be on her record, for life, Logan. Drop it."

"But—"

"I mean it!" His voice raised an octave.

Then Logan threw his arms up. A litany of curses spewed from his mouth as he shook his head. "This is bullshit. We don't have to play by their rules. So what if it'll go on her record. She can fight it. She's not running away. This is such a load of crap—"

Then Nate spoke up, "It's not your call, Logan."

"What?" He swung around. A snarl was fixed on his features and his chest heaved up and down.

Nate faced him squarely. His gaze never faltered, he never blinked. "It's not your call. This has nothing to do with you."

"I got shipped off because of it. This is my brother. She's my—"

"It's their relationship. It's her life, it's her mother. They eliminated you from the equation because you support them, but right now you might be hurting them more than helping."

"But—"

"Stop!" A whisper escaped my lips. I couldn't hear any more of it. I couldn't bear it. I clapped my hands over my ears and turned away from everyone. "Stop, please."

I could only hear myself breathing. I was panting, not breathing. I couldn't get enough oxygen and everything suddenly hurt in my body. All my limbs, everything hurt and I collapsed onto the chair by the desk. I had no idea what was going on behind me. I couldn't hear it. I couldn't sense it, but it didn't matter.

I had torn them apart.

My mother had torn them apart, like she tore my own family apart.

I clasped my eyes closed and bent over. With my head buried in my lap, I hugged my arms around my legs and started to rock back and forth. I kept going. The movement kept me from breaking down.

CHAPTER ELEVEN

At some point, two strong arms slid underneath me and lifted me from the chair. I curled into Mason's shoulder. I didn't need to look; I would know those arms anywhere. He carried me to the bed and set me down gently. As he pulled away, I reached for his shoulder in protest. I didn't want him to go. I couldn't be without him anymore.

"Ssh." He pressed a soft kiss to my forehead. "I'm just going to lock the door."

It wasn't long before he was back. The light was switched off and I heard him undressing before he lifted me back up and slid both of us under the sheets. Then I rolled over to him, my eyes were wide, and there was a gaping hole in my chest. Only he could fill it. It was cheesy, but it was true. As his eyes caught mine, he held still for a moment. His chest rose in the air and I pressed my palm over it. His heart picked up its pace at the touch as I kept my hand there, and Mason closed his eyes. Then he caught my hand with his, bent his head to kiss my palm, and gently placed his other at my hip. He moved me over some more before turning to tug me into his arms. Our legs intertwined together and I rested my head on his chest.

This was it, this was home.

Analise might try to take this away from me, but I knew that somehow we would stop her.

"What's wrong?" He felt my tension.

I shook my head. I didn't want to talk about it, but found myself mumbling, "My mom…"

He drew in another deep breath as he tightened his arms around me. I felt his head rest on top of mine; his breath tickled my hair. He brushed back some of my hair from my forehead and shifted so he could press a kiss to it. His cheek rested there again. "I called my uncle. He's a lawyer."

I sucked in my breath and pulled away to look up. When he didn't meet my gaze, I grabbed his chin and made him. I saw the torn look in his depths and I froze.

No, she couldn't win…

"Mason," I whispered.

He clasped his eyes closed, his mouth twisted, but then he opened them again. Pain flared in them, bright and clear, before he sighed. "Your mom's right. I could be charged with statutory rape. And if I was found guilty, I'd be labeled a sex offender all my life. He said there's a seven year limit on pressing charges from when the act was committed."

I felt punched in the gut. "Are you serious?"

He nodded before his head dropped to my shoulder.

My hand went to his shoulder, I don't know what for. To soothe him? Reassure him with a massage? My touch felt insignificant compared to the burden that'd been placed on him, but then I shook my head. My mom was not going to get away with this. I pushed him back. She would not do this to him.

"Sam?" He cupped the side of my face.

He looked so sad, and that broke my heart. But it made me even angrier. She had done this, and why? Why was she doing this to me? To him? Mason didn't fold to anyone—that was one of the reasons I had fallen in love with him. But my mom had gotten to him, and she held something over his head that he couldn't ignore, evade, or scare away from her.

I sat up and cupped both sides of his face.

"Sam?" he asked again.

I shook my head and ignored the tear that fell. "I won't let her do that. I will make this go away, I have to, Mason."

A myriad of emotions flashed over his face, wariness, sadness, anger, darkness. He sat up and scooted against the headboard, and then he took both my arms. He'd been scared before, but now he let me see his fury.

My stomach wrapped in knots. Oh yes. There was the guy that I'd fallen in love with. I saw the danger lurking in his gaze. I had a sudden thought to rush from the bed and hurry to my mom, to get to her before he did, because as I continued to hold his gaze I knew he was capable of things worse than what I was going to dish out.

"Your mom is becoming crazy—" He stopped suddenly and looked away. As his chest rose and fell at a rapid pace, he was trying to keep control. When he looked back, the fire had diminished, but only slightly. "Your mom's going nuts because she's lost you. She knows it and she's blaming me. What happens when you're eighteen, Sam?"

"I'm gone." The words ripped from me, from my vehemence. She couldn't do a thing to me then.

He nodded. "Exactly. You're gone." Then he waited for me to figure it out…

When I did, my eyes went wide and surged forward. "She doesn't want to lose me—" Like the last time she had lost something and the last time I saw that look of madness in her eyes. I shivered at the memory.

The blood was everywhere as I pushed open the door. My mother was slouched on the floor. She sat with her back to the tub and her nightgown was soaked in sweat and something red. As I pushed the door wider, the pool of blood sat beneath her. It grew slowly. The red on her gown was blood. She was covered in it.

"Mom," I whimpered. I was frozen in the doorway. My legs trembled, I couldn't move. Then something trickled down my leg. It was warm on my skin, but I barely felt it.

I no longer had to go to the bathroom.

"Mom…" I tried not to cry. Her eyes were closed and she was so white, as white as her nightgown—but no. It was red now. All of it was covered in blood.

My cheeks were wet and I raised a hand there. I couldn't have—oh—I was crying. Those were tears, I wiped them off roughly. She couldn't see me cry. She'd get mad.

Oh god.

"Mom." I couldn't leave her, but she wasn't answering. Then I looked back to the hallway. Was dad awake? I should go to him, but my knees were knocking against each other. Because I couldn't stand, I fell to the ground. My knees touched the blood now... oh god...I couldn't stop crying. She wouldn't want me to make any sound. She never wanted me to make a sound, but this...I tried crawling to her.

"Mom..."

"Hey!"

Mason was crouched on the bed, on top of me. His legs straddled me as his head was bent low, eye level to me. He'd grown pale, but when I gasped, he visibly relaxed. He didn't move from my lap, his head fell low to my chest and his hands clasped my waist. His thumbs rubbed back and forth, a fresh set of tingles went through me. As he pressed a kiss to the dip between my breasts, his shoulders shook.

I lifted my hands there. Was he laughing?

No. As I bit my lip, confused at what had happened, he lifted his head again. His concern was evident as he lifted a hand to run his finger over my lip and cheek. Then he cupped my face again and breathed out, "Where did you go? I almost crapped my pants, Sam."

I let go of a long breath. As it rushed past my lips, my insides clenched together. The horror from that night was back. I couldn't get it out of me. I had forgotten it, pushed it down, and numbed myself, but it was back.

"Hey, hey," Mason soothed in a quiet tone. He pressed his soft lips to my forehead. "What's wrong? What's happening?"

I couldn't tell him. I hadn't told anyone, not even David. He should've been told long ago.

"Sam!"

I cried out, still held prisoner by those memories, but then I shook my head. My hands were trembling.

"What's wrong? Tell me. Please."

Everything was quaking in me, my legs jerked against his; I couldn't lift my arms because they were shaking so much. I knew my voice was going to break so I kept quiet and laid my head against his chest. I couldn't do anything. I waited, hoping he would let it go. I couldn't tell him, and after awhile his arms swept around me again. He lifted me above the sheets and curled me into his lap.

It was going to be okay. He was going to push that nightmare aside, he always did.

He murmured, "I have no idea what just happened, but you scared the shit out of me. You're going to have to tell me, Sam. Sometime, you're going to have to tell me."

But not today, not yet.

I closed my eyes and I burrowed even further against his chest. I wanted to curl into a ball and disappear.

"Sam, do you hear me?"

I nodded as I clung to him.

Then he relaxed, slowly, as he sank down into the bed. The memory was still with me, I felt its dirtiness on me as if I were actually back in that bathroom again so I tried to concentrate as I told myself I wasn't there. Her blood wasn't all over me and I was with Mason, I was safe. After a while, a long while, my heart slowed to a regular pace, and then exhaustion kicked in. Mason pulled the blankets back over us.

The sounds of the party were still loud, but in his arms, as his warmth sheltered me, I didn't really hear anyone else. It was just him and me.

It was early in the morning when I woke, but it didn't matter. The security cameras were up, the code had been keyed in. I was screwed. Analise would know where I'd been since she knew I would never spend the night with Adam Quinn.

Adam.

I sighed. Crap. What was I going to do about him?

Mason shifted in the bed. His arm lifted as he reached for me, but instead of letting him pull me back down, I sat up on the edge of the bed. Everything seemed harsh as I slipped away from the warmth of the blankets. The morning seemed brighter than normal, and it was damn cold.

I didn't slide back under the covers. I couldn't close my eyes and burrow into him anymore. When he rolled back over and continued sleeping, I decided that this was the day everything either went to shit or everything went fine.

With my mother, everything was probably going to go to shit.

I ducked inside the shower before I dressed and headed out. I hoped to find someone still awake downstairs that could give me a ride back home, but if not, then I would wake Mason. I just didn't want to. If he took me home, he would come inside and the confrontation would be worse.

My hair was wet and I had Heather's clothes in a bag, grateful that Mason took some of my clothes with him to Nate's earlier. I thought his foresight had been ludicrous, but he hadn't. He was convinced I would be there sooner rather than later—he'd been right on two occasions already.

When I slipped from the room, I didn't look at Mason. I couldn't or I would've crawled back with him.

People were everywhere. Some had fallen asleep near the stairs, a few at the bottom of the stairs. As I circled around the set of couches on one side of the house, I saw a lot of people I didn't recognize. When I crossed over the center area and bypassed the square set of couches there, there were a few from my school. Then I smelled the coffee and a big smile came over me.

That smell would pull me anywhere, but then I turned around. "Oh."

Adam gave me a sheepish wave. "Hey."

My stomach dropped. "Morning."

He gestured to the coffee pot and slid his hands into his front pockets. The green polo and pants were wrinkled.

When I glanced around to see who else was awake, Adam misunderstood. "It's six in the morning."

"You stayed here last night?"

Of course, he had. I flushed at the stupid question.

He hesitated before he surged forward a step. Uncertainty was all over him as he cleared his throat, "Hey, uh, they're wrong, you know. I don't like them. I almost hate them, but not you. I don't want to hurt you. And I really meant it when I said I want to be friends. I...I told you about my dad, Sam."

I didn't move. I didn't say a thing, but I waited. He had something to say so I would listen...I also needed a ride home...

"I apologized for what I did and I came clean to Becky long ago." He jerked a tight shoulder up in a shrug. "She hasn't come to you, even though I told her that I came clean to you. That's on her; I'm more worried about my friendship with you. I do care about you and yeah, it might not be in the strictly platonic way, but I'm above that...or I'm trying to be above that. I'd never hurt you and I know hurting him would be hurting you too. I'd never sue. I don't want Mason and Logan to get between our friendship. I really do want to be your friend."

He sounded sincere. He looked sincere, and I sighed. I hoped he was sincere because I needed a favor. "Can you give me a ride home?"

He paused. Then he rapidly blinked in surprise. "That's it?"

I shrugged. "What do you want? We already had our heart to heart."

"Oh." He fell back against the counter. He seemed dumbstruck.

I waited. I wasn't going to pour my heart to Adam. I had cared about him before and he'd been a friend at times, but I was desperate. Mason would be pissed that I snuck out, but I really needed to get home before he got there. Everything could be destroyed if I didn't get there first.

"Look," I cleared my throat. This was going to sound awkward, but here went my best shot. "I—uh—as far as you and me, I figure we're good." As his shock deepened, I expanded, "I mean, I get it. You don't like Mason and Logan. You don't have to, but I knew that you wouldn't sue."

Well, he might've, but that wasn't the situation at that time. My situation was at my house, where I needed to get. Now.

My hands lifted in the air in a rolling motion. I needed this to hurry along. "So can you do me a favor?"

"Ugh." A beat passed as he struggled to comprehend the sudden turn of events, but then he shot up from the counter. "Yeah, I uh, yeah." He raked a hand through his hair and looked around, then felt his pockets. "My keys…"

He lost his keys in this house? With this amount of people? Panic started to rise up again…

"Oh, wait!" He patted his back pockets and pulled them out. He gestured to the door. "Lead the way."

CHAPTER TWELVE

When he pulled into the driveway, I couldn't move. I had convinced myself that Adam could lie for me again. He would say that I fell asleep at his friend's house, where there were only Academy students at. But I couldn't bring myself to ask him to do that. I couldn't owe him any more, not after Mason almost beat him up.

But the problem would still exist.

Mason said there was a seven year limit. She could file charges within the next seven years and have that over our heads long into our adulthood. Then I remembered his other words—she didn't want to lose me. When an image of the blood flashed in my head, I pushed it away. I couldn't keep going forward if I remained in the past. This wasn't then. This was now. Things were different.

And, not really feeling the bravery that I was trying to convince myself I was, I thanked Adam for the ride.

I felt like I was going to throw up.

He frowned. "You okay?"

No. "Yes."

His frown deepened. "Are you sure?"

No. "Yes."

"Oookay. Uh." He was at a loss for words. "Well, I guess I'll see you later? What are you doing tonight?"

I jerked back in my seat as I saw the front door open. My mom poked her head out as she lifted a hand to shade her eyes. I knew the exact second she saw me in the car and when she saw who was with me. Her shoulders visibly dropped two inches, and then she gave me a small wave before she went back inside.

I let out the breath I'd been holding.

"Sam." Adam touched my arm. He had turned to face me completely. "Are you sure everything's alright? You said things weren't good with your mom and your relationship with Mason. Is there more to it? Things seemed heated in the room last night. I don't think I'm overstepping my role as your friend by being worried here." He stopped, then slumped back in his seat. "I'd really just like to help."

"No, I'm sorry." I tried to give him a reassuring smile. "I've gotta take care of something right now, but hey, I'm working at Manny's now if you ever want to come for food or something."

"That bar I picked you up from last night? You work there?"

I nodded, but shrunk back. I hadn't explained that to Mason yet either. He still thought I'd been alone at a bar before. Ugh. A headache was threatening to come, but I pressed my hands to my temples. It couldn't, not now.

"I'll see you later, Adam." As I shut the door, I gave him a small wave.

I didn't wait for him to leave; I turned around and regarded the mansion. It was as intimidating as it had been the first day we moved in, but this time it was from my family inside, not the Kades. When I went inside, I saw the green light on the security system and figured Analise had turned it off for the day. It'd been red when I headed out for the second run/two hour walk.

"Hi, honey."

I stiffened in the doorway, but went further towards the kitchen. Her tone was cheery, too cheery. When I rounded the corner there was a pile of mail in front of her. She was sorting through it as the coffee was brewing behind her.

What the hell?

My mom was the epitome of the perfect housewife, make-up all done, hair sprayed into place, and a sexy white robe that showed off the lacy nightgown underneath. There was a good hello peek at her cleavage.

I narrowed my eyes. Then I realized that she thought I had been with Adam all night. Anger rushed through me. Adam was okay, but Mason wasn't? Why was that? But I kept it from boiling out as I asked, in a controlled voice, "What are you doing?"

"Oh, nothing. You want some coffee?" She turned for the cups.

"No."

Nothing. She didn't pause. She only grabbed one for herself and then added some creamer to it.

I waited as she rested on one of the stools, and then went back to looking through the mail. A big fat envelope was plopped on the table. She pushed it towards me.

"What's that?"

She shrugged. Drops of the sun could've dripped from her voice. "Oh, nothing. I think that's a college application."

"What?"

It said Columbia University, with a New York address in the top corner. What the hell? "I never requested an application from them."

"Maybe I did."

Her head came up now and there was an underlying message there. Our gazes caught and held. I found myself unable to breathe as I tried to sort through what she was doing. Then it clicked. And I couldn't believe it.

My voice was soft, so soft, "You're going to pay for my college tuition there?"

She picked up the coffee mug, smooth and smug now. "Maybe." Then she took a sip. Her eyes never wavered.

Bitch.

I drew in another breath. I couldn't believe this was happening. "You're bribing me?"

Her eyes narrowed to slits. Her hand tightened on the handle, but she didn't stutter. "Yes."

"Because?"

My heart started to pound now. The thumping sounded closer together, harder against my chest.

"I know where you were last night, Samantha. Do you think I'm an idiot?"

A choked laugh ripped from me. "Things would be a lot easier if you were."

She drew in a soft breath. Her knuckles were now white as she gripped the mug. It started to shake from her hold. "Are you fucking with me?"

Something shifted in her gaze and the wall fell down. Malice and meanness shone through and that was the mom I remembered six years ago. She was the one I heard as she destroyed our entire house. My gut shifted at the reminder.

"It's your fault!" she screeched with wild eyes before she lunged at me. Her finger had pointed at me, but then it turned into a fist. I closed my eyes as I braced for the impact—

I spat out now, "You heard me."

The mug shattered on the floor. She never moved, not an inch, as her eyes were glued to mine. Outrage poured in them, but then the fury gurgled up. A strangled scream started from the base of her throat—

"Honey?" James appeared from around the corner.

The scream stopped short and she blanched. She fell back two steps as everything was stuffed back into place. The warm and sunny façade she had when I got home was back in full force. She was sugary sweet again. "Honey! Good morning."

I felt punched in the stomach. I stumbled backwards.

"Sam?" James sent me a frown. "Are you okay?"

With a hand over me, as if she really had kicked me, I couldn't look away. I was disgusted. This was my mother. This was the woman that gave birth to me, tried to use me to keep Garrett, and then found another man to raise me as his own. Had she ever loved David?

I saw her now with James and I thought she really loved him. I thought that was why she left David for him, but now I wondered. Did she even love James? She couldn't have, not if she was going to turn Mason in for statutory rape. She had to know that he would be irate with her. She would've ruined Mason's life. That was his son. I didn't know James that well, but I knew he loved Mason and Logan. I knew he would do what was right, what he thought was right. That was why he supported her and sent his sons away. He thought he was doing the right thing for her relationship with her daughter, because he understood from his own point of view of being a father.

My mouth fell open as I studied her.

She frowned at me, behind James.

Oh god.

I gasped and I knew what she'd been planning on doing. It couldn't wait, not when he was there. I had to do what I could to foil her plan. I blurted out, "She's going to press charges against Mason!"

A fierce frown flared over James. He turned, slightly to Analise, who paled at my words.

I pointed a finger at her. My voice rose because I was so sure of it now. "You were going to press charges against him and then you were going to try and take it back, weren't you? When he found out, you knew he would've been furious so you would pretend that you hadn't thought." I could hear it now. She would cry, acting desperate and so despondent. My voice hardened, "You would've told him that you hadn't thought it through, that you were so desperate to keep me from him. You were, weren't you? That was your plan. And you were going to go and try to drop the charges, but you know they can't do that. I bet that once you make a claim like that, they can't drop it. They have to pursue it and you wouldn't be blamed for it at all."

I felt sick.

From the rage in her eyes, I knew that had been her plan. My mother was sick, she was not right. Oh god. How could she have done that?

James whirled around to her. His back was to me now, but I staggered to the table behind me and sat down. I couldn't move; I could only sit as he drew to his fullest height. But he didn't say anything, not a thing. The room was so tense, my heart continued to race.

"Honey—" She tried, but she stopped.

Slowly, so slowly, he turned and left the room. And that was enough.

I'd just broken what love he had for her.

"Get. Out."

I fell off the chair. Her tone was ferocious, and as I saw the enraged eyes, the fisted hands, I knew she was close again. The robe fell open, and she was braced in front of me. The nightgown was white, like the one from that night, except this one wasn't drenched in blood. A part of me fell away and slipped back to the memory. She'd been so quiet, almost dead, in the bathroom with the pool of blood beneath her. Her eyes had been murderous days later.

My mother took a step towards me. She drew in her breath, as the veins on her neck stood out. One of her hands started to shake back and forth, but it wasn't from fear. I stood now, numb suddenly, and looked at my mother.

"OUT!"

I flinched, but I couldn't move. She wanted me to leave? But—

"GET OUT! NOOOOW!"

"Analise!" James rushed back into the room. "Do not speak to her like that!"

My heart picked up again, I couldn't breathe once more, and I fell against the wall behind me. It was all closing in around me. This wasn't how I thought it was going to be. She wanted me gone, actually gone... I cared. I hadn't known that I cared.

When I heard a thump, she was on the floor. A hand was to her chest and she was out cold.

"Oh my god." James dropped to his knees beside her. He skimmed his hands over her body, checking for anything wrong with her. When there was nothing, he pressed his fingers to her neck and felt her pulse.

She was breathing. I watched as her chest moved up and down, but I saw it from the distance. I had detached from myself. I was floating away, to somewhere safer than in that room.

"…911 now!..."

"Huh?" I looked at him through a fog now.

"911, Samantha!"

I frowned. 911? She was faking, didn't he know that? But I couldn't speak. The words never came as he rushed past me for the phone. It was attached to the wall behind me, and as he grabbed and lifted it to his ear, he accidentally pushed me backwards.

I reached out for something to hold onto, but there wasn't anything. It was just wall and then I fell to the floor. I scooted up against the wall and sat there as he spoke on the phone.

Everything happened in slow motion. It was surreal. I was watching a movie played out in front of me. The ambulance hadn't taken long. Two EMTs checked her vitals and interrogated James with questions. When they couldn't find anything wrong, they loaded her onto a stretcher and left.

James went with them. He glanced back at me once and asked me a question, but I couldn't make sense of it. I saw his mouth moving, but I couldn't hear him. There was a buzzing sound in my head, it drowned out everything else. When I only looked at him, he gave me a small frown, but grabbed a set of keys from a drawer. He left after that.

I was like that when I heard pounding on the door.

I couldn't move. I knew I should get up to see who that was, but I couldn't. But then—no. I had to get up. She'd been faking it. Why was I in shock about that? So, slowly, I pushed myself up and then went to the door.

I turned the lock the whole way and the door was shoved open. My hands braced against it, and I was thrown against the wall. Before I could fall or steady myself, Mason grabbed me. He hauled me close.

I gasped, everything came flooding back.

God, the buzzing sound was still there. It felt like someone was stomping their foot on my head.

"Where'd they go?"

Logan rushed past Mason into the kitchen. He came back a second later and lifted his hands. "They're gone." He looked at me. "Did they go to the hospital already?"

I shook my head. "She was faking it." She had to have been.

Mason clutched me tighter against him before he pressed a rough kiss against my forehead. "Are you okay?"

Logan stepped closer, concerned as well.

What were they so scared about? She was faking.

"Sam." Mason cupped both sides of my face. "Your mom collapsed. Dad called us. He said you were in shock. Are you okay?"

"She didn't," my voice cracked. I shook my head. Why did everyone believe her? "She's faking." I knew it, she had to have been. The convenient timing, how dramatic it had been. All of this was nuts. It was over the top, how Analise liked to live. I shook my head clear of the shock and my voice became clearer. "I told your dad what she was going to do, that she was going to press charges against you and then pretend she hadn't been thinking straight. She saw it, she saw his face." I hadn't. His back had been turned to me, but how he'd grown quiet, how he had left the room. I'd been so sure that it was done, that they were done. How could he have stayed with her after knowing that?

"Huh?" Logan scratched his head.

Mason cursed under his breath. "Nothing."

"Wait, that's not nothing." Logan stepped closer. "What aren't you telling me?"

Mason stiffened, but when I knew he was going to feed him another lie, I spilled the beans. "My mom was going to press charges of statutory rape against Mason. It's illegal to have sex with a minor. He's 18. It would've stuck."

Logan's eyes went wide. He sucked in his breath and gaped at us. Curses spewed from him as he shook his head. "And you weren't going to tell me? What the hell, Mason?! What the fucking hell?" He stopped abruptly, but then his gaze shot back to us. "Nate knew, didn't he? When did you know about this?"

Mason cursed under his breath.

My hand found his and I held tight to it. "She told me the same day you guys left. I was coming to see Mason and she was waiting for me. She knew I would." I swallowed over a knot. "That was the ace up her sleeve. It would've ruined his life."

"Fuck."

Mason let out a soft breath behind me. His hand wrapped around my waist, and he tugged me back against him. As he held me, I watched Logan from his shelter. I waited for his response, whatever it was going to be. It wouldn't be good. I knew that much. He'd been lied to.

"Fuck you!"

I closed my eyes. There it was.

"Fuck you! Seriously." He scooted away from us, all the way to the back wall.

I started for him, but Mason went instead. He stood close to him as he lifted his hands up, as if to his shoulder. Then he dropped them. "What would you have done?"

Logan glanced up, his gaze stormy. "I would've done something."

"Exactly." Mason sighed. His hands found his waist and his head hung down. His voice came out soft, "You would've come over here and threatened her, or you would've done something worse. You've been asking every day to tie her up and scare the crap out of her."

Logan gave a weak laugh. "I wouldn't have really done that."

"I don't care. This needed to be handled the right way and I had no idea what to do, not until last night…" He lifted his gaze to me.

I realized that he wanted me to confront her. He knew that I was the only one that could've. Shame flared through me. I should've done this sooner. Now it was all a mess.

I sighed, "She kicked me out."

"What?" The surprise was clear with both of them. Then Mason turned back to me. He asked again, "Does she really want you gone?"

I shrugged. "It seemed like it."

"Are we sure she was faking?" Logan frowned. "Are we completely sure that there wasn't something wrong with her?"

Mason started to reach for his phone, but I stopped him. I put my hand on his arm. "She's done this before."

"What?"

Logan poked his head around Mason. "What?"

"She lost a baby…before…" But as I said it I realized the truth, I realized why I had spoken up in the first place. "No, she killed her baby."

CHAPTER THIRTEEN

"Dad!" I ran down the hallway and shoved open their bedroom door, but there wasn't anyone inside. The television was on so I circled around the bed and threw open the bathroom door. Still no one. "Dad?"

"Sam!"

I jerked and my bag went flying across the room. I cursed.

Logan laughed from the doorway, a bag slung over his own shoulder. "You ready?"

Was I ready? I looked around my room, it'd been my home for the last five months and now I would move into another one. No, I wasn't ready, but I was at the same time. A sigh left me. "Yeah…"

"Oh, come on." He sauntered in the room and threw an arm around my shoulder. As he pulled me tight against his side, his hand spanned the rest of the room. "Think of it this way, your next room's going to be orgasm-friendly. That's good feng shui, right? Heh? Heh?" He wiggled his eyebrows at me, chuckling. "That's all about natural bliss and stuff like that, isn't it?"

I shrugged off his arm and grabbed my two bags. "Come on, let's get out of here." I went to the door. He didn't. I looked back. "What?"

Logan had an odd look on his face. He glanced to me and then back to the room. Then he took a breath. "Did you want to go to the hospital?"

"Why?"

I knew why. I wasn't stupid, but god, I wasn't going to give her the satisfaction.

"You know," he hesitated. "I know Mason went there to make sure that she really was faking, but did you want to go too? To make sure that what she was said was legit? That she's actually kicking you out? I mean, I don't know, Sam. Your mom's crazy, certifiable, but she's nuts about you. Since we all got close, your mom's gone off the deep end because she's scared of losing you."

My stomach clenched as I remembered the murderous look in her eye, the one I saw before she collapsed today.

"Being kicked out is a big deal. You might act like you don't care now, but you will. I'm sure of it."

The sincerity in his voice had me blinking back tears. My throat swelled with emotion and I clasped my eyes shut.

"Hey."

I shrugged out of his hold. He had no idea. His dad had cheated, but he wasn't crazy. James had always and would always love his sons, and while their mom was intimidating, I knew she loved them as well. He had no idea.

"Look," his voice grew gruff. "I didn't say that to make you cry. I only meant that it sucks to be on the outs. You know? I've gotten kicked out of the house a few times and I always acted like I didn't care, but I did. I cared a lot. I think the only person who might not care would be Mason."

I chuckled, but it sounded more of a whimpered sob.

"So…did you want to go to the hospital and make sure this is the real thing? That you're actually being kicked out?"

I needed to pick up the pieces and move forward. I shook my head.

Logan put his arm around my shoulders and flashed me a grin. Pulling me into his side, he dipped his head down. He breathed out against my forehead. "Think of it this way. You no longer have to go to the party. The party will come to you, so that makes you the party…in a way. I guess." Frowning, he murmured, "No, that doesn't make sense either."

Another soft chuckle escaped me. Relieved by the brief respite, I thumped him on the chest. "Thanks for distracting me, but you know that I'll never be considered the party."

"You might, if you got really really drunk and started stripping." His eyes narrowed. "No, because then my big brother would sweep you up and take you for your own private party. You only would've been considered the party if you never knew us and still got really really drunk and then stripped. Then you would definitely be the party."

I rolled my eyes. "So I'm only fun if I had never met you guys?"

"Yep, sounds about right." He wiggled his eyebrows at me and flashed some charm. "So what do you think? Break up with Mason and go get wasted?"

"Are you serious?"

"No." His smile remained, but the laughter faded from his voice. "Not really. Kind of. Do you want to?"

"What kind of brother are you? You're encouraging me to break up with Mason."

"Not really."

My eyebrow arched high. "Really?"

"No, no. In this world we're all friends, no romance at all. That stuff's just too much drama anyways. In this world, you can go off and forget about your mom. Forget everything. Get drunk, or not since you don't really drink, but do whatever you do to take the edge off."

"I run."

"Not that," he said. "I want to be a part of this fun that I'm envisioning for you and that means that I'd have to run. I don't like to run, not unless I'm chasing someone or someone's trying to kick my ass. Then I'd run with you, but not in this world."

"This world? Your world, the one where you're not considered delusional?"

"Yeah." Logan's smile doubled. His eyes sparkled from anticipation. "I might be delusional, but what about Vegas? That sounds like a perfect world to go to. We can do all sorts of forgetting." Tugging my hand, he led the way out of my room, out of the house, and then he drove us towards my new home. My next home.

We were almost to Nate's when I frowned at him. "Were you serious about Vegas?" I didn't dare ask him about the other part, I did not want to know if he'd been joking or not.

At my words, his shoulders dropped and he let loose a deep breath. "Damn."

"What?"

"Ten minutes."

"Huh?"

"You forgot about your mom for ten minutes. That wasn't very long at all, Sam." He winked at me. "You're going to have to do better than ten minutes. Maybe Paris? Let's dream about going to Paris, you and me. What would we do there?"

Laughing now, I joined in. What the hell? "Not Paris. We wouldn't go to Paris if it were only you and me. That's too romantic."

"Ouch."

Ignoring him, I mused, "We'd go…"

"Yes?…"

"Germany." I nodded to myself. That sounded right. "You could drink all the beer you wanted."

"Damn good beer."

There was a silly grin on my face, but I didn't want to think about it. Then it'd go away and it'd been so long. But I couldn't help to ask, "Why only you and me? Why not Mason too?"

He rolled his eyes as he turned the car onto Nate's Road. "Because he's the real deal for you. You and me, all fantasies. Only fun, no drama."

"No drama?" I teased, "What about the twins?"

He grimaced. "Too much drama. We can't have any of that. None whatsoever."

It sounded like heaven, but then we pulled into the driveway and heaven fell back to earth. There were six other cars beside

Logan's Escalade. I never would've been concerned if it had been Mason with me—I knew he would've smiled in greeting at their friends, taken my hand, and gone upstairs with me. But it wasn't Mason with me. It was Logan, and Logan was the social butterfly. I knew it wouldn't be long before I'd be upstairs and alone while more and more people joined the party. This was Nate's home and now Mason's home. Of course, the party would be there.

"We don't have to stay long."

"What?" I looked over and found that Logan had been watching me. There was no humor or spark. He was only serious.

He repeated, "If you're worried about Will and James, they left this morning. My aunt called and wanted them back home, but we don't have to stay long. We can put our stuff away and head to the hospital right away, if you want."

Did I want that? No, that was why Mason went. He would get to the bottom of everything for me. It was why I asked him to go. Logan and I stayed back to finish packing whatever we needed since now all of us had been kicked out of the house.

Faintly, I murmured, "I think I'm going to go for a run."

He frowned. "You sure? You don't have to, you know."

I did. Oh my god, I really did. I gave him a fleeting smile. "It's okay. I need to get out and stretch my legs."

"Okay," but his frown lingered. I felt it follow me as I headed inside and veered up the stairs. When I got to the bedroom, I closed the door, heaving a deep breath as I rested against it for a moment. This day might've been the hardest in my life. Then I thought about it, nope. I had a lot of days that sucked.

I put my two bags beside the closet and started to search for my running clothes when I felt my phone vibrate in my pocket. A thrill went through me when I saw it was Mason calling. "Hey!"

"Hey," he was tired and tense.

I straightened abruptly. "What happened?"

He hesitated.

"Mason."

Then he gave in, "Your mom's a class act, Sam. And my dad's a clueless bastard. I can't believe it, but he's buying everything she said."

"Are you serious?" He couldn't be, but my heart sank. I had already known that James was going to believe her. He loved her, he had to.

"Yeah, but listen, she's faking. Even some of the doctors think it too. I heard one of the nurses talking about it in some office. They didn't know I could hear, but they were laughing at some diagnosis the doctor gave her. I guess it's given to headcases when they can't find anything wrong. They all recognized her from the ER trips she took during our road trip."

"Did you talk to my mom?"

Again, another strained silence before he admitted, "No."

So many emotions flared in me—disappointment, hurt, relief, and so many more.

He added, "I'm sorry, I really am. She banned me from the room. What I got from talking to my dad was that she's sticking to her story that she collapsed. She's saying it's because of all the anxiety we're giving her."

Of course.

I looked down. When would I learn? She was never going to change.

"I told my dad that you and Logan are going to move into Nate's. He agreed that it was for the best." I heard noises from his phone and knew that he had stepped outside. There was a rustling sound. Then there was a ding, a slam, and complete silence again. It wasn't long before his engine started and the rustling stopped. His voice came from far away, "Sorry about that, I'm on my way home now."

Home. Despite all the stress, a tingle of excitement flared in my stomach. My heart picked up its pace. He was coming home to me, with no parents, no hiding. We were living together, like a normal couple.

"I'll see you in a bit. Do you want me to pick you up something to eat? I was thinking of grabbing some food."

I was already shaking my head when I responded, "No. I'm going to go for a run. I've got enough time before I have to get back and head out again."

"Head out? Head out where—"

But I didn't hear him and hurried out, "Bye. See you later." Tossing the phone on the counter, I rushed to get dressed. I felt the old itch start up and knew that I wouldn't be able to quell it until I was sweating, panting, and sprinting on the road for an hour. Before I started out the door with my earbuds already in, I spied the phone and nabbed it quick. When I went down the stairs, I stashed it in a pocket, but I didn't worry about keys.

A large group had congregated to the back patio. As I went outside, more cars had accumulated so I knew I'd have no problem getting inside the house after my run. I had a feeling everyone would be there long until the next morning.

But then I stopped thinking and I started to salivate at the idea of a new running route. There'd be new roads, new parks, maybe even a running trail that would turn into a wooded maze. I couldn't help myself. I was sprinting by the time I got to the end of the driveway. After an hour I slowed down to a fast jog and kept that going for another hour. I figure two hours was good enough since Heather had already told me she needed me from five till close for my second day of training. As I started back, it didn't take me as long as I thought it would, or I ran faster than I realized, so my adrenaline was still pumping through me when I turned into the driveway.

The cars had multiplied. I wasn't surprised.

When I went inside, they were still on the back patio. The sounds of splashing and cheers told me they were in the pool. A few girls were in the kitchen and looked up as I came inside, panting and sweating. They were covered in string bikinis with long tanned bodies, holding frilly drinks. I stopped, grabbed the end of my shirt and used it to mop the sweat from my face. Their noses wrinkled up and were giggling as they went through the open door to the patio.

"Hey!"

I had turned for the stairs, but stopped. My knees buckled as Mason strode away from the group. God. My mouth watered, my drool mixed with my perspiration, and I was one wet girlfriend. As he walked towards me, I noticed that he had lost a little bit of weight. When had that happened? He'd been muscular before, but the slight leanness made the muscles on his arms even more striking. His shirt clung to his chest. It molded over the muscles that looked like an intricate map, one that only I got to explore. At the thought of tracing each and every dip with my finger, I grew wet between my legs.

Goodness.

"You okay?" He stopped before me, but the slight smirk that flashed at the corner of his mouth told me that he knew exactly what was going on with me. "I know how running can spur you on. I never knew it could turn you on too."

"Smartass."

The smirk doubled and his eyes darkened with desire as he stepped even closer. His chest brushed against my front, he was intimately close, and his lips lingered on my lips. "Goddamn Sam, you looking wet makes me hard."

My throat jerked in reaction and his eyes were glued to mine. Then his hand curled around my waist, and he tugged me closer. One of his legs slid between mine, hoisting me off the ground so I was straddling him as we both stood there.

"Mason," I whispered.

He bent forward, going slow to draw it out. My eyes widened, I hungered for him. At the thought of his lips on mine, my mouth parted. Eager. Then his hand slid around my neck and cupped the back of my head. He anchored me in place as he slowly, so slowly, leaned down until I felt the soft tip of his lips against mine. A deep groan left me, I heard it from a distance, and then I opened my mouth further for him. His tongue swept in and everything flared inside of me. I gasped at the feel of him and surged upwards against him. When my legs tried to climb higher, he grabbed under my thighs and lifted me. I wrapped my legs all the way around his waist. As my arms held onto his shoulders, I clasped my legs tighter around him and then sunk down.

Mason grunted from the contact between us but deepened the kiss even more. His touch was commanding and I didn't want to stop it. In the far distance of my consciousness, I felt us moving and then a door closing behind us, and a moment later, I felt the hot torrents of water spray down as he stepped inside the shower. He pressed me against the wall and slid a hand under my shirt to cup my breast. When his finger caressed the tip, I fell back against the wall gasping.

"God, Sam, I love you," he whispered as his touch grew more demanding.

I loved him. I needed him.

I needed *more*.

"Wait." He pulled away, panting, and rested his forehead to mine.

I felt him trembling under my hands and reveled in the power of it. Sliding my hand under his shirt and over his chest, he drew in a deep breath. I leaned forward and pressed my mouth there, he quivered under my kiss. Then I flicked my tongue and he gasped, surging into motion at the same time. I was pulled from the wall, and after he kicked open the shower door, he plopped me on the counter before his fingers hooked inside of my shorts. They were whisked off the next second. Heated, I reached for him. My fingers couldn't undo his zipper. I cursed, but Mason helped me. As soon as he sprang free, he clamped a hand under my thigh, arching me back and slid inside with one smooth movement.

A gasped scream ripped from my throat at the sudden contact. It was intoxicating, but not enough. I pushed up from the counter and moved in motion with him as he thrust in and out. The speed picked up, he went deeper and rougher with each thrust until I couldn't think. I could only feel as I rode with him in every movement, every back and forth, climbing closer to climax. When we were nearly there, he didn't linger. He thrust in one last time, the deepest yet. I exploded as I went over the edge with him, my body arched into the air. His penis touched the back of me and another burst of spasms coursed through me.

Before I fell back down, Mason scooped an arm around and held me to his chest. My body trembled and a second orgasm ripped through me. Crying out, I clamped onto his shoulders, still shaking in his arms.

He held me there, cradled in his arms, as he brushed a hand down my back until I stopped quivering. Weak from the climaxes, the adrenaline I had from running melted into exhaustion and I didn't protest when Mason carried me to the bed. When he slid us both under the covers, my head hit the pillow and I let out a contented sigh. Then his arms slid around my waist, he pulled me back against him, and I was home.

CHAPTER FOURTEEN

I woke up and lunged for the nearest thing that told time. 4:45—
holy shit. I rolled out of bed to my feet and was in the shower faster
than I could've imagined. I impressed myself, but when the door
opened, I met Mason's lust-filled gaze and dropped the shampoo. I
was going to be late for my second day of work.

My back hit the wall again as music started blaring below us.
When he slid inside, he kept rhythm with the bass underneath. We
were both climaxing during the bridge of the second song. As he
let me back down, he braced an arm above me and gasped a few
shuddering breaths. I grinned at the feeling of intoxication. Being
with Mason was something I would never tire of, no matter the
drama, no matter the obstacles. He made me alive. When I slid a
hand up his chest and around his neck to draw him down, I pressed
my lips to his and felt the same power over him that he had with me.

It was liberating.

"Hell, woman," he grunted as he braced a hand against the wall
behind me so he could lean over me. "You're going to kill me."

A grin teased the corners of my mouth, but I held my breath
as he moved down, closer and closer, until he was a hair's width
away from me. His breath fanned over me while I waited for his
touch with my heart pounding. Just like that, even after we had
been together, I still felt the intoxication sweep through me again. It
was powerful and heady. When he didn't press his lips to mine, my
eyes flicked up. His had darkened with desire, and he slammed his
mouth on mine, melting the world away.

Once more, I was swept off my feet as he picked me up and carried me to the bed. When he slid me back down, I caught sight of his clock—6:00. Panic overtook me like a bucket of ice thrown on us, and I shoved him away.

"Wha—what are you doing?" His first question fell away as I scrambled off the bed and hurried to my bag.

I grabbed the first thing my hand touched and threw it on. As I hopped around, trying to get my shoe on, Mason moved to sit on the edge of the bed. "What are you doing?"

"I'm late." *Where the hell was that other shoe?*

"You're late?"

I glanced up, distracted, but crashed into the couch as I saw the blood drain from his face. His eyes were wide with horror. It clicked with me. "No, no, no. I'm not pregnant."

"OH!" His shoulders slumped with relief. "Thank god."

Ah ha! I spied my other shoe and pulled it on right away. "I'm late for work. Gotta go." I grabbed my purse, my keys, and flew out the door. The crowd had moved to the center area around the fountain. I raced down the stairs and jumped over a girl who sat on the bottom step.

Mason followed, standing in the bedroom's doorway, shirtless with a pair of unzipped jeans. He hollered after me, "You have a job?"

"Yeah!" Ignoring the stares and sudden lull in conversation, I yelled back, "Manny's. Started yesterday. See you!"

I was out the door and in my car within seconds but had to slam on the brakes when I looked in the rearview mirror. There were cars in front of me, on the side of me, and behind me. I was boxed in.

"AH!" My forehead hit the steering wheel from frustration. I was never going to get there. Heather was going to fire me on my second day.

What was I going to do? But I didn't have the time to consider my choices—she needed to know what was going on so I looked through my purse for my phone when I heard a tapping on my window. Glancing up, a heady rush went through me when Mason bent down and had his set of keys dangling from his hand. He was still shirtless. I wasn't going to complain.

He said through the closed window, "Come on. I'm not blocked in. I'll give you a ride."

When I got out, he led the way and I had a good view of his backside. Goodness. I forgot how he was just as well sculpted in the back as the front. The only times I looked at his back was when I pressed against him. It was his front side that always held my attention. I blushed as I remembered the reason why I was late for work and at how wanton my behavior had been. I should've been used to it, but when he sauntered to his Escalade with a natural grace that only the best athletes seemed to possess, I knew I never wanted to get used to our times together. I wanted every time to feel like the first.

"What's the hold up? You coming?"

Oh god. I had paused beside his door and was staring at him, lust in my thoughts. My head ducked down as I hurried around to the passenger side. I rolled my eyes. I was like a schoolgirl crushing on the local god. But I was, and he was, and we were together. My shoulders came back up at that thought. When I slipped inside, he gave me a questioning glance but pulled out and veered around the cars in the driveway.

"You good?"

I nodded, biting my lip. His jeans were still not zipped up, but he was only dropping me off. "I won't be done until the bar closes."

"You help out in the bar too?"

"Yeah." I gave him a sheepish look. "I'm sorry I didn't tell you, a lot of stuff happened today, but I meant to."

"It's no problem. I'm just surprised."

"Really?" For some reason, I had thought he would've been upset that I got a job. But now as I saw that he didn't care, I relaxed.

A small flutter started in the pit of my stomach, but it was a good flutter. I wanted a job; it hadn't been all about avoiding my mother. Correction, I wanted this job. I liked working at Manny's. I liked working with Heather.

He grinned as he glanced at me from the corner of his eye. "Yeah, why? You think I'd be pissed or something?"

I shifted in my seat. "Well…yeah…" But why? That'd been a ludicrous thought, but then I understood. My mom would've been mad. She would've hated the idea, she always did. I slumped even further in my seat. Mason wasn't my mother. He wouldn't want to keep me only to the house or out with the only friends he approved. Lydia and Jessica had gotten Analise's stamp of approval. That ended with disaster. Then a sick feeling came to me, and I looked back over at Mason.

"What's wrong?" His voice was so quiet. He glanced from me to the road, but he could tell.

I took another breath. Could I even say this out loud? "My mom liked Lydia and Jessica. Do you think—" I hesitated. I couldn't say it.

"Do I think…what?"

But I knew I would always wonder. "Do you think she liked them because they were like her? I mean, they were mean and didn't really care about me."

His eyes widened a fraction of an inch, but that was his only reaction. The air seemed tense, though, and my gut twisted. I knew why it had changed as soon as I said those words. It was true, and Mason knew it but didn't know how to say those words to me. I shook my head and looked away. "It doesn't matter. I know what you're going to say."

"No, you don't."

I nodded. Drawing in a painful breath, I leaned my forehead against the window. I'd been so blind. She had made comments. She always knew that Jeff was a cheater—could she recognize it in him because she was one too? Was that why she liked Jessica most of all? Because she was like her? She hadn't liked Lydia as much—was that because Lydia cared the most for me out of all three of them?

It was sick. I didn't want to think about it anymore.

"Hey," Mason spoke. He was cautious.

My shoulders tightened and bunched around me. "I don't want to talk about that. I really don't."

"Well, you need to. You sure you have to work tonight?"

I swung around at his gruff voice. What was he mad about? Even though his eyes weren't on me but on the road, I saw the glimmer of fury there. His jaw clenched and his grip tightened on the steering wheel. I asked, "Are you mad at me?"

"What?" He whipped his gaze to me. Then spat out, "No! I'm mad at that bitch you call your mother. Did she pick your friends for you?"

My stomach dropped. She had.

He saw my answer, and a disgusted sound came from him. "I can't believe her—no, I can. She's controlling and possessive. That's why she never liked the idea of you and me, because she couldn't control me and because she knew I cared about you. You want to know my guess as to why she liked those two for you?"

Did I? No, but I knew I needed to.

He continued as his voice grew savage. "Because she wanted people around you that would hurt you. She wanted them to hurt you because then you'd stay with her. You would never know what else was out there, that there are good people out there. I'm not a saint, I know that, but when I love someone, I love them with everything." A curse ripped from him, and he pulled into Manny's parking lot in a rush of gravel before he braked to a stop. Then he was on my side of the car. His eyes were fierce, but his hands were gentle as they turned me to him. He pressed his forehead against mine. I felt how he was keeping himself in control. He expelled a deep breath. "I want the best for you. I don't want to keep you imprisoned to me. I want you to reach your fullest, find friends who really care about you, get a job that you like. I want you to go to my school and get a track scholarship. I want you to do all of that in spite of your mother, because if she had her way, you'd never go anywhere. She would ruin it."

I closed my eyes. She would. The truth stabbed me in the gut.

His hand cupped the side of my face and lifted me up. He whispered, "Look at me."

A whimper escaped me. His eyes burned with love. The emotion was there, an extra layer to the windows of what he felt. It hurt, but it was the good hurt. Something unlocked inside of me, that was him. I had everything boxed inside, kept away so I wouldn't feel, but with Mason, all I could do was feel. That was because of him, because he loved me. I whispered back, "Thank you."

"For what?"

"For loving me." For giving me what my mother should have—unconditional love. That hurt to admit. Another whimper slipped out, but I was lifted into his arms and held against his chest. He rocked me back and forth with his head tucked down. I didn't want to be anywhere else.

When I walked into Manny's, much later, Heather was behind the bar counter. She wore a similar red shirt from yesterday with ripped jeans that stuck to her like a second skin. With a towel and glass in hand, she dried and placed it back behind the counter. She picked up another as I went over. One of her eyebrows lifted in the air. "I hope this isn't a pattern because, girl, if it is we have to rethink this job for you."

"I'm sorry, I am. My mom collapsed this morning. She was rushed to the hospital."

Her mouth dropped. When an apology flashed over her face, I looked away. Mason told me the lie would work and it had, but there was a ball of guilt on the bottom of my stomach. I only hoped to work it away. That meant showing up on time and no more afternoon quickies. Mason never let them last as quickies. They grew into full-blown afternooners.

"I'm sorry, Sam. I figured something happened from last night, but I didn't think it was your mom." She nodded towards the door. "I saw Kade drop you off, it looked intense in there."

I flushed. She had seen that?

"Uh, yeah." A sudden rush overtook me. I wanted to tell her all about it, but I couldn't. Well, I could, but she wasn't my friend. I had never trusted any of my friends, but after only knowing her a day, I wanted to confide in her. Confused by that, I pushed it away. I was here for a job. "Where do you want me today?"

She gestured to the back of the bar. "You can stay here with me today. It shouldn't be too busy until later, but Brandon will take over by then."

As I settled beside her, there were some customers I recognized from last night's party. A few older couples were there as well, along with a young family.

"Jason!" a mother hollered as her two-year-old darted down the hallway, giggling. He pumped his chubby legs harder and his giggles increased.

Heather and I shared a look of amusement as the mother raced past us. "They come here every morning, and little Jason loves going to the back office to see my dad."

"They come here every morning?" I grabbed a towel and glass to dry.

She nodded as she picked up another. "Yep. Coral and Jeff, her husband, have opposite schedules. He's on the road with his job at night, so they meet here for some time together. It'd probably be easier if they did it at home, but I think Coral enjoys the break from watching all three of their little ones. My dad dotes on Jason." She nodded to the table where a girl and another boy looked the same age. Food was plastered over their faces and hands. Their dad wore deep bags underneath his eyes as he tried to feed the baby. Heather chuckled, "Jake and Jenna too."

"Triplets?"

"Yep. They're almost a part of the family now. Coral keeps trying to set up Brandon with her co-workers. She's a nurse, she'll go in for a twelve hour shift."

Watching that table and hearing the fondness in Heather's voice, I felt slapped in the face. That was what a family was. They cared for each other. Her dad came out of his office with the two year old in his arms. His mother followed behind, cooing and smiling as Jason flailed his arms over Manny's shoulders at her. Another chuckle came from Heather as her dad sat at their table. The other two flocked to his lap, and soon all three of them were crawling all over him.

They weren't blood, but they were family.

"You okay?"

I jerked from my thoughts, but caught the glass before it went flying from my hands. A full face flush was coming. I ducked down and grabbed another glass to dry. "I'm good. Do you need me to grab some more glasses to shine?"

I was aware of the skeptical look she gave me but ignored it. When she remarked, "I suppose you could polish some of the silverware—" I had that tray in my hands before she could finish her sentence and scurried to a far table. It hurt to watch that loving family.

CHAPTER FIFTEEN

Brandon arrived and went behind the bar so Heather and I could help Lily and Anne, the other two servers from the diner. After the third hour of full tables with more people still streaming in, I asked Heather if it was always like this and she nodded with a rueful grin on her face. "Why do you think I get so pissed at Brandon for banging my friends? They quit after he breaks up with them. I can't keep losing anymore girls."

"Watch out!" Lily called as she hurried towards us and collapsed a bin full of dishes on the counter. "Whoa. I almost dropped that. Manny would have my hide."

Heather snorted, "Yeah, right. My dad? He can't even bring himself to squash a ladybug. Your job's safe if you break a few dishes." When the door opened and a bunch of guys walked in, she groaned but started towards them.

Lily grinned as she turned to watch her beside me. "She's right, you know."

"About?"

"About her dad. He's a softie, that's why so much of the other stuff falls on Heather and Brandon's shoulders. They do the firing and hiring. If anyone would fire me, it'd be Heather."

When the guys folded around a table in the back corner, Heather stood with pad in hand. All of them stopped and scanned her up and down. She shifted her weight to one side so her hip stuck out and lifted her chin up. They looked up with cocky smirks already starting, but those fell away as soon as they caught whatever expression she wore. A few cleared their throats before snatching up the menus she plopped on the table.

I chuckled. She had stopped their flirting in its tracks. Heather was not someone I wanted to mess with.

"So what's your deal?"

"Huh?" I looked over. I had expected Lily to leave the dishes and hurry away again, but she had been watching me as I watched Heather. "What do you mean?"

She shrugged. "Heather likes you, a lot. If another girl had shown up two hours late on her second day, she would've been sent away at the door."

"Oh." I shifted around and reached for the bin of dishes. I could wash them, anything to get away from this line of questioning. I liked Lily and Anne from the night before. Both were on the heavy side with friendly smiles, but I grew uneasy at the keenness in her eyes now. It hadn't been there the night before. "It's nothing. My mom went to the hospital today. I was late because of that—"

"Oh my gosh!" Her hand clamped on my arm.

Startled, I let go of the bin, and it landed with a thump back on the counter. "No, it's okay. I mean, it was a shock, but my mom will be fine. I think it was—"

"Logan Kade just walked in here," she hissed. Her hand tightened on my arm. I gritted my teeth against the pain from her hold but processed her words. Sure enough. Logan waltzed through the front door as if he owned the place. His eyes were narrowed, but the same cocksure smirk was there as he scanned the room. When he saw me, he paused in question, but I shook my head so he nodded and turned to the bar. He lifted a hand in the air. "Yo."

"Kade!" Brandon boomed from the bar. "Get your ass over here, man!"

The two bumped fists together when Logan claimed a stool at the bar. The two acted like long-lost best friends. It wasn't long before they were having shots. After an hour, the enjoyment of each other's presence wasn't fading. I was mystified. Logan never sought me out. He seemed content to swap stories with Brandon, who I was reminded had played football with Logan and Mason a year ago. That startled me as well. Heather's brother owned and ran the bar, but he had only graduated high school a year ago. That was a lot of responsibility, but he seemed to handle it fine, like Heather did with running the diner.

Just then, she slapped a hand on the counter beside me. "I need a smoke break. You game?"

"Game?"

She jerked her head through the back door. "Come with? You're up for a break soon, aren't you? Lily and Anne can handle our tables for awhile."

"Tables? You mean my two and your ten?"

She flashed a grin as she reached for her purse under the counter. "Come on. This'll be interesting."

"What will?"

But I didn't have to wait long. The second we went through the door, Logan popped out behind us and shut both doors so no one could see or hear us. He claimed a chair on the other side of Heather since I was next to the door.

She lit her cigarette, took a drag, and leaned back to watch us.

"You don't want to talk to me in there?" Logan leaned forward on his elbows. He'd been happy inside, he was intense now.

I ignored that question. "Mason told you?"

"You yelled it across the room."

"Oh." I flushed as I remembered. With Mason shirtless, I hadn't noticed anyone else. But he wasn't there to question me about my job. "What's going on?"

He expelled a breath and glanced at Heather.

She blew out a long puff of white smoke before she lifted the cigarette again. "I ain't going anywhere, pretty boy. This is my place. This is my break. She's my friend now. You got something to say, share it here or keep it till later, but I ain't going anywhere."

He frowned and then shot her a dark look. "Whatever."

She rolled her eyes and took another long drag from her cigarette. "Logan."

His eyes jerked back to mine. "Right. So." His eyebrows furrowed together.

"So?"

He chewed his lip for a second before bursting out, "Why didn't you say anything about what your mom was going to do? You told Mason, he told Nate, but no one told me. What's up with that?"

My stomach clenched in knots. I leaned forward and lowered my voice, "Why didn't you bring this up in the car, when it was just you and me?"

He shot me an incredulous look. "Because your mom *just* went to the hospital. You were doing your numb shit."

"My numb shit?"

"Yeah." He jerked his head in a quick nod. "When you don't want to feel all your crap or your mom's crap so you shut down—but it wasn't working then. You were feeling it and you were freaking. I could see it. Remember? I distracted you."

I rolled my eyes. "That would've distracted me too, and it would've been a lot more private."

Heather snorted but turned her head and blew out her smoke again.

"Or tonight too. You could've waited until tonight."

Logan snorted this time. "Yeah, right. Like I could tear you away from my brother. If you're home and he's home, you two are always with each other." His voice went low, almost threatening. "It sucked being a third wheel before, but I don't appreciate being a fourth wheel now."

I sucked in my breath. What was he saying?

"If Mason doesn't tell me, you should. Don't kid yourself, Sam. Nate's not here for you or me. He's here for Mason. If my brother wasn't so straight with you, I'd think those two were a happy gay couple. They're so giddy living together and making their plans for college." Logan kicked up a leg to rest on the edge of my chair. He pushed his chair in the air so it rested on the back two legs as he grumbled, "I forgot what those two were like when Nate actually lived here."

I sighed. What the hell did I do here? Logan was hurt, that was obvious. Mason had been shutting him out lately, but why? Was it my place to intervene? As I considered that, I remembered the party two months ago when Mason and Nate worked together like a slick team and manipulated Logan. He meant to protect me while Mason wanted to protect his relationship with his brother as well as with me. It worked. The threat had been silenced, and Miranda never even knew she had hit the one button that could've unraveled the brothers' relationship.

I was seeing another button now, the tight bond between Nate and Mason. Logan was hurting because of it, and he was right. If Mason wasn't going to look out for him, I would. He'd done it for me too many times to count.

I leaned over and touched his arm. "I'm sorry, Logan."

"For what?" He had tensed under my touch but didn't take his eyes away from me.

"For not telling you. I don't care what Mason says, I'll tell you from now on."

Some tension left him, and his shoulders relaxed. "Thanks, Sam. I know he does it to protect me, but it pisses me off."

I bit my lip. What would happen if Logan ever found out how they had manipulated him? A knot formed in my throat at the idea of that day. I knew it was coming. All secrets came out, no matter how long or deep they were buried.

Then Logan switched his gaze to Heather. The cocky smirk slid back into place. "So, how's Channing?"

Heather froze, but then threw him a seductive look and blew a puff of smoke into his face. "Oh, you know. He's probably still sleeping from all the sex we had last night."

Logan's eyes lit up. "Yeah?"

"Oh yeah." She nodded. Her voice lowered to a husky tone, full of promises. "I tired him out, especially when I brought out the handcuffs. I hope I remembered to uncuff him this morning." She feigned concern before her lips curved into a sultry smile. "I'm sure I did and if I didn't, I'll have to make it up to him tonight."

"You're into handcuffs?"

"Oh, I'm into a lot of stuff, Logan. A whole lot of painful dominatrix sort of things, only the good kink that every couple wishes they could do. You know what I mean."

I caught the wink she sent at me behind her hand.

Logan licked his lips. "Oh yeah. I love it when a girl lifts her legs like a pretzel. Do you do that for Channing?"

"Of course." Her voice lowered even more as her finger slid from her throat to the front of her shirt. She paused in the valley between her breasts, above where she had knotted the ends of her shirt together. "He loves it. He really does."

Logan sucked in a breath; his eyes enraptured where her finger paused.

Then she snapped them together in front of his face. He jerked back, startled from the sudden movement, but Heather calmly grounded out her cigarette. "Anyways. Break time is over for me. Enlightening, Kade, every time you come here. It's always so enlightening." She caught my gaze. "You can stay for awhile if you'd like. You never took your half hour for supper."

When she went inside, I was surprised to see Logan grinning.

"She was joking."

He lifted a shoulder. "I don't care. Jax can be hella hot. I forgot how much fun it is to mess with her."

"You were friends with her?"

"Somewhat. She was best friends with Tate."

My gaze shot to his. "What?"

He nodded as his grin thinned.

"Tate as in the Tate that you dated for two years, that you loved, that tried to cheat on you with Mason?"

He nodded before yawning, "Yeah, that Tate. She wasn't always the prissy bitch you met a few months ago, Sam. Tate was cool. I wouldn't have dated anyone who wasn't cool. Her and Heather had been friends for years."

My eyes widened. "Did she used to work here?"

His lips pressed together, but he didn't say anything.

"Oh god. She did, didn't she?"

Then laughter boiled out of him. He slid further in his chair with a wicked smile. "Yeah, she worked here. She quit after she'd been with me for a year, that was when she became the bitch you met a few months ago."

"She wasn't before?"

"Nah, not until she became obsessed with Mason, then she became one." The wicked glint in his eye depleted as memories rolled over him. His voice grew softer. "Tate was really laidback at first, but she wouldn't stand for any bullshit. She never let the guys mess with her, not even me. I think that's why I liked her. She knew what she wanted and she went after it."

"You?"

The humor was gone now. "No, Mason. She wanted him. I was the means to get to him. I should've recognized the signs earlier than I did, but I don't think I wanted to see them. She talked about how Mason was the alpha male at school. She'd say things about how every person needed their other half, that they were supposed to be equals. That's about the time that she started to become more of a bitch to everyone. She tried to become the female alpha that was his equal, I guess. When she became friends with Kate and Parker, that crew, her and Heather parted ways. Tate was awesome in bed. I was getting great sex so I didn't put two and two together until Mason called me from his room." His jaw clenched.

I could see the anger and hurt still there.

"She used me. That girl used me, straight out. She was a cold bitch the first time we slept together. But to give her some credit," he winced, "I don't think she counted on me actually falling for her. But that first night lasted to two, then three. I was taking her on dates, coming here to hang out with her."

"That's why you and Brandon acted like long-lost friends."

He nodded. "I guess. I don't know. I always liked Brandon. He was cool to hang out with." He flashed me a dimple. "He got us free alcohol, you know. Even when we were sophomores. I think his older brother was running the bar then, but Brandon still snuck a keg for us." He paused. "Or two."

The door opened then and Brandon popped his head out. "Hey, Sam. My sis needs your help."

"Okay." With a small smile at Logan, I headed inside. I wasn't sure how I felt about everything he had revealed, but I couldn't dwell on it. As I stepped through the door, my eyes got big. The crowd had doubled. Then I saw Mason and Nate come in through the door. Great, they brought the entire party from the house here.

Brandon was still in the doorway, but I looked around him to Logan. "Everyone from the house is here."

He sat up straight in his chair. "Everyone?"

I nodded. "Yep, Mason and Nate brought everyone."

Oh joy.

CHAPTER SIXTEEN

When the dishwasher had to go home for a family emergency, I offered to take his place. I wanted to avoid the extra attention. Time flew after that. Bins of dishes were pushed through the window. I hurried to wash them, get them dried, and back into place for the cook. After two more hours, it didn't look to be lessening, and I heard Heather sigh as she picked up the phone. She was calling in reinforcements. Another girl came in to be a server, and there was another cook in the kitchen. At one point, Heather stuck her head through the window to where I stood and asked if it was okay if I did dishes for the rest of the night.

I nodded. Hell, I was relieved.

At one point, the new server that I hadn't met snapped at me. I'd been stacking the dishes and didn't get out of her way fast enough. I ducked back into the kitchen, but heard Lily hiss, "Watch it, that's Mason Kade's girlfriend."

"What?" the new server exclaimed. "Are you kidding me?"

Lily whispered to her, "Don't worry. She seems really nice."

"Oh." The girl mumbled something else to her, but I couldn't hear anymore. They moved away from my window.

"I thought you were a waitress?"

Mason stood in the back doorway with an odd grin. As he came closer, he reached for an apron and tied it around his waist. His eyes were glazed over.

I snorted, reaching for more plates to pile on the crate. "You're drunk."

He settled beside me and sighed. "Yeah, a bit." Then he bent down and placed a soft kiss on my shoulder.

I wanted to melt into him, and I did, for a second. Then I pulled away and began lining up the plates in their slots again. "Frank had to go home so I volunteered to take his place. What are you doing back here?"

He narrowed his eyes at me. "You like it back here, don't you?"

"Yeah," I confessed. "I kind of do."

He reached out and brushed some hair back from my forehead. When he leaned close again, I felt his lips there and snuggled against him.

"Employees only, Kade!" Heather rapped on the window. "Out."

He wrapped an arm around my waist. "Make me, Jax."

"Are you serious?" She shifted and one hand went to her hip.

I hid a grin at the movement. After watching her yesterday and today, that was what she did when she was all business. She'd shift back on her left heel, her hand went to her hip, and she narrowed her eyes at whoever was giving her trouble. Her elbow stuck out when she really meant business. She did it all now, but then threw both hands in the air. "Fine. Fine. Just actually help your girl. If you distract her and we get behind because we have no dishes, I'm throwing you out."

"Whatever."

"Don't think I won't call a few of Brad's buddies. They're bigger than you, Kade."

He chuckled but sighed when she narrowed her eyes again in a warning. "Fine. Yes, I'll help her. Why do you think I'm here?"

"You're here to see your girl. When your posse came in, she went back there so then you had to go back there to see her. I'm not a moron, Kade. I know why you're back there, and I don't want any sex going on in my diner. You hear me?"

"Yeah, yeah."

"My diner, Kade!"

"I get it," he barked back now. "Your diner, your job. My girlfriend."

She stuck out her chin at him. "She's my worker and she's my friend."

Mason grew stiff beside me. I wasn't surprised when his next words came out as a threat, "I already told you I'll help her back here. If you keep talking to me like that, you and I are going to have a real problem."

I knew neither of these two would back down so I moved Mason to the back end of the dishwasher. Ignoring Heather's hawk-like scrutiny, I lifted the door and pulled out the crate that'd been washed. "You need to wait until they're all dry and then stack them in those places over there."

He glanced to where I pointed and nodded. All the other dishes were easy to see. As he started to dry, I went back to loading more dishes onto the crates to put through the washer. Heather hadn't moved.

"Sam," she started.

My hand shot in the air. "Don't. If I was dating Logan and he were back here, you wouldn't care. I know you don't like Mason, but I love him. He's being a good guy right now. If you think that I would let my relationship interfere with my job, then I need to show you that's not who I am. I am sorry about being late today, but you have my word it will never happen again."

Her hand fell from her hip again and her shoulders dropped. "I'm sorry. I was being a bitch." She chewed on her lip for a second before she gave me a sheepish grin. "I kind of think I'm in love with you myself. I get it now. I see why those two care so much about you." Her eyes twinkled in humor. "If I were a lesbian, I'd want you as my girlfriend. I have a straight boner for you, Sam. Hot damn."

Mason cursed behind me.

Her smile widened even more before she left.

When I heard a groan behind me, I turned. "What?"

Mason had a towel in one hand and a bowl in the other. He glared at me now. "She's going to be your new best friend, isn't she?"

I straightened at his words. Was she? Then I shrugged. "I have no idea. Would that bother you?"

He rolled his eyes. "Your friends are either scared of me, want to screw me, or think I'm an asshole. Can't you find some girl who is *just* a good friend to you? Who doesn't care that I'm your boyfriend?"

A snort came out of me. "Please. Do you realize how ridiculous that sounds? One, you are an asshole. Two, a lot of girls want to screw you. And three, if they don't fall into those two slots then they're going to be scared of you, like Becky was."

He grimaced as he reached for another mixing bowl to dry. "I just don't like feeling that I can't be around my girlfriend. I'm sick of having to jump through hoops and sneak around to be with you."

My voice softened. "If what you say is true and Heather and I become good friends, she might turn into that girl who doesn't care about you. She's looking at you through the same lens as everyone else right now. She hasn't seen you with me enough to know how good you treat me. And she's not my mom."

His shoulders relaxed. "Yeah, I know." Then his eyes shot back to me again. "Things aren't done with your mom, you know. We're just in the waiting stage while she regroups." He moved to put the dishes away. When he came back, I pushed another load out of the washer for him. He picked up a plate and leaned back against the wall as he dried it. "My dad's suspicious of her now so she'll focus on him and play nice for awhile. Once she's got him brain-dumb again, she'll start back on you."

I felt stabbed in the gut. I'd always be her second priority. The man was number one.

"Hey," Mason called over, his voice soft again. "You okay?"

I nodded, but I couldn't speak. The emotions were choking me again.

"I said something wrong?"

I shook my head, turning to load more dishes onto the crates. When the washer beeped another cycle, I avoided his gaze and pushed another crate through. He didn't push me, and slowly the emotions started to settle down again. We worked in silence for awhile, maybe an hour, before I noticed that the dishes had stopped piling up so much.

"What the hell, man?" Logan's voice made us both jump as he boomed through the window. "You're both back there? I want to go back there."

Mason came up behind me. I felt his heat as he pressed against me, but he didn't slide his arms around me how I expected. Disappointment flared in me. Then he spoke over my shoulder, "Where's Nate?"

Logan bristled, "Who cares? I don't know. He's with Parker, I think."

Tension replaced my disappointment. Those girls were here too? Did everyone go where Mason and Logan went?

Mason's hand splayed out on the small of my back. I knew he felt how stiff I became at the mention of those girls, but he didn't say anything. For that, I was relieved. Instead, he asked, "When's everyone heading out?"

Logan rolled his eyes and threw an irritated glance over his shoulder. "I think they're all waiting to see what we do. What are you thinking?"

His arms slid around my waist, and I was finally pulled back into him. I breathed a little easier. As he spoke, I felt the rumbling through his chest. "Tell Ethan to have the party at his place."

Logan's eyebrow arched.

Mason's voice had an edge to it. "Why do they always have to be at Nate's? That's our home too. We only had people over to the house when we wanted them."

"Nate initiated the open-door policy."

Mason bit back a growl, but his hand clamped tighter on my waist. "He only did that for us. He'll do whatever we say—"

"Whatever you say, you mean."

"Whatever!" He growled now at his brother. "What's your problem? You've been pissy all day."

My eyes went wide. I knew Logan was just waiting for an opening to start something and Mason had given it to him, but now was not the time or the place. "Okay." I turned and shoved Mason back, then gave Logan a meaningful look. "Get everybody out of here. We'll come to the party when I'm done with work, but I would enjoy a quiet house tonight."

"Yeah. Okay," he grumbled before he glowered at me. Then he sighed and left to do my bidding.

"What was that about?"

I glared at Mason. "Not now, and you know what that was about. Don't play stupid with me."

His head reared back, but a slow smile grew across his face. His eyes darkened, and he licked his lips when he took a step towards me. "I forgot how hot you can get when you're mad at me. You sure about the no sex at work?"

"Mason!"

He laughed but moved back to finish the dishes.

When everyone left and the kitchen closed, Heather assigned me two tables in the bar section. That was fine with me. The other server and Anne were released to leave for the night, leaving Heather, Lily, and me for staff alongside Brandon, who was still behind the bar. As the night drew to a close, I grinned as Mason, Brandon, and Gus watched a game on the television. A few girls remained, all whom were captivated by the guys at the bar. When they wandered over and perched on seats, I knew why Mason chose to sit near one end. The girls were on the other side of Gus, who choked on his drink when the first smiled at him. The other two craned their necks around to see Mason, but he was the good boyfriend. His gaze remained trained on the game, even when two of the girls started a conversation about the game. Brandon was the first to join. He poured their drinks and answered each giggling question they sent his way. Gus piped up too, and when my last customers left, I couldn't stop from watching the show.

"Ah." Heather jumped on the stool next to me as her last table left. "Gus loves when we close. He comes in late sometimes and hangs out with Brandon because he knows that's his best time to get a girl. They're so drunk by then, and he thinks that Brandon makes him look better for his chances. He's in heaven tonight, sitting beside the god-like Mason Kade."

I heard the cynicism and frowned. "You really don't like Mason, do you?"

She hesitated, but then shrugged. "I...I'll be honest, I can't be objective with him. He's the reason Tate isn't around and why she and I stopped being friends. But I like you and you like him and he likes you, so I'm woman enough to say that maybe there's more to him than the asshole everyone says he is."

"With a referral like that, who wouldn't want to get to know him," I teased, but sat up straighter when one of the girls took a deep breath and walked around Gus. She approached Mason, who still hadn't taken his eyes off the television. As she slid onto the one open stool beside him, he still didn't look over. He yawned, instead.

Heather choked on a laugh. She hit her chest and bent over, her shoulders shaking. "Man, if that's not a burn then I don't know what is. The girl is stupid."

Lily stopped on the other side of the counter with a washcloth in hand. "I think she's being brave." Her eyes met mine, and she gave me a timid smile. "I know he's your boyfriend, but a lot of girls don't believe it. She's being brave. She's going for it."

Heather snorted, "She's going to crash and burn. Mason has never been open to cold approaches. Logan, on the other hand, doesn't give a damn, but not that Kade. That Kade has whipped out some doozies for rejections. You know how many girls I've found crying in the bathroom?"

We all grew silent when the girl touched his arm and opened her mouth. There it was. The pick-up line was coming, but then her mouth dropped in shock. Mason stood and threw some money on the counter. He tapped the counter and said something to Brandon before he looked for me. When he saw the small audience, he smirked as he came over.

The girl watched him. When he pulled me into his arms, her mouth snapped shut. I saw the glimmer of anger in her eyes, but then her other friend tugged on her arm and they hurried out of the diner. The door had just about shut when it swung back open and the girl stomped inside. Her hands were on her tiny hips and her mouth was twisted with disgust, but Heather stepped forward. She folded her arms over her chest and lowered her head. As she stood in front of Mason and me, her stance told everyone not to mess with her. It worked. The girl faltered, then wrinkled her nose at us, and glared back at Heather before she turned on her heel. She stormed out once more and slammed the door.

The diner was quiet for a moment before Brandon tipped his head back in laughter. "My sister, the bulldog! Don't mess with a Jax!"

Heather's arms fell to her side and her shoulders came back up. She shook her head, but I heard a soft chuckle escape her mouth. Then she hollered, "Brandon, get Gus out of here and finish cleaning."

"Yeah, yeah."

Lily chuckled behind us as she wiped the counter off. I picked up the other washcloth and it was a half hour later, after the money had been locked away and the last floors were mopped, when everyone filed out to the parking lot. Lily and Brandon sat down on the patio chairs, so Mason and I did the same as everyone waited for Heather. She was the last one.

When she came out, she locked the doors. "We had triple the business tonight than a regular night."

Brandon gestured to Mason. "Because of him and their friends."

I felt my hand squeezed, and Mason whispered in my ear, "I'll wait for you in the car."

I nodded. As he left, Brandon stood up. "I'm tuckered out. See you ladies tomorrow."

Lily called out goodnight to him, and I gave him a small wave as he disappeared around the side of the bar towards their house. As he went, Lily gave us a small smile and wave of her own before she went over to her car.

Heather pulled out a cigarette. When it was lit, she gestured to Mason's Escalade. "He didn't want to stick around and hear our thanks for the business?"

I shrugged. I had no idea. "Ethan Fischer is having a party tonight. We said we'd go. You want to come?"

As she took a drag, she paused for a second. "Are you kidding me?"

I frowned. "No, why would I be? You went to the one last night."

"Yeah, but we shouldn't have gone there. Channing had been opposed the whole time."

"So why did you?"

She took another drag off her cigarette. "Can I be honest?"

Her eyes found mine and fixed there. I felt her studying me in the same way Mason would when he wanted to read my mind. "Sure." But I didn't know why she wouldn't have been honest?

"I saw you last night, after we closed. I waited around because I wasn't sure if you had a ride or not. I know you told me Kade was your boyfriend, but I had my doubts. Then I saw that other guy pick you up and I don't know." She inhaled, and then exhaled. Her head fell down. "I went to the party to see if you were there and if you were okay. I figured any girlfriend of Mason Kade's would be at his party so…"

"You went there to see if I actually was his girlfriend?" Disbelief slammed into my chest. I wasn't used to that reaction. Most girls hated me when they learned the truth, but Heather's reaction was almost refreshing.

"I went there to make sure you were okay."

"Oh."

"Look," she stood from the wall and took another drag. "They haven't told you so I guess I have to. I'm good friends with Channing."

"Okay." I nodded. "Why's that such a big deal?"

She didn't answer again, not right away. But when she did, it all made sense. "He goes to school in Roussou."

CHAPTER SEVENTEEN

Coach Grath met me at a park near my old home where David lived, if he still lived there. I didn't ask why my new coach picked that park, but it was fine with me. This was one of my normal running routes. When I got there, he pointed to the grass, "Stretch out."

He was all business.

Coach Grath had a gruff face. His square jaw gave a no-nonsense vibe and there were no wrinkles around his mouth, like he never smiled or laughed. He was dressed in a crisp-looking track suit with the Fallen Crest Public school colors, red and black. A whistle hung around his neck, and he held a clipboard in his meaty hand. As soon as I was done stretching, he grunted, checked his watch, wrote something down on his clipboard, and gestured to the walking trail. "Keep to the right, circle the park, and come back here. It's one mile. I'm recording your time." He paused before his eyes went flat. "Go."

The abrupt command startled me, but I started off. I wasn't sure what he wanted, but I wasn't going to go my fastest, not until my muscles were looser. When I came back around, he checked his watch again, wrote the time, and told me to go again. As I hauled off, he yelled after me, "Go faster this time."

So I did.

That was my training routine—each mile was timed, and with each lap, he told me to go faster. After I had been running for 90 minutes, he asked how much longer I could go.

"My longest run has been four hours." All at one time with no breaks, but I didn't share that bit with him.

He nodded, wrote something more on his clipboard and pointed at the trail again. "I want you to go your fastest now and don't stop until you're out of gas."

My eyes widened. Did he know what he was getting into? But then he said, "When you're done, remember the time and distance. Report back to me tomorrow, same time, same place. No late nights. Start buying almonds, whole-grains, oranges, and vegetables. Don't carbo-load the night before your long runs."

"I never have."

He had started to leave, but turned back. He didn't blink. "What'd you say?"

"I've never loaded up on carbs the night before. I don't want to change my eating habits, sir."

"Coach."

"Coach."

Then he frowned. "What do you usually eat?"

I shrugged. "Chicken, a bagel every now and then."

He nodded. "Chicken's good. Salmon's better, but don't stretch your bank account. Do what you're already doing for this month. Next month we'll try it my way and see which one has the better results."

I stepped back. "Excuse me, sir?"

"Coach!"

I winced. "Coach. Are you challenging me?"

He folded his clipboard against his chest and tucked his chin down as he gave me a long searching stare. Then he sighed. "Strattan, you came to me. If you want a scholarship, you'll play by my rules. I'm not challenging you, I'm pushing you. You're going to be the best damn runner you can be and if you stick with my rules through the track season and cross country season next fall, you'll be going to a school with a full ride."

"Cross country?"

"Running's a solitary thing for you. It's like that for the best runners, but you better start getting used to not doing everything your way or no way. You're joining both teams whether you like it or not. Make sure to stop at the school sometime this week and fill out all your paperwork. We run at 6 in the morning, every morning."

He didn't wait for my response. As he got inside his car, he hollered back to me, "Run, Strattan! Time and distance, Strattan. Time and distance."

I stood there, not sure what to think so when he tapped his horn once, I got to running. Even though I knew I would be dead for the rest of the day, I did what he ordered. I ran until I had no gas left, and then I ran some more. By the time I was done, I collapsed on the grass and waited until my heart would stop pounding. Then I remembered he said to mark the time and distance. The numbers didn't make sense to me, not much did at that moment, but I knew that I had to stretch and I needed to call for a ride.

Stretching was torture, and by the time Mason arrived, I had fallen asleep.

"Sam." He touched my arm.

I opened my eyes, frowned as he was bent over me. Then I let out a deep groan, "Oh my god."

I couldn't sit up. I tried. I failed.

Mason caught my arm and pulled me to my feet. When I would've fallen back down, he scooped me up and carried me to his car. It wasn't long before he had me buckled in and was in his own seat. Then he pointed to my car. "You want me and Logan to come back and get that?"

I nodded, feeling weak. Why had I run so much? I croaked out, "What time is it?" But my eyes were already closing. I needed sleep, just sleep.

"You have two hours before your shift."

I cursed under my breath. Why the hell had I run so much? But I remembered Coach Grath's barking orders and knew the look on his face would be worth it. His gruff exterior pissed me off. I felt like I had to prove myself to him. No matter what he said, I still felt that he didn't believe in me. I wondered if he was meeting with me as a favor to...I looked sideways. Mason seemed clueless to my thoughts as he drove to Manny's.

Wait, to Manny's? I sat up. "What are you doing?"

He wheeled into the parking lot and turned the engine off. "You're eating. What else would I be doing?"

My mouth fell open. "Mason, I stink! I can't go in there. Everybody will leave because I smell so bad."

He grinned but shook his head. "With Gus as close competition? I doubt it. Come on, Sam. You need to eat and we don't have anything good at the house."

My head fell back with a thump. He went inside. My ass did not. He was nuts if he thought I was going in there. But I did, after he came out and carried me inside. Lily grinned when she saw the state I was in. And after our food orders were taken, I glanced around. I hadn't before, I didn't want to see the reactions to my messy appearance when Mason walked through the diner, but couldn't stop myself now.

The place was full, but Mason chose a corner table for me. There was a fan beside me, so I dried off quickly, and it was pointed out the side door. All my sweaty fumes went that way. Still, while I wanted to be invisible, I knew whom I was with. Mason attracted attention, and with him beside me and how I looked, we were getting a lot of attention. It was unavoidable.

Heather came over with our water, but instead of leaving, she dropped into the chair beside me. "You want to tell me why you look like you ran a marathon?"

Mason grunted but reached for his glass.

I slunk further down my chair. "That bad, huh?"

"Sammy, don't tell me you ran a marathon? You're on shift in two hours."

"I know, I know." I opened my mouth, ready to start explaining how my new coach was a potential ass, when the door opened and more people strolled inside. "Where did all these people come from?"

"Oh." She jerked a thumb towards Mason. "You can thank your boy here."

"Huh?"

He narrowed his eyes, but didn't say a word.

"Mason?"

"Or maybe it's because of you." Heather studied me again.

Mason gave me a strained smile before he stood up. "I'll be back in a few."

I watched him walk over to a table in the back section, close to the bar, before Heather pulled my attention back by saying, "My dad's over the moon."

"Huh?"

She nodded in Mason's direction. "Word got out that Mason and Logan Kade were both here last night, then word got out that their stepsister works here, and everybody put two and two together. Judging from the crowd we had this morning and how it hasn't let up since, I'm figuring my baby is the new hang-out."

Dread formed in my gut. I liked this place because it was small and private. That was gone now. Then my eyes widened again as I saw the section by the front door. "Academy students are here too?"

"Yeah." She turned to look too. "Those some friends of yours?"

Definitely not.

Jessica shot daggers at me while Lydia sat beside her. Across from them were Becky and another guy who was bouncing in his chair. Jeff sat on his other side, laughing at something he said, but it was the table next to them that had me surging to my feet. Adam was the closest to Becky. He had a hand out to her chair and the two were conversing while the Academy Elite sat around the rest of his table. Miranda's lips thinned as she scanned the diner. The other three girls had spotted me and converged together. When their hands came up to block their mouths I knew the whispering gossip had started. Again. The only two who seemed semi normal were Peter and Mark, but when I caught Mark's gaze for a second, I flinched and turned away.

"...he wants to break the news that he thinks his mom and Coach are going to get hitched, but he doesn't know how to."

I couldn't deal with that. I couldn't think about David and his mother together. Was that the reason my dad had stopped calling me? Adam said that to me two months ago, which now feels like ages ago. Mark was going to be family to me. I felt a burning in my chest. It was tightening, suffocating me. I jerked away from my table, but ran into someone.

"Okay." A strong hand took hold of my elbow and pulled me through the crowd. I couldn't see anyone. I had no idea where Mason was, he had left me. The door was kicked open and we were outside. Barely registering the fresh air, I was pushed down in a chair and my head was shoved between my legs. "Breathe, Sam. Jeez, just breathe."

I took gasping breaths and my eyes closed against the visions that assaulted me.

I pushed open the bathroom door, but he wasn't in there either. "Dad?" Where had he gone? Mom needed him. Mom was bleeding. I hurried back around the bed, but tripped over something. There was a bag on the floor — no, it was a suitcase. Mom was going somewhere? A sob came up in my throat and I whimpered, "Daddy."

His clothes were in the suitcase. Some of his other clothes were spread all over the room. They'd been thrown like that. Why would he do that? He wasn't like that.

Mom was bleeding. I had to go to her.

I pushed myself up, stepped over the suitcase, and hurried down the hallway again. As I neared it, I slowed down. I didn't want to go in there. She was so still and so white. I had only seen another person that white before, when my dad picked me up after I fell off our patio. He took me to the hospital — mom needed the hospital. I turned and went for the phone.

"Hey." Mason's calming voice brought me back as he picked me up and held me in his arms. Then I felt him turning away.

"Where are you taking her, Kade?"

His voice was rough as he threw over his shoulder, "She just needs a minute. She'll be fine. Don't worry."

"Come on, Kade—"

He twisted back around. "I said, she'll be fine. Leave it, Jax."

The edge left her tone. "Take her to my house. It's not the Grand Ritz you guys live in, but it's private. She can shower there. I have a pile of clothes next to my bed. I lent some to her before; she can pick what she wants to wear."

He stiffened underneath me. I knew he wanted to take me home, but enough reason had filtered back to me that I lifted my head from his shoulder. My voice was still weak, "That's fine, Mason. I have to work. I can't miss my shift."

"You sure?" His eyes searched mine.

I nodded but started to tremble at the look of concern in his depths. There was so much love. I lifted my hands to his face and cupped it. His eyes closed and he drew in a ragged breath. My thumb caressed over his cheek. He was so handsome. Perfect. And he was mine. I pressed a kiss to his lips. He hesitated, but I whispered, "I'm fine. I'm fine." Then his mouth opened underneath mine, and he took over the kiss.

I pressed closer, but he had already gentled the kiss by the time he stepped around the back of Manny's. As he put me back down on my feet, he indicated the house. "This is the place?"

"Uh…" I could only focus on how much I wanted to feel him, only him. "Yeah, I guess."

He stepped onto the squeaky patio and opened the screen door. I followed when he went inside, and he stopped to peruse their small living room and kitchen. The stairs were straight ahead with an open door beside them. I saw now that it led to a bedroom. The same boxes of liquor were inside, along with clothes, and dirty dishes.

I gestured upstairs. "Her room's up there. I'm going to shower and change. You'll be okay down here?"

He hadn't stopped looking at the living room. A ratted couch was covered with a bed sheet. The table in front of was covered with magazines, dirtied plates, and cans of beer and soda. Against the wall, their large screen television was the only thing that looked expensive. Mason took a step around the couch and lifted one of the remotes. When he saw that I was waiting, he nodded, "I'll be fine. You're okay up there?"

I nodded. I knew he was really asking if I'd have any more panic attacks, but it hadn't been a full-fledged one. Or maybe I was becoming used to them. "I'll be fine. I'll hurry down."

"No, no." He waved a hand at me. "Take your time."

"You sure?"

"Yeah. I'll be fine."

"Okay." I grinned as he stood in the middle of the living room, searching where to sit. There was a loveseat next to the couch, but it was covered with a similar bedsheet. He bent down and removed a pile of magazines from one corner and perched on the edge. When the television turned on, I headed upstairs.

CHAPTER EIGHTEEN

I heard raised voices when I got out of the shower and ran downstairs. My body was tired. Actually, my heart was tired. But when I heard Mason, a jolt of adrenaline burst through me. I grabbed a towel on the way and had it wrapped around me when I skidded to a halt at the bottom of the stairs. Mason had his back to me. His shoulders were tense and bunched forward. His hands were in fists at his side, and I knew he was a heartbeat away from a fight. When I took another step down, my eyes widened. Heather stood in front of that guy, the model with tattoos. He was in the doorway and had a similar stance as Mason's, but her hands were braced to his chest. A snarl was on her face until she threw a look over her shoulder and saw me. Her eyes bulged out.

"Chill, Chan. Seriously. There's the evidence, smack dab in a towel. You see her?" She shoved her friend back a step. Then she swung an arm and pointed at me. "He was here for her, not me."

Mason glanced back and bit out a curse. "Sam." He stepped up to block me from view. "Go get some clothes on."

"But," I searched around him.

The guy had visibly relaxed, but Heather was still in front of him. Her arms were crossed, and I knew from the tension in her shoulders that she was glaring at him.

"Go." Mason's hands gripped my hips as he urged me up a step.

"Go with her," Heather spoke over her shoulder.

"Better idea. Let's go."

"What was going on?"

But he wasn't listening. When I didn't move, he scooped me up in his arms and carried me up the stairs. His arm wrapped around the back of my legs and my body kept straight so I watched over his shoulder. Heather glanced at us and shook her head. She rolled her eyes, but the guy said something to her. As she looked back at him, she swatted at his shoulder. And then I couldn't see anymore as Mason stopped at the top of the stairs.

"What happened down there?"

"I'll tell you when you've got some clothes on."

"Oh."

"Exactly."

I'd forgotten about my state of undress. I giggled. And then I really thought about the situation. I had a mini-panic attack, Mason brought me here to regroup and shower, and then I walked in on him about to get into a fight with only a towel on. Goodness. The swift change of events had me feeling light-headed as I sat on Heather's bed.

"What's wrong?"

I shook my head, still dazed. "I take it that guy didn't like that you were here?"

He grimaced and then sighed. "Where are those clothes? I'll feel better when you're dressed."

"Okay." But I didn't move.

"Seriously?" He raked a hand through his hair, the little he had with his crew cut. His eyes widened and irritation flashed over them. His shirt lifted from the movement. I caught a glimpse of his abdominal muscles, sculpted with perfection. The oblique muscles had been hardened and stuck out as they disappeared under jeans that hung low on his hips.

I licked my lips. God, those muscles. I wanted to touch them. I wanted to—his hand caught mine and he hauled me off the bed and into his arms. I found myself staring into heated eyes, lined with suppressed anger and more. A groan escaped me, and I started to close my eyes as my head bent down. I needed him. His kiss before had sparked the flame, but now it raged inside of me. I couldn't bank it down now.

"Are you two kidding me?"

Heather's voice was like a bucket of cold water being thrown over us. I shoved back from Mason. I would've pulled him down to the bed. Even if he had protested, I knew that I would've made him forget where we were. Goodness. I drew in a gaping breath as I clutched my towel, the only thing covering me still.

I croaked out, "Heather."

She was in the doorway with a fierce frown on her face. Her arms were crossed, but she jerked a thumb over her shoulder. "I brought your food over here, figured you'd need some grub in you." Then she looked at Mason. "I'm sorry about Channing. He's a bit protective of me, and you're…you…"

He clipped his head in a nod but didn't say a word. As he turned to look out the window, he stuffed his hands into his pockets.

"So…" Heather watched me now.

I flushed and grabbed some of her clothes. "I'll put these on and head downstairs."

She waved at me. "Take your time. I wanted to check on you, didn't realize what I'd be walking in on. But whatever. Logan showed up and filled me in on some things. Your friends are all still there so you're going to be dishwasher again tonight. I hope that's okay."

Relief washed over me. I nodded, unable to speak for a moment.

"Frank went home. His wife is coming in. I was going to have you cover a full section tonight, but I get what's going on. Rosa will fill in for you. When things get crazy busy like this, you can go to the back. We'll figure it out as we go. Sound good?"

I nodded again. It sounded perfect.

Her eyes lingered on Mason before she looked back to me. Her concern was evident. "You'll be okay for the night?"

"Yes. I mean it." I did. Determination spread through me. I wasn't going to disrupt anyone else's life because of my issues. "I can sit if I need to in the back."

Mason turned around, now more in control. He said in a soft tone, "I'll help her too."

Heather nodded. "I figured you might want to."

His jaw clenched. His eyes touched on me for a split second, but he turned back for the window. When his tension didn't leave him, I nodded to Heather's unspoken question if he would be alright. She frowned, but left a second later. As soon as she went down the stairs, I shut the door. "What's going on with you?"

"Nothing."

"Mason," I sighed. His answer had been short, too short. "I'm sorry that I freaked out before—"

He swung around. This time he didn't hold back his anger and I was startled from the fierceness of it. "You're sorry? What the hell happened? I never have any idea when you're going to flip out or sprint off for one of those long-ass runs you do. They're not healthy, Sam. I've been quiet for a long time, but you need to start telling me what going on with you."

"Mason," I started.

"I mean it." His jaw was clenched tight, and his eyes glittered with emotion. He'd had enough.

I saw it then and knew that my hiding was done. I slumped down on the bed and hung my head. This was going to be painful.

I took a deep breath. I was going to need it. "I've been having flashbacks to that night with my mom."

"Your mom? What night?"

"The night she lost the baby—"

His shoulders loosened a fraction, but he remained by the window. "You said she killed her baby."

I nodded. A storm of emotions swirled inside of me, but I couldn't deal with them, not now. "Yeah, I know. She did, but I didn't know then and I keep remembering it in bits and pieces."

"Oh."

I needed to tell him more. I needed to explain it all to him. So I rasped out, "I saw Mark Decraw in the diner and it sent me into a tailspin. I'm sorry. I really am, just the sight of him reminded me of his mom, who might be married to my dad now and…" I drew in a shuddering breath. The pain ripped through me, stabbing me in the gut. "I have no idea if he married her or not. He hasn't reached out to me at all."

Mason sat beside me on the bed and picked up one of my hands. He held it in his lap. "David's not married to that woman. The divorce isn't even finalized with your mom."

"Oh."

I blinked in surprise. I should've known that.

"Logan told me about that before, but I didn't realize you bought into it. Decraw has no idea about your parent's divorce. He's a dumbass. Don't listen to anything he says."

"Oh."

"Was that it?" He frowned at me.

I couldn't get over how stupid I'd been.

"Sam."

"What?"

He narrowed his eyes and studied me again. One of his fingers tipped my chin up so I was looking him straight into the eyes. I couldn't look away. While his eyes held mine captive, he asked further, "What else happened before? Your dad being a neglectful asshole didn't push you over the edge. You had a flashback again?"

I nodded. My throat was full as I remembered it all again. I couldn't explain how the reminder of David took me back to the night he had left me again—no, when he left me the first time. I shook my head as tears leaked out. I didn't want to tell him that I called for an ambulance, all on my own, or how I sat beside my mother. I sat in her blood.

He should've been there.

That thought raced through me, along with a bolt of anger. My jaw hardened. He should've been there. I shouldn't have had to do that on my own. I'd only been eleven. A goddamn eleven-year-old and I had to call 911 for my mother.

"What are you thinking right now?"

The words slipped from me, "It was the first time he left, Mason." My chest lifted. A dull ache started in my gut. "She tried to kill the baby on her own and I found her. I went and looked for him, but he wasn't there. I think," I drew in a deep breath. "I think they had a fight or something. His suitcase was on the floor and his clothes were everywhere. I don't know what happened, but I remembered hearing them before. They'd been fighting. He was going to leave her…" I couldn't finish. I didn't want to remember anymore.

"You okay?"

I couldn't tell him anymore. It was too painful. But then I didn't have to. Mason slid an arm underneath my legs and he lifted me again. He folded me onto his lap, and I curled into him. His hand smoothed up and down my back. It was a comforting motion, one that I needed so much, but after we sat in silence for awhile, I needed to pull away. I had to work soon and he couldn't keep holding my hand every time I felt like I was going to break.

My eyes shot to his, bleak and exhausted. He mirrored what I was feeling. "What was going on downstairs? That guy thought you were here with Heather?'

He jerked his head in a nod. His body stiffened underneath me. "Mason."

With gentle hands, he deposited me back onto the bed but didn't move away. I was relieved. Instead, he held my hand and rested his arms on his legs. "Heather brought the food over. She'd been here two seconds before he showed up. He went berserk when he saw her and me together. We weren't even on the same couch or anything. She was in the kitchen and I was in the living room, but he saw me in her home and connected the wrong dots together."

"She told me that he goes to Roussou. It's because of that, isn't it? I know you guys hate that school."

"There's more to it than that, but yeah, he's from Roussou. He doesn't run with the same crew as the Broudou brothers, but he knows my history with them. I'm sure that's part of it."

"The Broudou brothers?"

Mason nodded. His shoulders had filled again with tension. "Yeah, there are three of them. Two are seniors this year, twins, and they have a third little brother in your grade. But all of them hate me."

"Why you?" Other than the normal high school football rivalry, I meant. I remembered the first night I saw them and knew I'd be moving in with them. Two cars had pulled up and an instant fight exploded, then they lit their cars on fire.

"Those three hate me because of their sister."

Blank.

Uh, what?

"Huh?"

He chuckled at my reaction. "Don't worry. Nothing happened with me and her, but that's not what she's told them."

"So what do they think?"

"That I met her at a party, slept with her, and never called her back. They think I treated her like trash."

I blinked again, startled. Mason wasn't always the nicest to girls, but he wasn't known to sleep around. But I knew he hadn't been a monk. "Did you?"

"No!"

I held up my hands in surrender at his glare. "I'm sorry. I had to know for sure."

His eyes narrowed. Instead of the tension leaving him, it increased. "I would never touch a girl like that. She tried to seduce Nate first, but he threw her aside. Then she tried Logan. Even he didn't want anything to do with her. We all knew who she was."

"When did this happen?"

"Two years ago. Logan had broken up with Tate, and because that had just happened, I swore off girls. I didn't have a great view of her gender already and then Broudou started saying that I slept with her and dropped her. Her brothers demanded that I do right and date her, but like hell I was going to do that. I wasn't going to do a goddamn thing anyone told me to do. I was sick and tired of people trying to manipulate me."

Oh god. My forehead fell against his arm. I already knew how he must've handled that. "You didn't kill anyone, did you?"

He chuckled. The sound of it sounded foreign from the tension in his body. "No, but I wanted to. I wanted to kill her. I'll be honest. After Tate, then her, I had a piss poor opinion of girls."

I sighed. "What happened after that?"

"Nothing. She still claims the same story. Her brothers hate me, have hated me ever since. And you know the rest. Things aren't exactly friendly whenever we have any interaction with someone from Roussou."

And that was the reason for Channing's reaction downstairs.

"I'm sorry."

"For what?" He looked down at me. The anger was still brimming within him, but it had softened. "You had nothing to do with that."

"Yeah, but I always thought you guys were jerks before. I didn't know the history with Roussou, but I judged you before I even knew you."

A grin curved up from the corners of his mouth. Then he shifted so he could pull me back into his lap. He smiled at me. "Well, you said it before. I am an asshole."

"But not that time, not with her."

He shrugged. "I'm not going to let some shady bitch affect me."

I could've pointed out that she had, but I held my tongue. Mason didn't think of it that way, and I knew if he did, I would have reason to fear what he would do because that girl, whatever her name was, had changed things for him and Logan. I didn't know all of the ramifications, but I had a feeling they went deeper than even he realized.

"What's her name?"

"Why?" He shot me a look.

I smiled at him, to show that I didn't have an agenda. "No reason, but if I run into her, I'll know to go the other way."

"Oh." He frowned, but then replied, "Shannon Broudou."

I didn't need to commit that name to memory. It was already seared in, permanently, but I had lied to him. I very much had an agenda, and if I ever met her, there was no way I was going to go the other way. For the first time in a long time, I knew that was a confrontation that I didn't want to avoid. That was one that I wanted. She had hurt my family.

CHAPTER NINETEEN

That night set a pattern for the rest of my break. I ran in the mornings for Coach Grath and worked at Manny's in the evenings. I didn't run as much as I had that first time, but when I reported my time and distance the next day, he blinked. It wasn't much of a reaction, but as I started to get to know my coach over the next week, I realized that had been a huge reaction for him. He pushed me to beat my times each day until I told him that I was on my feet the rest of the day at my job. So, then he told me to beat my times on the days I didn't work, which I planned to do anyways. I was already salivating for my next day off.

"Hey, baby girl."

Heather broke my reverie, and I jerked the dishwasher head so it sprayed all over me. "Ah!" I dropped it and jumped back. As it twisted from the cord, it sprayed her in the window and she yelped. "Turn it off, turn it off!"

I scrambled for the faucet and rotated it to the side. The water stopped, but the damage was done. Both of us were wet from head to toe. Great. I had to work in these clothes for the rest of the night, seven hours left to go.

Laughing, Heather jerked a thumb over her shoulder. "I'll grab you some clothes. This will suck when the rush comes."

"Thanks."

Lily glanced in, and she grinned from ear to ear. "It's a good look. Those Roussou guys will enjoy it."

My eyes went wide. Roussou?

Heather froze for a moment. "Oh, uh…" Then she turned to me. There was a warning there.

Oh no. A deep knot formed in my gut. This couldn't be good.

Lily cocked her head to the side. Her long black hair had been pulled high into a ponytail, and she caught the end over one shoulder. She twirled it in one hand as her smile dimmed an inch. "Joke, guys. That was a joke."

Heather twisted around. Her shoulders stiffened before she whipped back to me and her wet hair slapped Lily in the face. With white knuckles, she gripped the window's edge and leaned close. "Brett and Budd are here. You don't leave this room, not one foot out there, you hear?"

Everything had gone numb at her reaction. If Heather was this scared…I gulped. I didn't want to finish that thought.

"Text your boy. Make up some lie. He cannot come here tonight."

"I—"

"They'll jump him, Sam," she hissed. "They'll do worse to you if they find out who you are." The warning heated up in her eyes. "I won't let them hurt you, but they must know you're here. They wouldn't have come if they didn't."

"Okay." Lily forced out a laugh. "You guys are making me nervous. I was just joking before. I know you didn't get wet on purpose. What's going on?"

Heather's hand shot to her arm. She latched on with a death grip. "You stay with those guys all night. You smile, you serve, you make them happy, but you don't say a word to them about Sam, the Kades, or anything that has anything to do with them."

Lily's eyes went wide and she took a step back. "You guys are really starting to freak me out. Wait; is this because of the school pranks and stuff? I didn't think it was that bad."

"Just do what I say." Then she paused, frowning. "Where'd they sit?"

"In the back section. Anne already got their drinks."

"Take over her section."

"What about Gia? She's supposed to come in at 5:00 today."

A spew of curses came from Heather as she glared out at the diner. "I'll call her. I know she'll say something. I'll have Rosa come in for her instead." She turned and fixed us with a steely gaze. She meant business. "We good on the plan?"

Both of us nodded. My hand itched to salute her.

"Good. I'm going to run home quick. Be back in five."

When she dashed out, Lily looked back at me. "Is it really that bad?"

I took a deep breath as I gripped the rinse head in my hands. "Let's just say those guys hate Mason and if they hate him…" My eyebrows went up as she finished the sentence in her head.

She gasped. "You think they'd hurt you?"

I deadpanned, "Heather doesn't freak out for no reason."

She paled. "Oh, dear."

Oh dear, indeed.

I grimaced. Tonight was not going to be fun.

And it wasn't.

I had my suspicions, but I found out for sure that Brett and Budd's last name was Broudou. I figured, judging from Heather's reaction, but I wanted to know for certain. One time, I snuck a peek and saw two mammoth size linebackers at a back table. There were other guys with them and a few girls too. A short stocky girl with blonde hair had a similar face as theirs, square and tough, had me wondering if that was their sister. She glanced at me and I stepped back inside, but a part of me didn't want to.

I didn't want to hide from this girl, not when I knew how she had lied and caused so many problems for Mason and Logan. It wasn't the right time, though the need to say something to her was burning the back of my heels.

More and more customers poured into the diner and I eventually forgot about the Broudou siblings. I rushed to catch up with the dishes and even stepped out to load the glassware behind the bar. When my bladder was screaming for release, I shot past the table and hurried into the bathroom. It wasn't until I was returning that I remembered Heather's warning. Too late. I tried to slip past their table, but a muscular guy stumbled backwards, straight into my pathway. He would've knocked me over if I hadn't sidestepped him.

"Hey, whoa." Two meaty hands wrapped around my arms from behind. "Steady there, girl."

I wrenched my arms away and shot the guy a dark glare.

"Whoa," he said again as his eyes went wide. He stepped back.

It was one of the brothers.

A shrill feminine laugh peeled out, "She don't want your help, Brett. You're not good enough for her."

His eyes had seemed startled before, but now they darkened. A tinge of anger seeped in, and his jaw locked in place. Another chair scraped against the floor and the other mammoth stepped next to him. His eyes were already filled with dark intent. A cruel smile spread over his face before he cleared his throat. "Is that true, girly? My brother's not good enough for you?"

"Hey!"

Heather's shout jolted us. She stood behind their friend, the one who had stumbled in front of me, and wielded a long towel in one hand. A butcher knife was in the other. Her legs were planted apart. She looked ready to fight. My eyes trailed past her shoulder. Brandon was behind her. He folded his arms over his chest. Even Gus was watching the exchange with a somber expression.

Both of the brothers' heads shot up, but it was Budd who gave her a fierce frown. "What do you want, Jax?"

"Get away from her!" She pointed at me.

His eyes narrowed, and he sent me a long sidelong look before his chest puffed up. "Oh yeah? Why's that?"

"Budd." She growled in warning.

"Brett was only talking to her. That's it. What's all the fuss about?" But his narrowed eyes wouldn't stop flitting back to me. I could see the wheels turning. It was then that I knew he didn't know who I was. Relief washed over me. My knees almost buckled, but I caught myself and folded my arms over my own chest. I tried to quench the sudden trembling.

"I mean it, Budd. Let her pass."

His hand started to lift. I sucked in my breath. I knew he was reaching for me…

At the same time, he asked, "Why? What's she to you?"

In slow motion, I watched as Heather's stormy eyes filled with even more anger. She opened her mouth. I knew she was going to let it slip, she thought they already knew, but I had to stop her.

I grabbed Budd's hand and twisted it. In a flash, I wrapped his arm behind his back and yanked at his wrist.

A scream came from him. He buckled under the force I was putting on his wrist. I was a tenth of his weight, but in that moment I could've snapped his wrist in two. A strangled cry came from him as he cursed, but then I was pulled away from him. When I expected rough hands, I was surprised to feel a gentle touch as Brett lifted me in the air and took three steps from his brother and around their friend. He placed me on my feet in front of Heather. As he frowned at me, he said to her, "We didn't mean any harm, Heather."

Her glower slipped a notch, but she still glared. "She's my friend." She stressed the last word.

His frown deepened. "We figured. We didn't mean any harm."

A sudden light clicked on in her depths, and I stepped in front of her. I said to the hulk, "We're friends and she's protective because I work here too."

He nodded, his eyebrows bunched together. "I figured that too. Look, we didn't come to hurt no girl."

"Then why are you here?" Heather scoffed behind me. She was more composed now. "This diner's in Fallen Crest. This ain't your town, and it ain't your crowd. What are you doing here?"

"Truth?" He scratched the back of his head.

Her eyes narrowed to slits. "You'd lie to me now?"

"No, no. I didn't mean that. But," he twisted around and took in the varying emotions from his family and friends. "We came for a brawl. We heard the Kades hang here a bunch. We were hoping to see them."

Heather nudged me with her elbow. I gulped—I hadn't had time to text Mason yet. He didn't know to not come tonight. Again, oh dear.

Brandon stepped closer to our group. "Hey, uh, Brett, I think maybe it's best if you guys take off."

"Why?"

Heather snorted. Her hand found her hip and her chin jutted out. "Are you serious? You admitted that you came here for a fight? At my establishment."

Brandon coughed.

She amended, "At my family's establishment."

"That's better."

She rolled her eyes. "I'm not as nice as my brother. Get out. I want your whole brood out. No one's fighting here. You're not going to destroy my family's livelihood, and you're definitely not going to scare away our *regular* customers."

"Oh, um." He turned back to his group. "They want us to go."

The blonde gasped. She shot forward from the table and was in Heather's face within two steps. "Are you effing kidding me?"

"Hey, whoa, Shannon. She's—"

"Back off, Shannon!"

Heather sucked in her breath, but tattooed-model Channing stepped around Brandon and got in the Broudou's little sister's face.

It was confirmed.

This was Shannon. This was the girl that had caused so many problems for Mason and Logan. My eyes narrowed to slits and my head went low. I wanted to hurt her. I wanted to do more than that.

I wanted to hurt her like she hurt Mason. The need for violence was starting to sizzle deep inside of me. It was on a low burn, but the notch was turning up. It was going to be going full blast in a minute.

I was distantly aware that one of the mammoth brothers said something to Heather's model, who said something back. The Shannon bitch had melted once she realized who snapped at her. A seductive smile was on her face now. I felt Heather's tension beside me and touched her arm. When she looked at me, she gasped and then shuffled so she blocked me from their view. Her hands went to my shoulders and she whispered to Brandon, "Get her out of here. Now."

His hand grasped the top of my arm, and he dragged me out the side door. As soon as the screen door slammed shut, he closed the second door as well. Then he started towards the house and I went. Wait, no. What was I doing? I dug my heels in and pulled away.

"Stop."

"No." His hand adjusted his hold and he yanked me even further after him.

"I have to go back. That girl," I gasped. That girl had been the start of all of it. If I said something, if I told them what happened—

"Hey!" someone yelled from the parking lot.

Brandon cursed but kept going.

I twisted around and frowned as I saw dark silhouettes. Someone was running towards us, there were more behind him. As he drew closer, he yelled again, "Let her go!"

Adam.

Brandon stopped and turned to face him. "Look, man. You don't know what's going on."

Adam's face twisted in a scowl. As he caught up to us, he ripped Brandon's hand from my arm and pulled me away. "No, man. You don't know what's going on. You okay, Sam? What were you doing?"

But I wasn't listening. I had turned back. It was that girl. I had to get to her. I didn't care about the consequences. They'd know about me, but they were going to find out anyway. It was on my time, this way. I chose it. I chose how. I chose when. I decided what they would be told. I started back. I heard Adam and Brandon's voices behind me, but I kept going.

"Stop her!" Brandon barked behind me.

"Hey, whoa." Adam moved to block him. "Back off, buddy. I mean it."

"Adam?"

I was focused on the side door, but the soft voice made me pause. I turned, everything was in slow motion now, and I couldn't believe what I saw. Becky was there, in person, with frightened eyes. Her red hair was pulled back in some fancy braided hairstyle. She held hands with a scruffy-looking guy beside her. His eyes were glazed over and his hair stuck up in all directions. He wore a ratty tee shirt over baggy and torn jeans. When he noticed my attention, he gave me a blinding smile. It was soft at the corners, and the focus in his eyes dimmed. Then he lifted his free hand. "Heya there."

Becky was dating someone. I remembered Adam telling me that. She was dating someone from Fallen Crest Public. I sucked in my breath. This was him, had to be. A different kind of pain sliced through me. She hadn't stuck up for me when Adam lied to her. She hadn't stuck beside me, and when he told her the truth, she still hadn't come to me to apologize. This was the one friend I thought would've stuck with me through everything. She hadn't. Now she had a boyfriend, and she never told me.

It was trivial to be hurt by that, but it stung.

I didn't notice her pale features until her voice trembled, "Sam?"

I stopped thinking. I forgot about what was going on behind me and what was happening in the diner. Someone that I had considered a friend was in front of me. So I opened my mouth and said the first thing that came to mind, "I have a new friend."

She reared back as if I had slapped her.

I kept going. My voice sounded distant. "She's tough. She's in there right now." I gestured towards the side door. "She's covering my back and you know what else?" I waited. Becky was looking everywhere but me. Then her jaw stopped shaking, and she made eye contact. Finally. "Mason and Logan respect her."

She flinched again.

Adam cursed behind me. "Sam! Seriously." He grabbed my arm and jerked me behind him. "Becky, go back to the car."

Her feet didn't move. Her head went down and her shoulders started to shake as if she were crying. The guy next to her stepped closer. A half frown was on his face, and he lifted a hand to her back.

Then Brandon moved forward. "You guys are friends with her?"

Becky's crying grew louder. She hiccupped now.

Adam grimaced. "Yeah. We are."

"Then get her out of here. Otherwise a massive fight's going to erupt."

I whipped my gaze from Becky as Brandon strode past us and yanked open the door. He went through and it slammed behind him. Then I heard a click and physically cringed from the sound of it. He locked the door. If I wanted in, I'd have to go through the front door, and I already knew Heather would shoo me out immediately.

"What just happened?" Adam frowned at the locked door.

My shoulders lifted in a deep breath. "I got the night off."

CHAPTER TWENTY

I didn't know where else to go, and I needed to find Mason so we went to Nate's house. In Adam's car was Becky with her boyfriend, Adam and me. I found out the boyfriend's name was Raz and he thought Logan was "neat-o." When we drove up to the mansion, Adam frowned and parked around the fountain. "No lights are on. No one's home?"

It didn't matter. I got out and pressed the code to the garage. As we went in, I flipped on the lights.

"Oh, wow." Becky spun in a tight circle as the mansion was flooded with light. "I didn't expect that."

Raz held onto her hand and blasted me a bright smile.

I frowned. The kid seemed off, but she seemed happy with him. He had comforted her in the alley and then made her giggle in the backseat. Everyone knew she'd been tense because of me. I wondered how long they'd been dating or how they got together, but then she glanced at me and I stopped wondering.

Her eyes were full of questions, along with something dark. She couldn't be sorry. She chose her fate. She had nothing to feel sad about.

I felt a swift kick to my gut again. She'd been the friend I thought would stay no matter what and she bailed.

The corner of her lip started to tremble. But I moved away. Becky wasn't my problem anymore. She stopped being my problem the moment she believed Adam's lie.

"Where's Kade?" Adam frowned at me.

I shook my head. "Hold on." I hurried up the stairs and to our bedroom, but no one was in there. No note, nothing. I wasn't sure what I was looking for, but I hadn't expected the empty house. Reaching for my back pocket, I cursed. I left my purse and phone at the diner.

"Adam," I called out as I went out to the banister.

"Yeah?"

"My stuff's at the diner. I left it all there."

He held a finger up. "Hold on." Then pulled out his phone and pressed a number. It wasn't long before we heard him ask, "Can I speak to Heather Jax? Oh, hey! This is Adam Quinn....Yeah, I'm a friend of Sam's...Yeah, we brought her home, but listen....yeah, her stuff's still there." He nodded a few more times, murmured 'yeah' again, and then said, "That sounds great. Thanks."

He looked up. "She's going to bring it over after closing, but she said there was a text from Mason. She read one and it said something about a family meeting with his mom?" He frowned. "You know what that meant?"

Relief rushed through me. They were in L.A. They were not headed to the diner. I nodded. "Yeah, I know. They won't be home till tomorrow."

Raz let out a whoop. "Hellsayeaha! Party in the Monson's bisnatch!"

Becky glared and slapped her hand to his chest.

He grunted and doubled over but peeked at her from the corner of his eye. When she rolled her eyes, he wrapped his arms around her and twirled her in the air. More giggles came from her with his laughter intermixed. The two disappeared down the hallway.

As I came down the stairs, Adam followed me into the kitchen area and sat on a bar stool. I started looking through the cupboards when he asked, "It's weird with her?"

I spied the rum and snatched it up. When I put it on the counter between us, I ignored his shock and looked for two shot glasses. I didn't like the hard stuff, but this rum was citrus flavored. This stuff I could drink just fine. Logan would be so proud of me right now.

"So it is weird." He nodded as he answered himself.

I pursed my lips from annoyance. I didn't want to talk about Becky. I didn't want to think about Becky, and I certainly didn't want to acknowledge that she was even in my home now. I put the two shot glasses between us and filled both to the rim. I slid one towards him and gripped the other. "Here's to not thinking about how we should go back to Manny's so I can beat that girl's ass."

Adam choked on his drink. "What?!"

I took my shot in one gulp. It was there. It was gone. I filled it again. As I tossed that one back, I started for a third, but Adam grabbed the bottle away from me.

His eyes were searching me. "What are you talking about? What girl?"

I wanted that bottle back. I needed it to help me forget. She had hurt Mason. I wanted to hurt her. I was starting to forget the consequences of going back and doing just that. What could her brothers do to me anyway? Heather could've been overreacting.

"Nothing," I clipped out.

"Sam."

I eyed the bottle in his hand, and when his hand relaxed, I grabbed it from him. I had my third shot poured within a second. He sat back with a defeated sigh so I filled a second one for him. Then I put the bottle between us as we both took our glasses and lifted them in the air. As he drank his, I leaned against the counter. Then I found myself saying, "There's a girl back there that did something to Mason. She caused a lot of problems for him and I really want to hurt her."

"Sam."

I grimaced against the sympathy in his voice and downed that third shot. It didn't burn. None of the three drinks had, but I didn't taste the sweetness anymore.

I pressed my hands against my eyes. What was I doing? I didn't drink my problems away. I wasn't that girl. I drew in a shuddering breath. What was going on? So much had happened and in such a short amount of time.

"Sam." Adam's voice was soft this time. He had moved around the counter and stood close as he pulled my hands away. "What's going on?"

"Nothing."

I pulled away from him, but he didn't release my hands. He kept them in his grip and he bent down so he could see me eye to eye. "Sam, talk to me. What is going on with you? I'm lying to your mom. Logan said about you running away and how they can't press charges against you? Then you took this job at Manny's, which I kind of understand, but now you're living here? What happened with your mom?"

"Sam?"

A whimper came from the doorway. I knew Becky had heard everything. Oh god. The secrets were out, but were they even secrets?

"Sam." Adam pulled me into him and wrapped his arms around me. He rested his chin on top of my head and smoothed a hand down my back. "You can talk to us. Becky messed up—"

She scooted closer. "I did. I really did. I'm sorry, Sam. I really am."

He continued after a deep breath, "—but she still cares about you. So do I, and I'm trying to embrace this platonic stuff here. I don't know what boundary is where and what line says only friendship, but you need to start helping out. I think if you talked to us, that'd be okay. Right?" He looked over his shoulder to Becky. "You'd ask this, right?"

She bobbed her head up and down. Her hands were folded in front of her as she scooted closer two steps. "Yes. I would. I'd want to know—"

I pushed away from Adam and rounded on her. "You don't get to do this."

Her eyes went wide. "Do what?"

"Come in here and try to get around your apology."

"My apology?" She gulped. Raz sidled up next to her, but he only took one of her hands in his.

All the anger, all the turmoil inside of me wrapped together as I lashed out, "You knew Adam was hurt by me. You knew he was angry, and you still believed him. What'd he even say, Becky? That I laughed at you behind your back? Does that sound like me? When have I ever laughed at someone? Ever! And you thought I was laughing at you, the only person who was my friend after what Jeff did to me, after what Jessica and Lydia did to me? Did you really think that I would laugh at you?"

Her head hung down again. Her soft, "No," was almost inaudible, but I heard.

It stung.

I reared back a step. I couldn't believe what I had heard. "You didn't believe him?"

"No." Her head came back up, and all the blood was gone. She was pale and trembling. Raz tried to stop both of her hands, but her legs were shaking too. "I knew you wouldn't have done that to me, but it hurt when he said it. I did believe him at first, kind of, but I didn't at the same time. It made sense to me. You were dating Mason Kade. You were friends with his brother. I mean, why would you be friends with me? I'm nothing." She stopped as her voice started to quiver.

I wanted to curse at her. She hurt me, and I was supposed to feel sorry for her? "Give me a break."

She gasped. Her eyes were wide once again. She visibly swallowed, clinging to her boyfriend's hand.

I shook my head. All the hurt and anger, I needed it out of me. I already had so much for Analise. I didn't need any more. It needed to be gone. But I couldn't deny what I felt. "You're not nothing. You've never been nothing. You were the only friend I had, even before I started dating Mason."

"You had me," Adam spoke up.

I snorted at him. "Really?"

He flashed me a tight grin. "Shutting up. This isn't about me."

"Thank you."

More tears had fallen over Becky's face, but she ignored them. "I'm really sorry, Sam. I really am. I was so stupid, and I was hurt."

"Why?" That made no sense.

"Because I felt left out. I knew you were close to the Kades, but it wasn't until that last party when I realized how tight you were with them. I mean, hello. Mason Kade is fighting for you, and then Logan snubs Lydia for you. She came onto him and he smacked her back and for what? For you. Those two care so much about you and when you're with them, it's like no one else matters except you three. You never even invited me to your home before, like I wasn't good enough or something."

"The four of them."

"What?" She looked at Adam.

He stiffened. "The four of them. Nate Monson's in there too."

"Oh yeah. I know, but he wasn't always around then. But that too. Look at this place. You're living at his house. He moved back, and now you're here with them. It's the four of you guys again."

I didn't know what to say. A part of me didn't care anymore. Her feelings were hurt? Well, she'd gotten me back. Good for her.

Becky hadn't stopped crying. Her boyfriend raised his skinny hand and wiped a few tears away. His thumb caressed her cheek and skimmed under her eye. The touch was gentle and loving. She was with someone who loved her. I could tell, just from watching him. I drew in an anguished breath. Becky was dating someone. She had someone who loved her. It started to really dawn on me. She had met a boy, dated a boy, had more dates with him, and hadn't told me. That was my job as her friend—I felt robbed of that.

I closed my eyes and turned away. I knew what I needed to do and it hurt. But it needed to be done.

"Sam?" Her voice dropped to a hoarse whisper. "Can you please forgive me? I'm sorry. I'm really sorry for believing Adam's lies."

I shook my head. I needed to forgive her and I knew I would, but she needed to realize something. I looked up with a tear in my own eye. "You wanted to believe him."

She flinched, like I had slapped her.

I pressed, "I didn't leave you behind. I didn't laugh at you behind your back. I wasn't using you. And you knew all of that, but you wanted to believe Adam's lie even when you knew it wasn't true. I think you did it because you were mad at me."

"But—" Her mouth hung open.

Adam frowned. "Why would she be mad at you?"

I shrugged, though my eyes never left hers. Then I saw it. Guilt. When her head went back down, I knew I'd been right. "She was mad at me because I had what she wanted. You were jealous, weren't you?"

Her head nodded up and down, but she didn't say a word.

"I had what you wanted, didn't I?"

As she looked back up, the anguish was all over her. More tears flooded her, her mouth was turned down in a frown, and she shook her head. "I'm so stupid, right? You went to the top, Sam. You got the guys that no one could get. I mean, you got both of them. Logan Kade worships the ground you walk on. You got what everyone wanted, not just me. Can you blame me for being jealous? Isn't that a human thing for me to do? To be jealous?" A sickened laugh bubbled out of her. "Yeah, I was mad at you. Yeah, I was jealous of you, but I was your friend. I'm sorry that I let myself believe Adam's lie. It was horrible of me. I know that and I really regret it. I really do, Sam. I really really do."

My heart sank with each word she said, but I couldn't argue with them. I knew there were more girls, a lot more, that felt the same as she did. Who was I to be taken in by the Kades? What was so special about me? I knew Becky wouldn't voice those questions to me. I knew she might never want to admit to those thoughts, but they were there. I had them too.

"This is bullshit," Adam cursed behind me. He moved next to me with disgust. "This is about the Kades? Again? Are you serious?"

Becky covered her mouth with her hand. More whimpers escaped her, and then she turned to her boyfriend. His arms came around her, and he patted the back of her head as he shot Adam a dark look. "Man. Respect it."

Adam rolled his eyes. "I'm so sick of this. Can we not have one night without talking about them?"

I hissed at him, "You're not helping."

He threw up his hands. "I'm not trying anymore. I didn't know all this boiled down to those guys again. What's so damn special about them? Their looks? I'm good looking. That they're athletic? I'm the freaking quarterback for FCA. I *was* the quarterback. Whatever! What's so damn special about them?"

Raz spoke up, "Dude, they're legends. Legit and smack dab. Legends, dude. That's all. Legends."

Adam snorted. "This is ridiculous." He turned to me, frustrated. "Are you okay?"

I nodded. Strangely, I was. When Becky sniffled and wiped her nose, all the hurt and anger was gone. She had admitted it, and that was what I needed. I guess…

"I'm going. I'm not sticking around to hear about how godly these douches are. See you, Sam. Becky, you two want a ride home?"

She looked at me, a deep question in her, but I slunk back against the counter. She could stay if she wanted. She could go if she wanted. This was her time to choose if she was going to be there for me or not. I wasn't going to tell her what to do.

"I…" She opened her mouth, then closed it.

Raz spoke up again, "She's staying. I'm coming. Let's go to the Hop-It. All this crying made me hungry."

He pressed a kiss to Becky's forehead and whispered something in her ear, which had her grinning. She relaxed in his arms, but then he skipped around her, swatted Adam on the butt, and led the way out of the room.

Adam followed behind him, "It's the IHOP, Raz. It's not the Hop-It."

Raz called to him, "It's always the Hop-It. That's what you do. You hop it, you get it?"

A long frustrated sigh came from Adam before the door closed behind them.

Both of us looked at each other, now alone in Nate's fortress. It never seemed larger than in that moment. A clock should've been ticking behind us. The awkwardness of the moment would've fit well with that idea. As I grinned to myself, she took the leap first. "Why are you living here, Sam?"

There was the old Becky, she was my friend again.

CHAPTER TWENTY-ONE

"So…"

She gave me a timid smile. There was a twinge of hope in there, but I didn't know what to do about it. I wasn't mad anymore, but I didn't trust her either. I gave her a small grin back and said the same, "So…"

Her smile fell flat. "Oh."

I sighed. "What do you want, Becky? Thank you for being honest and thank you for apologizing, but we can't bounce back to what we were before. I don't trust you anymore."

"You don't?"

I shook my head. "Nope."

"Oh." Her shoulders lifted up in a small shrug. "Well, I guess I understand. I wouldn't either, if I was in your place. I mean, well, I might've. I don't know. I've never had anyone be jealous of me before. I don't know what I would do."

"It's not about you being jealous. You believed a lie about me, even though you knew it wasn't true, to get back at me. You knew it'd hurt me if you stopped talking to me. Congratulations. You hurt me."

"I really am sorry," she whispered.

Then we heard the door open and someone yelled out, "Hey! Yo! I took off early, figured you'd want your phone asap. It keeps flashing that you've got texts, didn't know if they were important or not."

Becky froze, but I relaxed. It wasn't long before Heather strolled around the corner. She saw Becky and stopped in her tracks. "Oh. Hi?"

I sighed. Heather's eyes narrowed as she raked her up and down with a sneer while the other looked ready to piss her pants. "Uh..." I swept a hand between the two. "Becky, this is Heather. Heather, Becky."

Becky took a small breath. "You're the new friend."

Heather's eyebrows shot up. "That means you're the old one?"

I laughed.

Becky threw me a dark look.

"Sorry. I—sorry." I waved for them to forget me.

Heather snorted as she fished something from her pocket and tossed it to me. I caught it, my phone. When I glanced at it, my eyes went wide. She'd been right. There were a few from Mason.

Our mom called. She's pissed. Found out we got kicked out.

Family meeting called. Have to head with Logan. I won't be at Manny's tonight. You'll be alright? That one was followed with: **love u.**

I checked the rest: **Things got interesting, can't text for awhile.**

The last text was sent an hour ago: **Hoping you're ok and work is just busy. Not good here.**

"Things okay?" Heather was frowning as she lounged against the wall. Becky was against the opposite wall with her arms folded across her chest.

A raging headache was coming. I felt it at my temples and pressed my hands there for a moment.

"Sam?" It sounded like a whimper from Becky.

"What?" I tried to hold back my own glare. This wasn't about her and she was making it like that.

The pout twisted into a confused scowl, then a grimace. "Are you okay?"

"No."

"Where's he at?" Heather gestured to my phone.

I shook my head. "Family meeting. It doesn't matter."

"Aren't you in the family?"

"Not that one. It's with his mom."

Heather grinned. "I heard about the Wicked Witch of L.A. She's a pretentious socialite, isn't she?"

I shrugged. Helen was more than that in my opinion. "She's… confident."

"Confident?" The amusement on Heather's face didn't deplete. It doubled. She threw her head back as a smooth chuckle slid out. "I've never heard that one used to describe her, but then again," she eyed me up and down, "you are in that family so I hear ya. I gotcha."

Becky had been scowling as she looked back and forth between us. "What is going on? Your mom is confident? Your mom is mean, Sam."

"No," I sighed, but stopped. Maybe it was for the best if she thought we were talking about my mother.

Just then we heard the garage door slam shut. I held my breath; my heart racing when Nate turned the corner. Then a small hand appeared around his chest from behind, and a pair of tan legs slid between his as the hand groped farther south. A low moan sounded next. It ended in a feminine sigh as a pair of lips started to press against his arm and move upwards.

He stopped as he saw the three of us, but his eyes zeroed in on me. "What are you doing here?"

I jumped at the intensity from him. "What?"

All amusement fled from Heather as she turned to him, a scowl locked in place. "What's with the attitude, Monson? I thought she lived here."

His gaze went to hers, but the intensity was gone. He locked it behind a wall, and now he regarded her with a blank expression. I sighed. It was the same look Mason used on people when he wanted them to feel unwelcomed. It was a master tactic to make the other feel like scum beneath their shoes.

I gritted my teeth. He would not use that on her. "Stop, Nate. And what are you talking about, what am I doing here? I got off work early and Mason said he's at a family meeting."

The mask slipped a bit, and there was wariness instead. "Yeah, *your* family. Helen's out for Analise's blood."

The blood drained from my body. "What?"

He gave me a smirk now. It sent a shiver down my back, and not a good one like I felt with Mason. I was rattled to the bone when he said further, "They're at your house, Sam, with your mom. You're the odd-man out."

Shock started to form in my gut, but I heard myself mutter from a distance, "Why are you being a dick to me?"

His eyes went wide and his eyebrows shot up. "I'm not."

"You are," Heather retorted.

He frowned at her, but the girl behind him moaned in his ear, "Baby, can they go away?"

I narrowed my eyes. I recognized that voice. Everything slammed back into focus with me. Parker pressed against the front of him now. Her shirt had been tied around her neck, but it was undone. It fell around her waist, still on her as the knot hadn't been untied around her waist, but her breasts were against him. She wore no bra, and the jean shorts on her were loose in the back so they must've been unzipped from the front.

That's why he'd been a dick. He was with her, one of the four that still hated me. When I shared a look with Heather, I remembered her warning about the Tommy P's. It was her nickname for those four, Parker, her best friend Kate, and the other two whose names I couldn't remember. Jasmine and Natalie? Maybe. I preferred Heather's reference to them, the Tomboy Princesses. The name fit them perfectly, and the one trying to lure Nate away from the kitchen had been the worst so far.

"Parker." Annoyance dripped from his voice as he gripped her arm and held her away. Her breasts sagged, but she didn't cover them. She seemed shocked as she looked up. Disdain now filtered in as he finished, "Go to my room."

"But—"

"Go!"

She snapped to attention, but not before she sent me a loathing glare.

I lifted my chin in a challenge. The time would come when I'd need to deal with her and her friends, but it wasn't now. I thought about my new school and my gut dropped. It was her school; it was their territory. I was grateful for my job at Manny's. Heather would support me when I went there, as much as she could, as much as anyone could.

"Your girlfriend's a bitch," she informed Nate as soon as we heard an upstairs door slam shut.

"She's not my girlfriend." He shot her a dark look but then shrugged a second later and looked at me. "I'm sorry, Sam, if I was being a dick. I didn't mean to be."

It was who he'd been with. Her derision must've rubbed off on him, but I held my tongue. Heather bit her lip as she frowned at me, but then my phone beeped again. I read the text from Mason: **Can you come as soon as you're done with work? At the house. Your mom threw a bowl at my mom.**

"I have to go."

But I had no car—I looked at Heather. She grinned. "I'll give you a ride." She winked at Becky. "You too, oldie but goodie?"

"Huh?"

"Yeah." I latched a hand onto Becky's arm and dragged her behind me. "Her too."

Nate gave me a nod with a small grin as we swept out of the house. I knew it was his way of sending me another apology, but as I got into Heather's car, I wondered if that was the side of him that most people saw. He seemed nice and respectful, reserved even, whenever he was with Mason and Logan, but this Nate was different. Again, I remembered the comments about the trouble he and Mason would get into, the reason why his parents had him move away in the first place. But he was back…and I knew Logan already regretted it.

"Sam."

Becky was trying to hold back a smile.

My eyebrows shot up. "What?"

Then she handed me her phone.

"What is this?"

"Just look."

And I did, gasping when I saw the picture she had taken. It was a full frontal of Parker, when Nate had pushed her back. Her breasts were on display. "You snuck this picture?"

She nodded, biting her lip from excitement.

"Let me see." Heather held her hand out and took a quick peak. She busted out laughing and handed it back. "Your oldie but goodie is a sneaky one, Sam. Good one, back there."

Becky leaned back, pleased with herself. "I couldn't help it. She was so mean. They weren't paying me any attention so…"

"Don't do anything with that picture but don't delete it either."

"Yeah." Heather looked into the rearview mirror. "We might need that someday, but I agree with Sam. Don't post that anywhere or even show anyone else."

"Don't show your boyfriend, Becky."

Her grin was gone. "What?"

"Who's her boyfriend?"

"Someone named Raz?"

I looked at Becky for confirmation when I said his name. She nodded, but then Heather burst into laughter once again. "Are you kidding me? Raz has a girlfriend? That's great." Her eyes met Becky's once again. "Raz is a good guy, but I agree with Sam. Don't show that picture to him. He'd put that on a tee shirt and wear it to school. He doesn't get it sometimes."

"Yeah," Becky sighed. "You're right. But the picture was good, wasn't it?"

I nodded. "You did good, Becky."

"Thanks."

When Heather kept driving and she turned at all the right turns, I realized she knew where I used to live. I wanted to smack my forehead. Everyone knew where Mason and Logan lived. They had enough parties on the beach, even Becky had been there a few times, but never to the first floor of the house or the other two floors above. A few had been invited to the basement, but not to the top levels. That was reserved for a select few and when Heather parked in the driveway, her hand went to her seatbelt and I knew she had every intention of joining that small group who had seen the inside of the Kade museum.

"Uh," Becky watched as Heather got out of the car.

"Let's go." Heather slammed her door shut.

I was torn. Did I let them inside? I knew they wouldn't be welcomed, but Heather was already at the front door. She pushed it open and my decision was made for me.

I gestured at Becky. "Come on. Might as well see what's going on."

She grinned, and her cheeks flamed as she scrambled behind me. But then we were inside, and it was dead silent. Heather waited for us in the foyer. Her mouth had fallen open as she gazed around. Oh yes. I'd forgotten what the Kade mansion looked like to the virgin eyes.

"This place is an effing museum." She couldn't tear her eyes from the life-sized statue of a Greek goddess. "Is that real?"

I shrugged. My mom had bought it a month ago. She gushed over it when it was delivered so I figured it was real. My mom didn't know that Logan had taken a black marker to the backside of the statue and drawn a tramp stamp with an arrow pointing downwards that said, 'insert here.' The statue hadn't been moved since its arrival, but I knew when it was and Analise saw the added artwork, she'd go ballistic. I only hoped Logan would be here to see her reaction.

"Oh wow," Becky breathed out behind me. "This place is beautiful."

Heather snorted. "And we're not even past the foyer. You must think I live in a hole compared to this place and Monson's mansion."

"I liked your home."

It was the truth. When she searched me, Heather saw that I meant it. Her shoulders relaxed. "You're a good person, Sam."

I frowned. I was?

"I second that." Becky gave me a timid grin.

I was uncomfortable with the praise, but we heard a shriek from the kitchen, followed with the sounds of breaking dishes, and I chuckled. The uncomfortable feeling went away, and I was grounded again. I'd grown used to the chaos that surrounded Analise. "You guys should go. This could get ugly."

"Sam!"

Logan saw me and jogged down the hallway towards us. He grabbed my arm. "You need to come quick. Your mom's unhinged and my mom's making her fold. Helen's standing there, all cold as ice, and your mom can't shake her. It's awesome. Mason's stuck in the back corner. He couldn't get out, but we heard the door so I figured it was you."

"Sam," Heather called out.

Logan stopped and looked back. He was startled for a moment before a lewd grin covered his face. "Didn't see you there, Jax. Looking good." His eyes raked her up and down. "Real good."

Becky flushed beside her, but Heather rolled her eyes. "Eyes up here, Kade."

They stayed on her front, where her tight red shirt strained against her breasts. The black bra could be seen through the shirt and the longer his gaze stayed on her, the tighter her shirt became.

I knew she was getting annoyed, but then I saw some redness that started on her neck and traveled upwards.

Shock settled inside of me. Was there more than friendly annoyance between those two? But no, Heather was with that model tattoo guy…wasn't she?

She folded her arms over her chest. "Stop it, Logan!"

He grinned, cocky and so self-assured. "Heard a rumor about you today, Jax."

"Oh yeah?" She struck a defiant pose with her hand on her hip. "What was that?"

"That you and Channing aren't really an item, not yet anyway."

Her hand fell away from her hip, and she took a step back.

Was that true? Maybe there really was something going on between Heather and Logan, but I remembered Channing coming to my defense in the diner. He stopped the Broudou siblings from— from hurting Heather. In the moment, I thought he had come to my defense, but it had been for her. He always seemed to be there for her. I studied her and Logan for another second and then sighed. I hoped he knew what he was doing because I didn't want him to get hurt.

As Heather tossed her hair back and Logan's eyes lit up, something fell to the bottom of my gut. He liked her. I could see it, plain as day to me now, but I wouldn't let him get hurt. There was no way I would let Logan get hurt, not again, not like with Tate.

"Logan!"

I jumped at the shrill sound that came around the corner. Helen was calling.

He chuckled and grabbed my arm. "Come on, little Kade. Prepare to be entertained." Then he saluted Heather. "Off you go, Jax. You're always welcome in my bed, but not here. No fornicating allowed, her mom's rule. See you later."

Heather rolled her eyes and grabbed Becky's arm. "See you, Sam. Call me."

I nodded as she dragged Becky behind her. The door shut with a heavy thud behind them, but then Logan curved an arm around my waist. He didn't immediately take me to the kitchen. Instead, he held me in a hug for a moment and let out a deep sigh. His shoulders dropped and his head rested on my shoulder.

He'd been acting. The entire jovial side of him had been a facade. I hugged him back. "How bad is it?"

He flinched from the question but drew back. His wall fell and I reeled as I saw the torment in them. "It's not good, Sam. It's not going to get better either."

Oh no.

CHAPTER TWENTY-TWO

When I walked into the room, everything was wrong. I knew it. I felt it. I could see it. Helen was impeccable. She was dressed in a white business suit with a skirt and matching high heels, a lethal tip at the end. Her hair was swept up in some fancy bun to the side, but it was the pressed red lips and the cold ice in her blue eyes that sent the first reverberations through me. The second wave was sent from James as he stood between the kitchen and dining room. He leaned against a counter with his tie undone and his shirt pulled from his pants. The suit looked like it could've come from a GQ magazine, but it was wrinkled and wrung into knots as he lifted his hands to ring out his collar. From how it was already loosened, I knew he'd been doing that more than a few times. Then the third repercussion hit me from my mother herself. She stopped her pacing when she saw me, but it wasn't warmth that came to her, it was the lack of it. Even Helen noted it with a snort. She extended her hand to me. "And the root of the problem has made her appearance."

All jokes were gone.

Mason shoved his chair back and rounded the table. He took my arm and moved in front as Logan went and hopped onto the table. He flashed me a grin, more to reassure me than anything else, as he propped his feet on a chair in front of him. Then he leaned back on the table with his arms outstretched behind him, his eyes alert as he scanned the rest of the room.

That was the fourth.

Logan was alarmed. Logan was never alarmed.

The last reverberation was Mason as I touched his arm. It was cement. I felt his back and the rest of him was the same. He was rigid as stone. But he hadn't let me see it when I came around the corner. There'd been a look of amusement. I hadn't seen it when it fell away to the real emotion underneath. I'd been distracted by the tension in the room. Now I closed my eyes as the shock still rocked inside of me. Logan and Mason were both on edge.

I sucked in a breath. This wasn't going to end well. Then I opened my eyes and focused once more.

Here we go.

"Where were you, Samantha?" my mother clipped out. Her hands rested on her hips and her eyes bugged out. She looked ready to shriek again.

It clicked in me. I wouldn't fear her. The rightful anger was back again. She wouldn't scare me away no matter how intimidating she might've been. I wasn't eleven anymore. I shrugged as I moved to stand beside Mason. His hand curled around my waist. He anchored me against him.

She sucked in her breath. "Answer me."

"Why?" Logan sat forward on the table. His elbows rested on his knees now and his shoulders hunched down. He was getting ready for a fight.

"What do you mean why? She's my daughter."

He rolled his eyes. "Are you sure about that? You don't treat her like any family I've known."

"Logan," his father murmured, shaking his head. "Stop."

"Why?" Same question, same reaction. He wanted instant irritation.

A low growl came from Analise.

He was getting it.

"It's not your place." James sent him a pointed look and then transferred his gaze to Mason, who gripped my waist tighter.

I sunk into his side, grateful for the rock he had become for me.

Helen cleared her throat and refolded her arms over her chest. "This is not entertaining anymore." She fixed her ex-husband with a sneer. "Now that the prodigal daughter has returned, I'd like to continue our discussion as to why my sons got kicked out of your home and not *her* daughter."

Analise showed her teeth, it was so unlike the socialite she wanted to become since we moved into the Kade mansion. She resembled a caged animal, and it was the truth. My mom had been backed into a corner by Helen. We were all staring at her, waiting for her.

"Because." James hung his head.

"Because?" Helen tightened her mouth and lifted her chin another centimeter. "Just because? Are you toying with me, James? Our sons chose to stay here because of school. They didn't want to live in Los Angeles, and you agreed it was the better arrangement. A small town had a better environment for them. Then I hear from my sister that you've kicked them out? Mason is living with that Monson child—"

Logan grinned.

Mason bristled. "Don't start, mom."

"—and I hope to God that Logan's been with him the whole time because he hasn't been with me."

James looked back up. "I sent him to you."

She threw her arms in the air. "For one day! I got him for one day and then he took off with James and Will. They said they were going to Nate Monson's home. I thought they meant Calabasas. I had no idea they were coming here. I should've been informed when Nate moved back here." She turned towards Mason. "You should've told me."

He narrowed his eyes but remained silent. His hand on my hip turned into a fist, but his reactions stopped there. He had become a statue, or, as I shivered, he was biding his time and waiting for the right moment. I wasn't sure, but this felt like it was only the beginning.

James cleared his throat this time and wrung out his collar again. "Well, regardless, things have changed a bit in this house. I told Mason and Logan that if they didn't agree with my wishes, they would need to live with their mother. Logan was supposed to have been with you this whole time, but Mason is an adult. I cannot force him to do anything."

"You never could." Disdain dripped from her tone.

"You tell him, mom!"

"Shut it, Logan."

He hunched down. "Just saying."

Another deep sigh came from James as he stuffed his hands deep in his pockets. His shoulders hunched forward, "I understand that you're upset. I should've cleared everything with you—"

Analise gasped.

He froze for a nanosecond and then continued, "—but Analise and I made a decision together."

Helen's glare doubled with derision. She transferred it to my mother now. "I'm sure you did, by doing what she wanted for her reasons and not your own."

"You don't start," Analise rasped out. "This is not your family anymore—"

"This is my family! These are my sons and you threw them out like garbage." Helen's hands fell to her side and she jerked forward a step. Fury had replaced the cold condemnation and her eyes sparked with every bit the emotion that my mother was showing.

James glanced between them and swallowed.

"Garbage?" Analise started forward with a hand in the air. "Your son has treated my daughter like garbage. He had an itch and he used Samantha to scratch it. She was vulnerable. She'd just been dumped by her boyfriend and her friends turned their backs on her—"

"That is not true!" Logan shouted first as he hopped off the table. He started towards her, but Mason transferred me behind him and blocked his brother. As Logan bounced off him, Mason threw an arm out and shuffled him backwards. As they both moved to the farthest wall, I felt for the table. I couldn't see it anymore. Everything was rushing around me, my heart was racing, but when my hand touched it, I almost cried from relief. I folded into one of the chairs and pressed my palms against my temples. The raging headache had arrived.

My mom finished, "Samantha was convenient for him and he's made it worse. They've let her think that she matters to them, like they're going to protect her. She's my daughter. She's my family—"

"Okay, Lise. Stop." James held her with a firm hand. "Mason did not use Samantha like that and you know it. He cares for her."

My mother hit his arm down. She seethed at him, "You're blind when it comes to your sons. They're evil. You don't know the things they've done to me and now they've taken my daughter away from me. It was the last straw, James. I won't lose my daughter, not to anyone."

Helen laughed. The sound was shrill and harsh, and it shut my mother up. Her lip curled up higher. "This is so ridiculous, it's a comedy. You've lost your daughter to my sons? Is that why you banned Garrett from seeing her? Were you worried about an inappropriate relationship there as well?"

I went cold at her words. My heart slowed…

She continued, sounding like she was enjoying herself, "It's laughable! You're so nuts. Way to pick 'em, James. I thought you had a doozy on your hands with the fourth mistress. She was your secretary? No, that's not right. She was your assistant. And she hated me. I could always tell, but this one." She shook her head. "This one takes the cake."

Garrett had been banned? I started to stand up…

"Shut up, you bitch!" my mom shrieked.

Helen snapped her mouth shut, but her eyes glittered from suppressed anger. She shook her head again. "I'm the bitch? Look at what you've done to my family. You kicked my sons out. How dare you! And how dare you, James! When it involves my children, you bring me into the discussion. This relationship between our children makes it a family situation. I should've been brought in and brought up to date. I wasn't aware of the intimacy that they've reached—"

James barked out a laugh. "Are you joking with me?" He turned to face her squarely but kept Analise behind him with a hand on her wrist. His gaze settled on his ex-wife. "No, Helen. How dare you. You didn't know the level of intimacy between them?" His shoulders shook as more laughter poured out from him. "You walked in on them. And that was on your watch. He was at the hotel with you."

She sputtered out, "Not in my room. He had his own room."

"That you allowed." He pointed a hand at Mason, who was very still and very silent. "You know what our sons do. They have sex. They drink. They've both been in physical altercations. How many times have you bribed officials for them? I've done it a handful of times. I know you've dirtied your hands a few times, more than a few times. You can't stand there and spout that you thought Mason was this innocent son of ours."

"I didn't." Her jaw clamped shut, so tight. As she gritted her teeth together, the movement was visible. "I've never said that Mason and Logan are innocent little boys, but they're my little boys. You had no right to throw them out of the house."

"I didn't. I said they couldn't live here if they didn't comply with my wishes, and it's within reason to wish that my own son would not have sexual intercourse with his future stepsister, not under my roof."

Helen snorted. "Your roof? This was my father's home. Don't you forget that."

James raised his voice, "I got this house in the divorce settlement. It is my home. Let's not have you forget that!"

She threw her arms over her chest again and folded them. "It doesn't change the fact that you kicked our sons out, for any short amount of time or for any reason. You kicked both our sons out. Only one of them is sleeping with the girl."

"You didn't want Logan with you?"

"Of course, I did, but I wasn't given the chance to make sure that he came to me. He showed up one day, stayed a day, and took off with his cousins. I thought my son wanted to see me and I relished that time with him. I had no idea he was supposed to be there the entire break."

"He couldn't stay, not when he supports their relationship."

"Then kick the girl out!" Helen yelled.

She wasn't ladylike anymore, nor did she remain cold. The fury had taken over, and she was heated in anger. Her chest rose up and down at a rapid rate.

"She's my daughter," Analise yelled back. She started forward, but James crowded her back to the sink. "This is my home now. This will be my husband. My daughter will stay in my home. She has no other home to go to."

Helen reared her head back. "Are you kidding me?"

James closed his eyes.

Analise's eyes bulged out, even more enraged. She tried to launch herself forward, but he blocked her with his body. As she started to crawl over him, he turned to face her. He tugged her back down. She twisted around his side and snarled, "Get out of this house. Get out right now!"

"No," Helen clipped out. "Garrett told me about your quick little divorce, but as far as my private investigator knows, you haven't married my ex-husband yet. So, no, this isn't your home. You have no legal right to throw me out either, although I shouldn't be surprised. Isn't that what you do? Throw people out when they don't fall in line and pretend you're not crazy? Isn't that why you really kicked my sons out or why your own daughter isn't living here anymore?"

The room fell silent.

David and Analise were divorced. It was final.

I shook my head. I'd process that later.

Then Helen's cruel snicker filled the room. "I can't believe your nerve. You don't think I didn't come here with the facts? Do you not have any idea of who I am? You're going to be my sons' stepmother. You better get your act together, honey, because if you harm one hair on my sons, I'll slap you with a lawsuit. And you won't have any chance at winning because your insanity, Analise, has been well-documented."

"Shut. Up." But Analise paled, and the words said were whispered from clenched lips.

"Oh, yes, honey." Helen's control was back in place. She drew upright. Her chin lifted, her jaw squared into place, and her shoulders smoothed so her suit was impeccable once again. There were no wrinkles. She was a glossy version of an ice queen. "You don't think I'm aware of how you threatened Garrett from seeing his daughter? That if he even tried to make contact with her, you would take your daughter and disappear so he'd never find her again." Her eyes shifted to James. "I don't think there was much merit in that threat, but it scared the hell out of him. Or maybe," the cruel smirk on her face appeared again, "there was another reason Garrett would be scared for his daughter. Tell me, *Lise*, have you ever hurt anyone before?"

A cold sick feeling was spreading inside. I looked up in slow motion…Helen continued, but her voice sounded far away. I heard a whooshing sound, and it grew louder and louder. I shook my head. It was only me. It was only in my head. I needed to clear it away. I needed to hear what else she had to say.

"It's not like you've tried to kill yourself? It's not like a week later your daughter was hospitalized with evidence that she'd been beat up? You didn't do that, did you? My PI certainly thinks you did, but there was no condemning evidence and your own daughter was too scared to say anything." She continued, in a nightmare, "Where was your husband at that time?"

"Stop, Helen."

She ignored James. She was only getting started. "He had left you, but he came back, didn't he? She wasn't his real daughter. He had no way to protect her so he took you back. And the way you screwed him over later, cheating on him and getting James to fall for you. I should take lessons from you. No, I shouldn't because you're crazy. Your own daughter can't even be in the same room with you anymore. I know that you've hit her again. You slapped her twice four months ago. Have you done it since?"

All the blood was gone from my mother's face. She clutched onto James with white knuckles. Her knees buckled, but he held her up and looked over his shoulder. "Stop, Helen." He said it with more authority this time.

It worked.

Helen stopped, but she cast a wary look at me as I stepped up next to her. Then she added in a soft voice, "I'm sorry that you have such a bitch for a mother, but you might want to look into her divorce settlement. I think there'd be a few things that might interest you."

"That's enough, mom."

She turned around. "What, Mason? If you care for her as much as you say you do, you'd want her to know that the man who raised her isn't allowed to speak to her, not until she turns 18." She lifted an easy shoulder. "I would've gone for it too. He's being paid to stay away from his daughter, but she's not even his real daughter. He bides his time, waits around, and then he can talk to her all he wants. He's only got to wait another week and a half. And Garrett, who knows what she really threatened him with before he went back to Boston."

Garrett was in Boston?

Analise burst out laughing. "He left you, didn't he?"

Helen wheeled around. Her eyes narrowed to slits. "You don't know anything about that—"

"But I do." Analise's voice rose again. She felt in control once again. "He left you the week after we saw you last. And I know why." She giggled now. The sound was twisted and unnatural.

My stomach dropped as the sickened sensation spread through me.

"He went back to his wife. I know he did. He told me he was going back to her. Too bad for you, Helen. You couldn't hold onto him, and that was your only way of getting back at me. But I've got the life you wanted. I've got the man that you loved. I've got the home with your husband and your sons. And I've got a hold on Garrett that you'll never have. I have his daughter and as long as I have her, he'll never leave me, not like he left you."

Helen crossed the room in three steps. She lifted her hand and slapped my mother. It happened before anyone could comprehend what was going on, but the sound of it echoed in the air.

I jumped from the shock of it.

"Whore!"

"Mom!" Mason rushed around me and lifted Helen away as she raised her hand for a second slap.

James grunted, but held onto Analise as she shrunk back. She stayed there for a second and then launched forward. She raked her nails over his back, trying to find a foothold so she could get free from him. He yelled in her ear, "Stop, Lise!" Logan rushed and took hold of my mother's arms. He lifted them in the air and James wrapped his arms around her waist again. My mother was in the air as they tried to wrestle her down. Her entire body was convulsing back and forth, desperate to get free.

CHAPTER TWENTY-THREE

"How long does mom have to be in the hospital?" It must've been the third time I asked dad. It'd been so long, and she was still in there. He always said the same thing, another day, but it seemed longer than that. Two whole days had passed since he picked me up from Jessica's.

"She's coming home this weekend, honey."

"Really?"

"Really." He gave me a smile and hunched down for me. Then he cleared his throat. "Honey, I want to talk to you about that night you found your mom in the bathroom."

"Yeah?" I could tell he wanted to talk about it. Dad's voice always changed when there was something important he wanted to say, but I looked away. I didn't want to talk about that night. Mom was fine. Dad was back. Everything was fine. I knew it. I was fine.

"Yeah, honey." He cleared his throat again and folded up his sleeves over his arms. "Listen, Jolene called me from the hospital when she picked you up. That was nice of her, wasn't it? I'm glad the social workers found someone to watch you so quickly. Were you a good girl for her? She didn't have to go down to the hospital to pick you up. Wasn't that nice of her?"

I shrugged. "I guess."

His smile relaxed, and he expelled a deep breath. "Good. Um, do you have any questions about your mother?"

"She's coming home this weekend?"

He nodded. He didn't say anything.

Things weren't okay. When he stood and walked to his back office, I knew things weren't okay. I was eleven, I wasn't four. But mom was coming home. She'd make everything okay. She had to; I didn't want to stay at Jessica's house again. Her mom wasn't nice.

"Sam!"

I blinked suddenly when Mason touched my arm. "You okay?" He still had an arm around Helen, but she had calmed down and leaned against the wall. Her eyes closed as exhaustion settled over her face. Her hair had been yanked free from the bun. It spilled down, but she didn't smooth any of it back. It stayed how it fell.

"Uh." I blinked again, clearing the memories.

"Logan!" My mom shrieked. She tried to bat him away as he kept a restraining hand on one of her arms. James ducked his head into her side. A scratch was on his cheek, some blood already spilled from it. "Get away from me!"

He hissed when she swung down again, but jumped back. She sagged forward, crumbling to the floor before she slapped a hand to the ground and pushed herself back up. Her eyes were wild, her hair was a mess, and the front of her dress was ripped. A tan bustier covered her up, but the dress was in ruins. She started to grab it and rip it off, but I stepped towards her.

She stopped. Her eyes jumped to mine, widened, and her mouth opened.

"Stop."

She did.

As I took another step closer, Mason murmured behind me, "Sam."

I shook my head. He didn't move away, but he didn't stop me. Logan straightened as well. The adults grew still, but James spoke, "I don't think this is the best—"

"Shut up, dad!" Logan barked at him.

There was movement behind me. I sensed it, but I could only

stare at my mother. She was alone now, and her hand started to tremble. "Samantha—"

"I said, stop."

She clamped her mouth shut, but stood to her tallest height. Her chin lifted. Her shoulders squared back and the wildness in her eyes calmed down a notch. But she was still mad. I could see it.

I no longer cared. "You took them away from me."

She winced as if I had slapped her. "Honey—"

I held a hand up and she quieted. Then I shook my head. My stomach twisted into knots and the need to throw up was climbing in my throat. I felt it coming, but I couldn't deal with any of that. She made me sick. I'd never get that feeling out of me. My throat felt raw. "You took David away from me."

She grimaced again. Her head turned to the side as if I really had slapped her.

"You threatened Garrett from me?"

She didn't respond.

"Did you?"

She bit her lip. A sob convulsed from her, but she nodded once.

I gripped my stomach. The betrayal was there. I wished that she would've stabbed me. It would've been less painful than what I felt now. When would she stop hurting me?

I pressed on, whispering, "You kept him from me all my life."

"Sam," she choked out.

"Shut up, woman!" Logan surged next to me. "Let her talk."

Mason stepped closer to me. He didn't touch me, though I expected him to, but he was there. I knew he was there, in case I fell.

"You took my little sister from me?" Helen said Analise tried to kill herself, but that wasn't true. That had been the lie concocted to cover it up. She had committed murder.

"Oh god," she whimpered now. Her face crumbled, and she slipped to the floor. A hand held onto the counter, but it didn't help her. She held on, helplessly, as she curled into a ball on top of the tiles.

"Or did I have a little brother?" The question was ripped from me.

Her shoulders shook now and a sob sounded out. It was low and feral. It came from her core, but I didn't care. Not anymore. I knelt at her head, but she had it pressed into her knees. Tears and blood slipped over her skin. I didn't care where the blood had come from. I didn't even care that she was crying.

I whispered to her, "Did I have a little sister or a little brother?" It meant something to me. I needed to know. I had never asked. I had been too scared for too long, and then I had forgotten. "Mom!"

"Both!" she screamed. Her voice was muffled, pressed against her knees.

I stumbled back and fell. I could only stare at her in shock. Both? She was going to have twins?

She sobbed out, "Both! I was going to have twins. That's why there was so much blood loss. That's why I almost died. I wanted to die. I wanted to die…" Her shoulders shook with renewed frenzy as more sobs came from her.

Disgust flared within me.

Then I was being lifted back onto my feet. Mason had reached down and picked me up. He held me in front of him, but I shook my head. I wasn't ready to go so he waited. His hands never left my hips.

"You bitch."

Analise's entire body jerked from a tremor, but she didn't look up. She stayed in her ball and she kept crying.

No one went to help her.

I couldn't look away from her now. The great and almighty Analise was at my feet, literally. I'd been so scared of her for so long, then I had been angry at how selfish she was, but now I remembered so much more. She would never change. She had never been a mother to me. She never would.

There'd been so many questions swirling in me. How much had she paid David to stay away from me? No, how much had James paid. My mother had no money. She had nothing except for James and me, but she didn't have me anymore. I was done with her. But my little brother and sister. She had taken them from me. I gasped as the vomit almost came up. It was at the top of my throat. It wanted to spew out, but I pushed it down. I wouldn't let her see that reaction from me.

"Come on," Mason whispered in my ear. His hand curled around my arm, and he tugged me back.

I didn't move. I couldn't.

He bent and picked me up. I curled into his chest as he took me out to his car. As he placed me in the seat and clipped the seat belt for me, I couldn't move. I should've, but my insides had been gutted empty. She had done that—she had taken everything inside of me and ripped it all out. There was so much damage inside of me. I was damaged. How could anyone want to be around me? I was my mother's child.

As Mason shut my door and rounded to his side, I watched him through the glass. He was tense. His jaw was hard from repressed fury. The Mason I knew would've gone inside and wreaked havoc, but this one didn't. He was with me. He was taking care of me and being the stronghold that I needed.

He would wreak havoc another day.

He saw the small grin on my face as he got inside and started the car. "What's that for?"

A peace settled inside. His question was simple, but genuine. I heard his concern. I heard his love, and because there were no conditions to his love, it healed something inside of me. I knew it wasn't all of it, it wasn't even a sixteenth of it, but it was enough for now.

I reached over for his hand. At the touch, another little piece in me settled. I drew in a deep breath and held onto his hand tighter. The tears spilled now. I couldn't see anything as he pulled out from the driveway and started down the road. My throat was full of emotion. I couldn't say anything either. I just held onto him.

He drove for awhile, stopping for food a few times and even buying a coffee for me at one point. I took it, gratefully. As I sipped, the warm flavor settled my stomach a bit. That was when I noticed that he had turned his phone off. It sat in the console between us with no blinking lights. This was Mason. If it had been on, there would've been flashing lights. His phone never stayed silent for long. Someone was always calling or texting. Then I thought about my own and checked it. It was nearing midnight.

I sucked in my breath. What had happened to the night? Then I asked, my voice was raspy, "Where are we going?"

He shrugged. "Just driving. Where do you want to go?"

I settled back into my seat. It felt right—being with him, alone, in the middle of the night. It had started to rain outside, but we were protected inside the car. We could've driven all night and I wouldn't have cared. I murmured as much, "I don't care."

He nodded. "Do you work tomorrow?"

I shook my head. "First and last night off till school starts. I have to train in the morning with Coach Grath."

"Call him. Tell him you'll do the running on your own."

"Why?"

"We'll go back to L.A., to that apartment again. My mom won't think to even check the place."

"How would she do that?"

He shrugged again. "Call the front desk? Ask if we're there? I don't know. She seems to always find out what she wants to know." He grinned. "If she knows to look for something, she finds it. If she doesn't, she doesn't know about it."

"Someone told her about you guys?"

He nodded. "My aunt. I'm guessing one of my cousins spilled the beans. James was always an idiot. He probably said something without even thinking."

"And your mom came up here right away?"

He grimaced and tightened his hold on the steering wheel. Lights from the street flashed over him, illuminating the shadows on his face, before they slid away until the next light. My heart fluttered with each highlight. He looked like a dark angel, with beautiful features but a rough edge. He opened his mouth, "Yeah. She came up as soon as she heard. She'd been going after my dad for a long time before we came over. She called us, not him. I think my dad didn't want us involved."

"Or my mom?"

"Her too." A small smile graced his features. He glanced over with warmth in his eyes. "I don't think my mom realized how much of a hellcat your mom is." A low smooth chuckle sounded from him. "Helen likes to be cool, calm, and collected. Your mom put a stop to that today."

I remembered the harried expression on Helen's face. Her hair was a mess and she had sunk back against the wall, as if in surrender. "I don't think she realized how crazy my mom is."

"Yeah." Mason flashed me a grin. "Your mom is crazy, but mine's ruthless and cunning."

"So is Analise."

"In a different way."

I cocked my head to the side. "How so?"

He jerked a shoulder up as he turned back to the road. "Your mom is violent. She's tried to keep it together, but she can't. She's a loose cannon. My mom's not violent. She'd never do the things your mom has. I'm not stupid, Sam. I heard my mom and if a PI thinks you were beat up by your own mother, I believe him. You've never said it, but you're scared of her. You weren't as scared of her before, but something happened and now you almost pee your pants when you're around her."

Pee my pants? I folded my arms over my chest. I didn't do that…

He let loose another string of curses. "I don't know what happened back then. I know something happened and I know it was bad. I was keeping it together because your mom was already going off, so was mine, and you needed me to support you, but

I wanted to..." His knuckled wrapped around the steering wheel. They turned white as he fought to control himself. His jaw was rigid as he clipped out, "If I get the opportunity to hurt your mom and never have it bounce back to you, I'm taking it. I'm not going to lay a hand on her, but she hurt you. No one hurts you, Sam. I'm not okay with that."

I drew in a shuddering breath. A black hole had opened inside of me, and as I started to form the words, it grew and grew. But I had to say it. I had to say it to someone else. I had to get it out of me.

Mason had grown silent. He kept driving, and the silence of the car made me feel safe. This was the right place to talk about it. So I opened my mouth and the rest spilled free, "I was eleven and I had to go to the bathroom, but I was scared. I didn't want to wake her up, but I didn't want to go in my pants. She'd be so mad if I did that. I had, once. She slapped me so hard that time." My voice faltered. My head had hit a table on that occasion. Analise told David I'd been roller skating in the house again. The pain should've been overwhelming again, but it wasn't. As I remembered, I grew numb. "When I got to the bathroom, she was inside."

I drew in another breath.

"I didn't know what was wrong with her." I looked out the window, but I didn't see the lights. I didn't see my reflection. I saw my mom. "There was so much blood. She had on a nightgown and blood was coming from between her legs. I could tell. Her nightgown was soaked with it, and it was all over the floor around her legs."

I closed my eyes, but it didn't go away. The image became more vivid.

"I tried to say something to her, but she didn't answer so I went to find David." A tear slipped down. "I think that was the first time he left her. I didn't know it, but I figured it out now. There'd been a suitcase on the floor and his clothes were thrown all over. I think...I think they had a fight. Maybe he tried to pack a bag, but she didn't let him. I don't know, but he wasn't there. They couldn't locate him for three days."

I had stayed at Jessica's house for two of those days. The first night was spent at the hospital.

"I called 911, and the paramedics showed up right away. I was with her and they kept ringing the doorbell, but I didn't hear it. The 911 operator called me back and told me to open the door for them. I felt so bad that I made them wait outside. It was cold that night, or maybe it wasn't. I don't know. I was cold. But they bundled her onto the cot thing and took her out. It happened so quickly. I think they took her blood pressure and stuff. I don't know."

I stopped. I couldn't explain how it had been in the ambulance. Cold and alone. I was terrified. She never made a sound the whole ride. Her eyes never opened. Her hand didn't even twitch. The paramedic lifted it to feel her pulse. When he let it go, it fell with a thump back down. It was like she was dead.

"What then, Sam?"

I gasped from his voice. More tears came. I ignored them now. They slid down. I couldn't stop. But I continued, "They asked me where my dad was, but I couldn't tell them. I had no idea. I don't know how they found him. Jessica's mom came down. I think my mom had put her name on the medical forms so I stayed with Jessica until David came to get me. When he did, he didn't want to talk about it."

I stopped again. This was the worst part of it.

"They told David she tried to commit suicide or maybe that was a lie he told me. But there was a wire hanger next to her. I saw it when I went in the bathroom. One of the paramedic guys kicked it underneath a dresser in the bathroom. When David took me back to the house, I got it and cleaned it up. Then I threw it in the trash. I don't know why I did that. I don't think I wanted anyone to know what she really did. I realized now maybe he knew, maybe they all knew, but I wanted to protect her. I don't know why anymore."

I was eleven. I shouldn't have had thoughts like that at that age.

"I didn't want David to find out because if he did, I was scared that he was going to leave again. I couldn't handle being alone with my mom. She would've gone nuts, but she did anyway. Later…"

"Sam?"

I shook my head. I couldn't tell him what happened later. It was too painful, too much. I whispered, "I can't."

"It's okay." He reached for my hand and squeezed it. He pressed a kiss to it before he rested our hands in his lap.

That was good. He was warm. He was safe. He was strong. I breathed a little easier. I needed his touch. I needed to remember that it was okay now. I was okay now.

Then I said something that I never remembered before. "Mason."

"Hmmm?"

I remembered their voices one night. My mom's and David's. I had crouched outside of their door and stuck my ear against it. I'd been so scared he was always going to leave, but he never did. This was another fight. I hoped he wouldn't go, but I heard her scream. And I heard his response.

"Sam?"

"I don't think they were David's."

"What?"

I opened my eyes and turned to him. Another repulsive feeling started to grow. "They had a fight that night; she wanted kids, but he couldn't give her any. He told her he couldn't have kids. I remember it now." I stopped as I realized the extent of what my mother had done. "She had cheated on him. She got pregnant. Then she killed the babies."

"Because they weren't his?" His voice broke at the end.

I nodded. "That fight was before." Then I sucked in my breath. "That fight was *that* night."

CHAPTER TWENTY-FOUR

We didn't talk about our families after that. The only thing that we discussed was what would happen, but Mason just shrugged. Things were left unsettled. I couldn't be around my mother. I knew that much. I also knew that Mason and Logan wouldn't be moving back without me. So all the questions and decisions regarding my mother and his father were left unsaid, Mason said things would get settled one day so I left it alone. When we got to that extravagant apartment, the normal doorman wasn't there. Mason said he didn't work nights, but a young college kid was instead. After a substantial amount of money, he agreed that if anyone called, we weren't there.

When we got upstairs, Mason texted Nate and Logan to let them know that we went away for a night. He didn't tell them where, but I knew how close all of them were. I'm sure the other two could figure it out. When I asked what they were doing, Mason gave me a crooked grin and picked me up. He didn't say anything more and neither did I. The rest of the night was spent with moans, kisses, caresses, and the need to get as close as our bodies would allow.

I started to fall asleep when the sun began to peek through the blinds. Mason rolled over and pressed a kiss to my shoulder. A jolt of pleasure coursed through me, and I grinned into the pillow. I snuggled deeper into the blankets and drifted off with his hand on my back.

When I woke, the room was masked in darkness. After a shower, I left the shelter of the bedroom, and the sunlight blinded me. I'd forgotten the apartment had windows for its walls. No one could see inside so I wasn't worried about that, but the light that shone through was staggering.

"You'll get used to it." Mason's voice trailed from the kitchen. He grinned as he stirred something in a pan on the stove. With only a pair of sweats that rested low on his hips, my mouth watered as I took in the sight of him shirtless. His oblique muscles curved underneath his pants' drawstring, but his stomach and back ones rippled as he continued to stir.

Everything about him was perfect.

"I bought juice." He gestured to their refrigerator.

"Coffee?"

Grinning, he nodded to a cup on the counter. Steam rose from the small opening in the lid. "Figured you'd want that too."

"Did you?" As I went to grab it, I trailed the tips of my fingers across the bottom of his back.

He whirled in a flash. Before my hands could touch the coffee cup, I was lifted onto the counter beside him. He was between my legs in the next heartbeat, and his mouth was slammed on top of mine before anything else registered with me.

Hunger, deep and primitive, rushed through me, and I gasped. I needed more. Wrapping my arms around him, I clamped my legs around his waist. I held him tightly against me, urging his hips closer and closer.

His tongue swept in before he gasped, "I never get enough, never enough."

My tongue swished against his and he groaned. His hands pushed underneath my hips and he pulled me out for better access. I was throbbing between my legs. I tried to get him even closer, but his hand slid between us.

A groan ripped from the bottom of my throat. I needed him. I was blind with desire for him. Then his finger stroked me at the top. I shuddered in his arms. Two of his fingers slipped inside. I couldn't help it. I fell back, but he caught and lowered me to the counter until

I was stretched out before him. As he readjusted my hold around his waist, his fingers continued to slide in and out.

I groaned. Pleasure spiked through me. I needed him inside of me. That was all I needed.

As I closed my eyes, he smoothed his hand from my shoulder to my neck. He lingered on my breast and ran a thumb over the tip before he cupped it. Then he leaned down and I gasped as his mouth replaced his hand. He sucked on the nipple and ran his tongue around the edge. My hands slid through his hair to anchor him to me. He knew exactly what I liked. Teasing my nipple with his teeth, he murmured, "Open your eyes."

I did.

His fingers kept going in and out. I started to feel it building.

"Mason," I gasped. I couldn't close my mouth. He grinned at me while his tongue swirled around my breast again. His fingers picked up their pace. He pushed them deeper and deeper. Then his eyes changed color. They darkened as he watched me getting closer and closer. When I exploded on his hand, he withdrew, tugged me down even farther, and slid inside of me before I could catch my breath. I gasped as I fell back again.

He was hard and thick as he filled me. With the first thrust, he went all the way into me before he paused and slid back out, only to repeat the same motion. My hips moved in rhythm and a curse fell from his lips. He braced himself slightly over me while his other hand moved to my hip to hold me stationery. He continued to thrust into me, but his eyes never left mine. I closed my eyes once, but his hand left my hip to cup the back of my head.

"Hey," he murmured. His voice was low and hoarse.

My eyelids flew up. I gulped at the naked need in his depths. He didn't bank the emotion. Instead, it intensified as our eyes held and he continued thrusting into me.

I couldn't look away.

His hand fell back to my hip, and he thrust harder into me. My legs wound tighter around him, my ankles locking together as I urged him to keep going. When my climax started to build, I started to tremble. As it grew and grew, I could barely hold on. Then his thumb touched me again and I went over the edge. My body convulsed around him and he soon joined me as I felt him shoot inside of me before collapsing on top.

Our heartbeats raced and then settled into the same beat together.

When we were able to catch our breath, I swept a hand down his sweat-soaked back. He groaned against my skin. His lips reached out and brushed a kiss to the side of my breast before he lifted his hand and cupped it again.

I closed my eyes as he started to kiss me all over.

We didn't talk for the rest of the day or that night except for when I left Coach Grath a message. He sent me a text later and reminded me that I needed to register for classes before Monday. After another night in the apartment, our sanctuary, Mason and I headed back the following morning. It was the Friday before classes started again. I had three days until I would be in a new school.

When we drove back, I couldn't shake thoughts about David. I wouldn't see him again. He didn't coach at the public school, and I wasn't sure if I was relieved or disappointed. He'd been paid to stay away from me. What father would do that? But that was the problem.

He wasn't my father.

Pain sliced through me at the reminder.

"You okay?" Mason squeezed my hand.

I looked down at our joined hands. We hadn't stopped touching since we arrived at the apartment. There was always some contact between us. Even when I used the bathroom, he stood next to me brushing his teeth with our feet touching.

"Yeah," I sighed. I would be, because of him.

He wheeled into a gas station and turned off the engine. "You want food? We can get some here or stop somewhere. We'll be back in time to get to the school."

"We can stop somewhere." My voice was hoarse.

He grinned at me, pressed a kiss to my forehead, and hopped out. I stared at my hand. It felt so natural to always hold onto his. It wasn't long before he got back inside and turned the car onto the highway. Without a word, he reached for my hand again.

I closed my eyes at the natural fit and rested my head against my seat. I felt at peace.

When we got to the school, Mason went in search for his basketball coach. He left me alone in the office with the beady-eyed secretary. Her hair was swept into a salt and pepper bun with a pink cardigan tied over her shoulders like she was an Ivy Leaguer. The lady must've been 86, but she was thorough. It took me an hour to fill out all the papers. I didn't even know there were that many papers needed to switch schools, but when I told her that Coach Grath was the one mentoring me, everything got a lot simpler. The papers disappeared after that, and when she found out that I'd be 18 in a week, she waved me off and told me that I was done. I was registered for all my classes.

When I went back to the hallway, I had no idea where to go.

The school was huge, like a cathedral, and it was a foreign land to me. The only times I had been at their school were for football games. Those occurred outside, not inside. Fallen Crest Academy didn't play Fallen Crest Public in any other sports. FCP was in a higher competitive league and only played the football teams because of some local agreement. I knew their football coach respected my da—David a lot. They were all good friends, but I wasn't sure about the basketball coaches or the rest of the sports. I think it had more to do with David than anything else. He tended to have friendships with a lot of schools. I knew he was friendly with the Roussou coach as well.

I waited for Mason in the athletic hallway. Glass cases were mounted on the wall with trophies and team pictures inside.

"Samantha?"

Everything stopped.

A surreal emotion came over me and I looked up. Then my eyes bugged out. I clamped onto my other arm with a death grip and I stopped breathing. I saw his reflection in the trophy glass first before I turned. It was a struggle. My knees locked, and I almost fell into the glass.

David caught my other arm and pulled me upright.

"Thanks." A weak squeak came from me.

He was dressed in a tracksuit with the letters FCA above the Academy's emblem. A whistle hung from his neck, and he held a bunch of papers in his hand.

"What are you doing here?" My voice sounded strangled.

"Oh. Uh." He gave me a tired look and rubbed a hand over his jaw. "Coaches meeting. It was held here today instead of the normal place."

"Normal place?"

"Yeah, we usually grab lunch somewhere. Lenny asked if he could cater in for us. He had something else going on and needed to be back right away." Then he frowned. "What are you doing here?"

"I'm…" Could I tell him? Then I remembered that he'd been paid off. Did he deserve to know? I hadn't processed anything from that night. I didn't know if I wanted to process anything, but I heard myself saying, "I'm going to school here next semester."

"Oh." He took a step back, blinking in surprise. "O—you are?"

I nodded.

He glanced up and down the hallway as he took a deep breath. His shoulders lifted up and descended. It wasn't meant to be dramatic, but it seemed like it. David was 45. He looked in his fifties at that moment. There was no graying in his hair. It was the same dark brown, combed to the side like always, but he looked old. He looked defeated.

Then he sighed, "I see."

"What do you see?"

There was disappointment in his depths as he gave me a sad look. "Does your mother know about your plans?"

I didn't hold back the bitterness. "I don't think my mother has any say in my life. She's made it clear to me that she only cares about herself, and maybe James. She needs to keep one guy in her life. He has to bankroll her whenever she needs it." I scanned him up and down. "But then again, she might not even have him anymore."

He narrowed his eyes. "What are you talking about, Samantha?"

My chest tightened and I jerked a shoulder up. "What do you care? You got paid to not care."

He took another step back, as if blown back by a sudden gust of wind. He blinked rapidly as he rubbed his jaw again. "I'm not following you. Wha—what are you talking about?"

"She. Paid. You. To. Stay. Away. From. Me."

"Honey—"

He reached for my arm, but I yanked it away. "Don't call me that," I seethed. My teeth were clenched together. "Don't ever call me that again."

"Samantha." His arm fell, as did his voice.

"Did she pay you to stay away?"

I needed to know this answer; I needed to know it so much. If she had, I didn't know how I would handle it.

"No."

I jerked back.

His eyes were steady on me. He was imploring me to hear him. "I was not paid to stay away from you. I stayed away from you because I feared for you. Your mother's not healthy. She's not been in a right frame of mind lately. She paid me to sign the divorce papers and not fight anything. I didn't fight any of it. I didn't even read them because I don't want anything from your mother. The only thing I ever cared about was you, but I worried what she would do." *If she would harm you.*

I stumbled as I heard those unspoken words. They flashed in

my mind. I saw the same stricken look on him. He thought the same thing. A memory flared through me.

I was in the hospital room, in a nightgown. Analise had left, and I was crying. It hurt so much. Everything hurt. I couldn't breathe, but then David came in. He brushed my hair back and whispered as he kissed my forehead, "I will never leave you. I promise."

"You did leave me," I whispered.

He winced as if he'd been slapped. He nodded. Then he choked on a breath. "I'm sorry, Samantha. I really am. Your mother left me, and she took you with. I had no legal leg to stand on. I consulted with a lawyer, but I never adopted you. She was your mother, you were her daughter. I couldn't fight her, and then Garrett came into the picture. I didn't know what to think of him, if he was going to fight for you too. But you're seventeen."

"So?" I hissed at him.

"So." His shoulders drooped. "Any legal fight for you would've lasted a long time, possibly years. I didn't have years to fight. I didn't want to anger your mother. I didn't know what she would've done. I had no way of knowing what she could've said to you. She might've brainwashed you against me. I had no idea. All I could do was wait and hope that she wouldn't take you away from here."

"And if she had?"

His head jerked up. A fierce determination came over him. "Then I would've searched for you, and I would've fought for you. I wouldn't have given a damn what she had done or said, or how far she would've gone. I would've fought. But you are still here. You're still in town. You were still going to my school—not anymore, but you're here in town. You're still here. I can still see you, and you'll be 18 in a week."

"I moved out."

Surprise flared in his eyes. "You did?"

I nodded. "She threatened to leave James if Mason didn't stop seeing me; then she threatened to report him to the police because I'm still a minor. It was too much, all of it. And…" I shrugged and looked away. "It doesn't matter now. I moved out. I'm not moving back in." But even as I said it, I thought about Mason and Logan. They should live with their father. I was even thinking about James. He shouldn't lose his last few months with Mason before he went to college. And Logan, what about him? Where would we live in the next year? Nate would be gone. I wouldn't be able to live in his home, and Helen wouldn't approve of Logan being my only roommate if we rented an apartment.

The more I considered it, the more I realized that she would demand that Logan move in with her. That meant that he'd go to Los Angeles, or she would move back. But again, where would I go? She wouldn't let me live with them.

I glanced at David, but I knew I couldn't live with him. Too much had happened. There was too much distance between us.

My heart sank with that thought.

I would never get back the father that I had before.

He let out a breath of relief. "Well, that's good then. That's really good, Samantha. Would you—I mean—would you consider—where are you—" He struggled for words, but settled on, "What are you doing for your birthday?"

I waited, but when he finished with that question, I was dumbfounded. "What?"

"Your birthday is next weekend. I can imagine that Mason and Logan have a big party planned, but would you consider having dinner with me? We could go out? Or stay in? You could come back to the house." He nodded, so eager now. "We could make a homemade pizza, or no. I could order in. Chinese. You used to like Chinese. We could go to that restaurant you always liked when you were little."

"I…" I closed my mouth. I never considered my birthday plans. I'd been too consumed with the thought of being free from her, but that was done. And I was free now. So maybe dinner with David sounded like a good thing. That's what I'd been wanting, wasn't it? "Sure…"

My phone buzzed at that moment. It was a text from Mason. **In the car.**

"I'm, um, I'm going to go."

He nodded, a bright smile on his face. "Okay. That sounds good. I'm excited for your birthday, Samantha. I really am. I'm glad that there are boundaries with your relationship with Analise too. I've worried about you so much. You have no idea."

"I…" Again, I closed my mouth. I didn't know what to say to him anymore. Too much had happened. He wasn't my father anymore. Pain seared inside me. And what about Garrett? He was gone too. Both of them had abandoned me, maybe for good reasons, maybe not, but they were gone. I had survived my mother without them.

As I left, I didn't hear what else he said. I didn't care anymore. When I got into the car and shut the door, the shock was reeling inside of me. I didn't care anymore. I didn't care about David or Garrett. I had always cared, but not anymore.

"What's wrong?"

"I saw my dad."

"Garrett?" His eyebrows shot up.

"No." I shook my head. I was in a daze. "David. I saw him and…I don't care anymore."

He frowned. "What do you mean?"

I swallowed over a ball in my throat and turned to him. Everything seemed clearer now. "I thought that all I cared about was why he left me, why he wasn't trying to see me, and now I know that he was waiting. He was scared of what my mom would do."

He snorted. "Bat shit crazy."

"He wants to have dinner with me next weekend for my birthday."

"He does?"

I nodded, tearing up. Why was I crying now? "I can see my dad again, but I don't want to anymore."

Mason sighed and reached for my hand. He enveloped it in his strong hold and squeezed. "Things have changed, Sam. You're not living under your mom's thumb anymore. You don't have to be so scared anymore. You might care tomorrow."

"If I don't?"

He shrugged. "Then you don't. It's your life. You live it how you want. No matter the reasons, your dad screwed up. He stayed away. He shouldn't have. He didn't protect you."

"He didn't, did he?"

"No." His voice had a rough edge.

"Thank you."

"For what?" He narrowed his eyes as he frowned.

"For protecting me."

Mason smirked. "I didn't protect you."

"You didn't?"

He shook his head and leaned close. Then he whispered, his breath caressing my skin, "You protected me."

"I did, didn't I? I'm always protecting you." A smile came over me. As I looked up into his eyes, my heart constricted with love.

His grin widened. "Yeah, you do. That's what family does." Then his lips were on mine and nothing mattered besides that.

CHAPTER TWENTY-FIVE

It was the last Friday before school started again. When Mason and I got to the mansion, Logan and Nate were there with a few of their friends. I relaxed when I saw it was the guys from their school. I had only ever really interacted with Ethan before, but I was starting to recognize a few of the others. Strauss was one of them. He wore tight cowboy jeans with a big belt buckle and cowboy boots. I wasn't sure if his name was a nickname or his real name. I never asked.

They all gave us friendly nods, but Logan was the first one to reach us. He wrapped his arms around me and lifted me off the ground. "I did you a favor. Ask me what the favor was. Ask me! Come on!"

When he set me back down, I grinned. "What favor did you do for me?"

"I got your shift covered at Manny's!" He was so pleased with himself.

"What?"

"Yeah." He gestured to Nate, who came over and clapped a hand on Mason's shoulder in greeting. "We went to Manny's and asked who could cover for you tonight."

"Why?" My heart skipped a few beats. What had Heather said?

"Because we're having a huge party tonight. And I want you to be a part of it." He threw an arm around my shoulder and pressed me to his side. He bent close; the booze on his breath was strong. "So that Rosa chick said she'd fill in. And I invited all your friends to the party. They're coming after their shifts."

"Heather's coming?" She was the only one I wanted, but I doubted she would. She was too close to the Roussou side—and I remembered my brush with the Broudou siblings. I still hadn't told Mason about it. That was a conversation I wasn't eager to start. I didn't know how he would react, him or Logan.

Logan's grin slipped a bit. "Not sure about Jax. You know she runs with Channing."

Oh yeah. He knew.

Mason touched my hand and gestured upstairs. "I'm going to go shower." His eyes held the rest of his question if I was coming.

I nodded and followed.

It was after we had showered and were getting dressed that he brought Heather back up. He was in the closet with only a pair of jeans on, and as he was choosing which shirt he wanted, he said over his shoulder, "You like that girl, huh?"

I paused in my own dressing. I was wearing skintight black jeans that looked more like leggings and had finished pulling a sleeveless black shirt on. I tugged it around my waist and drew a deep breath. Here it was, the moment. "Yeah. I do."

He turned with a shirt in hand, but he made no move to put it on. He stared at me, long and hard. "She's Roussou territory, Sam. She's with Channing. He's a big player over there."

"But he's not the only one."

He narrowed his eyes. "No, he's not, but Jax has always been friends with that group. She's not going to change."

I sighed, "I like her." I needed a friend when I went to their school. Mason and Logan could only help me so far.

"She likes you. I know that. I've seen it, but I'm just preparing you. She's not going to start coming to our parties. Jax is fine by herself, but not the group she runs with."

What was this? A Jax intervention? I grumbled, "Why's she friends with them anyway? Why isn't she friends with you guys like all the normal girls at your school?"

"Do you know Jax? She's not a normal girl." Mason snorted before he pulled his shirt on in two movements. It fit perfectly over his chest, highlighting his muscular shoulders and trim waist. I couldn't stop myself from watching how his stomach muscles rippled and clenched. Even now, after we'd been together a record number of times over the last 24 hours, I still wanted him. The throbbing started between my legs again.

His eyes darkened, I knew he had caught my reaction. He stalked towards me, his desire strong. He bent and lifted me with one arm so I entwined my legs around his waist. His other hand rubbed up my back, holding me in place while his eyes held my gaze. Intense. Then he leaned forward, ever so slowly. His lips touched mine, gently at first.

I groaned. I'd never get enough of him.

That was all he needed. His mouth opened over mine commandingly. He wanted inside. I gasped against him, and his tongue swept in, claiming me.

"You guys are too horny. I don't think it's normal." Logan was propped against the doorway. He rolled his eyes and came inside as Mason shot him a dark look, helping me back down to the floor. "I feel like I should give you two the birds and the bees speech. You know, before she gets pregnant or something."

I laughed, but Mason froze beside me so I whacked him on the chest. "You know I'm covered."

He gave me a pointed look, reminding both of us about the apartment. It had been the first time he hadn't used a condom, but I was on birth control. We were both clean. I hoped the one time wouldn't produce a baby. I was sure it wouldn't, but he stopped for more condoms anyways. Mason liked to make sure everything was covered.

"We're celebrating, Sam."

"We are?"

"Yep." Logan nodded his head with a look of intent on his face. "Come on. You signed up for our school. It's all official and shit. I've got shots ready downstairs." Then he caught a look from his brother and held up his hands. "Just all in good fun, Mase. She'll be fine. Promise."

Mason rolled his eyes. His hand touched the small of my back as we followed Logan downstairs. "She'll be fine because I'm here, not because of you. You'll be hooking up with someone before the night is half over."

Logan flashed him a grin. "Yeah, maybe."

"Maybe?" I scoffed.

"Okay. Probably." A group of girls walked into the center area from underneath us. "Definitely."

"Shots," Mason reminded him.

"Right. This way." Logan weaved through the crowd that had already formed. He slapped a hand on the counter. "Six shots, Strauss. Give it to me, Cowboy man!"

Six shot glasses were turned over and filled with something pink. Logan pushed two to each of us and lifted his first. "To Sam coming to our school and to Mason always fucking her!"

"Logan!"

Mason laughed as he tapped his shot with his brother's. Both swallowed theirs at the same time before looking at me. Oh, fine. I threw mine back. We heard the same toast again with the second round. I couldn't help but shake my head as the alcohol went down my throat. Still, it didn't taste too bad. I turned for Mason and tugged on his belt loop. "One more."

His arms came around me to rest on the counter. He nodded to his friend. "Strauss, another round."

"Really?"

"I'm off. See you two lovebirds later."

Before we could look, Logan had already disappeared into the crowd.

Mason swung a finger from me to him. "Make that just for us two."

Strauss flipped over three shot glasses. As the pink stuff went into them again, he lifted one for himself. "I wouldn't dare make that same toast, but here's to your girl joining the gang."

"Nice." Mason grinned before he took his shot.

Mine was held suspended. Join their group? The girls hated me. "Sam?"

I shook my head. "Nothing." And down the alcohol went. It burned this time, for some reason. "Where's Nate?"

Strauss gestured towards the back patio. "He's out there with the guys. I think he's resting before Parker gets her claws on him tonight."

"Parker's been here every night?"

His friend lifted an easygoing shoulder. "I think so. According to her."

"What does Nate say?"

Strauss gave him a pointed look. "You know Nate won't say anything to us. He would to you, not the rest of us."

Mason frowned. "I haven't thought to ask. I thought he didn't want to make that exclusive?"

I frowned at the tension I felt from him. His hands moved to my hips in a strong grip. His fingers tightened into my skin, and he pulled me against him. As he pressed his hips into me, I didn't feel the usual bulge that Mason always had when we stood like this. Instead, I felt his anger.

Strauss frowned a bit but shrugged again. "I don't know. You don't want that exclusive?"

"It don't matter to me—not my relationship." But the bite that came from his tone said otherwise.

"Or is it a Parker thing? You don't want her having too much say with him?"

I became aware of Strauss's scrutiny as his gaze skirted back and forth from Mason to me. After the fourth stare, I straightened and rolled back my shoulders. I knew he was wondering if I had told them about the girls' vendetta against me, if that was his problem with Nate being so close with Parker. I shook my head. It was the tiniest of movements, but he caught it and his eyes widened even more. I couldn't tell if he was relieved or worried.

Mason's hands gripped me tighter and he pressed all of his body against mine. This time I felt the bulge and my eyes closed. The need for him started to rise in me, and the throbbing began again. As he brushed back and forth against me, I started not to care where we were.

Mason lowered his head to my neck. He breathed out, his nostrils flared, and I felt his possessiveness over me. His hand lifted one of my arms so it was entwined around his neck. My hand splayed out over the back of his neck as his other hand slid around to the front of me. Every inch of us molded together as his hand slid inside of my pants.

He never answered his friend's question, but it didn't matter. Before my eyelids dropped, heavy and laden with lust, I saw that Strauss had left. Then I was only aware of Mason lifting me and turning me around. I was placed on the counter and he was between my legs. His mouth was on mine, urgent and demanding.

"Don't you two breathe?"

We jerked apart, but Mason groaned and rolled his eyes as he saw who interrupted us. "What are you doing here, Tate?"

The tall leggy blonde looked fresh and healthy. She was dressed in similar jeans as mine, brown instead of black, and wore an off-the shoulder cream sweater that draped to give a glimpse of her lacy tan-colored bra. Her hair was swept to the side, and with a glow on her cheeks, she looked like she had stepped off the cover of a fashion magazine. Grinning like a Cheshire, she lifted her shoulders and flashed her dimples at him. "I heard about the happy couple. I wanted to congratulate you two."

Mason rested his forehead against the side of me as he glared at her. "Leave." His hand twitched on my hip. I knew he was holding back.

"Or what?" She widened her eyes in a dramatic fashion. "Or you'll make me leave?" She rolled her eyes. "You're going to have to get used to me. I'm moving back, Kade."

His eyes narrowed, and he sucked in his breath—just a little, but enough so that I felt it. My hand rested against his chest. I felt his heartbeat pick up as his muscles clenched underneath my touch. "Like hell, you are."

"I am." The smiling façade fell away. She stared back at him long and hard. "Get used to me. I'm not going anywhere." Then her grin picked back up, a slow malicious glint appeared. "I heard that you've been ignoring your precious Marissa's phone calls. Tsk, tsk, Mason. How noble is that? Was she your charitable donation at the time, an attempt to persuade yourself that you're not that bad of a guy?" Her eyes slid to mine. "But now that you've got the good girl you can screw, you don't care about the Saintly Marissa anymore? I saw her, you know. Her parents moved to my town, and she even cried to me one time at a coffee shop. You're heartless, Kade, but then again—I never forgot that about you." She gave him a withering look. "Now your little friend knows that side of you exists and she's all the more humiliated because of it."

Mason was a cement slab of stone. As he grilled her with his eyes, I touched the side of his face. Nothing. There was no reaction. It was as if he had forgotten I was there. It made me wonder if there was more to his loathing than just the Logan situation. Had something else happened between the two? Or maybe he had wanted her as she had him? But no. I sucked in my breath. That couldn't have been the case. Mason hated this girl because she hurt Logan. She had been the one person who had managed that feat.

It was enough for me. "You might want to leave before you're thrown out."

Her eyes snapped to mine. She seemed energized by the new target. "Oh really?"

"Really."

"I heard this isn't their house."

"No, but it is Nate's."

Her smile fell flat.

My own doubled. "You don't think he'll kick you out because Mason told him to?"

She straightened away from us and backed up a few steps. Her eyes went flat as she skimmed me up and down. "Look, I came here as a sign of respect."

Mason snorted in disbelief.

"I did." She glared at him. "I'm moving back. I don't want any trouble from you guys."

"Off on the wrong foot, don't you think?" I snapped at her.

She ignored me and transferred her gaze to Mason. Her tone softened. "I still love Logan—"

He released me in a flash and gripped her arm. "You never loved Logan."

Her eyes widened in fear, but she shot back, "Yes, I did. I made a horrible mistake. I was stupid and an egomaniac, but I loved him. I really did—"

His hand tightened around her arm. "Get out of here, Tate. Now. And stay away from my brother." He pushed her back. There would be an imprint from where his hand had been. It was already reddening on her skin.

She stumbled back a few more steps. Her eyes seemed in a daze as she took in the sight of Mason, but then she found her footing and straightened again. A wistful smile came over her. "Man, I forgot what you look like when you're threatened."

"I'm not threatened. I'm pissed." He stalked closer to her until he was in her face again. "I can make your life hell."

"Yeah." She nodded with a thoughtful look in her eye. "You can, but I can do the same to you." She glanced over his shoulder to me. "I think I'm the one of two people who could do that to you. You might not want to piss me off, Kade. I can take your brother away from you and you know it."

"Get. Out."

She looked ready to say something more, but at that moment, Nate entered the kitchen. He took everything in and wrapped an arm around her waist. Picking her up, he grunted when she started to struggle. "You're not welcome, Tate. Ever." Then he gave Mason a reassuring nod before disappearing with her. The crowd that had formed to watch was silent now.

Mason barked at them. "Get lost!"

They jumped back into action. The conversations doubled in volume.

Sighing as he came back to me, he raked a hand through his hair and growled. "I hate that bitch."

My hand touched the side of his jaw, but it was still rigid. Then I sighed. "Looks like the next semester won't be as much fun as you thought."

He grimaced and his jaw flexed against my hand. Then, because it had been bugging me, I had to ask, "Is she right?"

"About what?"

"Does Logan still love her?"

A wall slammed over him, and he turned away. That's when I knew it was true, and that's when I realized how threatening this girl really was to their relationship. Maybe it was karmic coincidence, but it was at that moment when I looked up and saw members of the Elite in the kitchen. They had stayed away from me since Logan dumped Miranda so long ago, but she was there. In Peter's arms, dressed all in white, laughing at something one of the others had said and looking radiant in her happiness. But she hadn't been, not after Logan screwed with her. She'd been humiliated.

Miranda had been a blip on Mason's radar from the one time she taunted him that Logan might've had feelings for me. If he had reacted like that to her, I had no idea how he would handle Tate. She was the real threat.

Chills went down my spine.

When Nate returned, he gave Mason a look. An understanding transmitted between them, just the two of them. My teeth gritted together. For some reason, I didn't like the closeness those two had, not anymore.

CHAPTER TWENTY-SIX

Later in the evening, I was on the back patio. Mason lounged next to me with an arm around my waist and his head next to my shoulder. He lay there as if he were a lion, resting for his next battle. Since Tate had left, he kept a hand on me at all times. It was a possessive touch, not the loving touch from the apartment, but I couldn't deny the reaction it was having with me. A primal thrill had been burning deep in me. It mixed with a sick excitement.

Everyone else seemed to react to this side of Mason too. They were more alert, a bit more silent than at other parties. Nate hadn't left Mason's side since Tate's arrival either and sat on the other side of him. One of his legs was kicked up to rest on the table in front of us while a few of their guy friends sat in the remaining seats across from us.

Logan emerged from wherever he'd been and joined us on the patio.

As if it had been practiced and scripted, Ethan, Strauss and another guy stood up and left. When a few girls started up the stairs, they blocked them at the bottom. Then all three of them got comfortable. They were the guard dogs.

Logan watched them too before he slunk into one of the empty chairs and stuffed his hands into his pockets. "What's going on?" His voice was guarded.

I sighed. He had closed off. This wasn't going to go well.

Mason leaned forward. Nate remained silent.

"Maybe I should go." I started to stand up.

Mason clamped a hand on my arm. He kept me in place while Logan rolled his eyes. "Stay, Sam. You're family."

So I stayed, but my chest swelled with a smidgen of fear. I couldn't deny it. As I watched Mason turn hawk-like eyes on his brother, I wondered why he seemed so upset. Logan hadn't done anything.

Then it started, "Your ex was here."

Logan's eyes flashed. The hands came out of his pockets and he straightened in his chair. "Are you kidding me?"

Mason jerked his head to the side. "She says she's moving back."

"Are you messing with me?" Logan's nostrils flared now. Anger started to swirl in his depths, it mixed with something else, something that sent chills down my back again. Danger.

He shook his head. "No. I wish." He gestured to his side. "Nate kicked her out."

"But she'll come back," Logan clipped out.

Nate swiveled his head over to look at him, but there was no reaction. Mason's best friend was like a Greek god statue, made of stone. He showed no emotion. He was there for Mason. Logan was right when he said that Nate was only there for Mason. He wasn't there for Logan and me. He struck me as another silent guard dog, but I sensed ruthlessness in him that I have never experienced before. It wasn't the first time that I'd been struck off-balance by him, but it was the first time that I was starting to fear him a little bit.

He spoke now, "She won't be allowed to any of my parties."

Mason frowned at him. "That's not the point." He turned back to his brother. "She says she loves you. She wants you back."

Too many emotions crossed over Logan before he shut it off. He collapsed against the back of his seat. His hands gripped the sides of it. "Whatever. The bitch took enough skin from me, she won't get any more."

Mason leaned back. His chest never relaxed; instead, it tightened even more. "You sure?"

He didn't believe him.

Logan shot back a dark look. "Back off. She hurt me, not you."

"She hurt my brother, that means she hurt me too," Mason whipped out, bristling from his anger.

The air was thick now, filled with tension.

The only one who didn't seem affected was Nate as he stood. "I'll be back."

Logan snorted and kicked his feet up on the table. He scooted down in his chair, restless and on edge. He reminded me a coiled cobra, ready to strike but without a target in sight. "What's with him?"

"Parker." Mason watched his best friend weave through the crowd with lidded eyes. As Nate grabbed the girl by her arm, he led her away from her friends and further inside. The frown on Mason's face showed his disapproval.

Logan grunted. "Not to be a dick to Nate, but he's always preaching against pussy. Look at him now. She's the most regular vagina he tastes. He's getting domesticated."

I frowned.

Logan flashed me a grin. "No offense, Sam. You're family. You're not normal."

"None taken?"

Mason jerked his head in a nod and the three guys from the bottom of the stairs filed back up. Each took a seat and it was back to being me with the guys. Mason lounged back and wrapped a hand around my shoulder this time. He pulled me tight against him.

Tingles reared inside of me. I didn't think they'd ever stop. He was claiming me. He always had before, but there were new threats tonight so he was showing it again. Adrenaline rushed through me when his hand started to brush against the back of my neck. His thumb rubbed back and forth. He would apply pressure under my ear so I would tilt my head, then he would press his lips there. He continued his soft kisses, and I could barely breathe an hour later.

The need for him was pumping through my blood, strong and urgent. I squirmed under his hand and I felt him grin against my skin. He knew what he was doing.

The guys ignored us. They chatted together while someone kept bringing drinks to the patio. Mason gave me a few more shots and I'd take them, but we never broke eye contact. His had darkened so much they looked black, full of promises for the rest of the night. I wanted that now. My body was demanding it and I started to raise myself so I was in his lap when Nate joined the group again. He was alone, thankfully.

"The girl happy now? Did you satisfy her?" Logan threw an empty shot glass at him as he took the old seat on the other side of Mason. His tone was jovial, but there was a dark underlining edge to him. As he glanced at me, I knew I wasn't alone with my concern about Mason's best friend.

Nate frowned as he caught the glass. He chucked it back. "What's your problem with her?"

"Nothing." Logan caught it with a quick grab.

The rest of the guys grew quiet.

He continued, "But for the guy who doesn't like girlfriends, you seem to have one."

"Parker's not my girlfriend."

"She know that?" Logan goaded.

"It's none of your business, Logan. Stay out of it."

A few of the guys shared looks, but Mason seemed unaffected. His hand rubbed up and down my back as he scooped me into his lap. He nuzzled my neck and I closed my eyes. My bones melted into him. I couldn't leave, no way. But he didn't seem to mind. His arms wrapped around me and his hand rested low on my stomach. His thumb caressed me there, back and forth in a normally soothing motion.

Now, however, it was anything but soothing. I squirmed in his lap from the desire pulsating through me. The flames of lust had been lit before, but now they were a fire. I'd be a bonfire if he kept up his ministrations.

"*You* stay out of it," Logan retorted. "I'm getting sick of Parker's attitude. She prances around here and brings her friends over like they own the place."

"No, they don't." Irritation was evident on Nate's face. His eyes flared in anger. "Why don't you say what you're really pissed about? I doubt it's anything to do with Parker." He paused a beat. "Maybe you got a girl on your mind, one who actually was your girl. Is she what this is about? Your panties all twisted because Tate made an appearance tonight?"

Mason's lips left my shoulder and he looked up. His hand continued to rub my stomach. It shifted further down and slipped underneath my pants, but stayed there. I was burning up.

"Shut up about Tate."

Nate leaned forward. "Shut up about Parker then."

"I'm not fucking Tate."

"And I'm not fucking Parker." He paused again with a wicked grin. "Right now. I'm sitting here. Right now."

Logan rolled his eyes. "So funny, Nate. You're a riot."

"You think you're the only funny one here?"

I frowned; the burning from Mason's caresses had started to ebb. Nate and Logan were scowling at each other from across the table. The other guys were silent, their eyes darting back and forth as they listened to the argument. Everyone waited to see what Mason would do. He could speak up, end it, or he could let it keep going. For now, he had stilled underneath me. He was listening, but he wasn't tense yet. I knew he wasn't going to step in yet.

"You're saying that you can be funny with that stick up your ass?"

I sucked in my breath, so did the others.

Mason tensed beneath me now and I tensed with him.

Nate grilled him with a warning. "Back off, Logan, about this.

I'm the only one containing the girls. They haven't done shit to Sam because I won't let Parker do a thing—"

Logan's eyes flared. "What?"

One of the guys moaned, "Fuckkk mee."

Nate clamped his mouth shut when he realized what he let slip.

Mason was like stone beneath me now. He turned to me, a mask over his face, before he looked back at his best friend. "You want to explain that comment?"

Nate closed his eyes, cursing himself, but when he opened them again, they were strained. "I'm sorry, Mase. I should've said something earlier—"

"—Yeah," Mason interrupted him. "You should've, but you better explain it now." His hand kept me on his lap with an iron hold. I couldn't even squirm. His other hand formed into a fist.

Nate's eyes were on that fist as he started, "The girls haven't been too welcoming to Sam."

"Since when?"

"Since," his eyes shot to mine. He flashed an apology in them. "Since you started dating and bringing her around. They don't like her at all."

"Why not?"

"Why not?" Nate laughed softly. "You're kidding, right? You know those four. No one gets in unless they put the girl through hell and misery. You think they're going to let Sam into the group without the same conditions? It don't matter if she's with you. Probably makes it worse, you know, since Kate's the ring leader."

"Kate was nothing to me." A dark scowl had formed on Mason. It grew with each word Nate added.

"She knows that *now*. You threw her aside." He hesitated, choosing his words with caution. "She's boiling because you dropped her. They're all boiling mad because you don't give them the time of day anymore."

Mason leaned back. He kept me on his lap. "They're not my friends. They're yours. They're the guys' friends, they aren't mine."

Logan cursed.

Ethan spoke up, "The girls don't look at it like that. They think they're friends with you."

Mason narrowed his eyes. "I could give a shit about them. I'm not friends with girls anyway, much less now when I'm with Sam. The only female friend I had was Marissa."

Nate spoke up, "Yeah and look at what happened to her. She had to leave school because of those girls."

"That was because of Tate."

"And who was she friends with? The four of them. You know what they're like with new girls. You didn't think about how'd they be with Samantha?"

"She's with me." Mason scowled at him.

Logan added, "And she's family. She's my family."

Nate shrugged. "That's why no one's spoke about this to you guys. They knew how you'd react."

Logan's eyes switched to mine. They were dark and angry. I stiffened as he asked me, "Why didn't you say anything?"

"Because it's my problem, not yours."

Mason exploded now. He lifted me in the air so I was straddling him. Grabbing my chin, he peered into my eyes. "Are you kidding me?"

I gulped at the rage from him, but I tightened my resolve. "It's my problem, not yours. I'm the girl coming into their group. I'm the one who's going to have to deal with them in the locker rooms or the bathrooms. You can't protect me everywhere, Mason."

"They won't touch you. I won't allow it."

I stuck my chin out and folded my arms. "I can't earn their respect if you're the one that's demanding it. I have to demand it. I have to earn it from them." I waited a heartbeat. I was too scared to breathe. "You know I'm right."

Mason was locked in a stand-off against me. He knew I was right. I knew I was right. His intimidation could only go so far, especially with these girls. These four girls were at the top of their school. They were tough. They weren't afraid of getting dirty, and they were loyal to each other. If I didn't want to go to school with fear every day, I would have to stand on my own against them. Mason would be gone after a semester; then it'd just be me and Logan. I needed to do this now.

He sighed and leaned back. He grumbled, "This is bullshit, Sam."

Relief burst inside of me. It was overwhelming, and I almost slumped against him, but I kept myself sitting up. My thighs tightened around him and I sucked in a ragged breath. I couldn't believe it had been that easy.

But it wasn't.

He lifted his head and met the gazes of his friends, one by one. "But the girls are exiled." He turned to Nate. "Is that going to be a problem with you?"

Logan let loose a whoop, but covered it up with a cough. The wicked grin couldn't be hidden.

Nate groaned, "Fine. That's not a problem."

"You sure?" Mason asked, heated.

"I'm sure. Like I said, Parker's not an exclusive thing. Might be good if she starts to realize that sooner rather than later."

Mason looked across the table. "Is that a problem, Fischer? I know you and Jasmine hook up."

He lifted his hands in surrender. "No problem at all. I knew it'd come to this anyway." He gave him a crooked grin.

The two other guys nodded their agreement, and it was done. Just like that. Whatever Mason meant by exiled, the rest of the guys would follow through.

After another hour on the patio, I grew restless and needed a bathroom break. Mason looked up, silently asking if I needed him with me, but I shook my head. I needed to start handling the girls on my own; besides, I had spotted a few of my friends below us.

Adam was there, and I knew Becky and her boyfriend wouldn't be far. I spotted Lily and Anne from the diner as well, so I wanted to say hello.

As I weaved through the crowd, I caught sight of Heather. She looked out of place. Her eyebrows were bunched together in confusion. Two guys stepped into her but she swung to the side and evaded their drunken steps. That was when she saw me and her face cleared of all anxiety.

"There you are."

As she drew close, I frowned. "Hi. What are you doing here?"

She was shoved forward from someone, but she rounded with a growl emanating deep from her throat. They were already gone. Her shoulders dropped and she turned back. "I wanted to make sure you were okay."

I continued to frown at her.

"I didn't know if you had told Mason and Logan about the Broudou siblings?"

"Oh yeah." It all flooded back to me, but I shrugged. "A lot happened that night. I haven't even gotten around to telling Mason about those guys."

"You haven't?" Her eyes went wide.

"Yeah." I grinned, ruefully, and led the way for the bathroom. "Like I said, a lot has happened."

"Like what?" Interest sparked in her.

"I'll tell you later, much later. It's a long story." We grew closer to the bathroom. I didn't want to use mine since Mason kept the doors locked during parties so I picked one in the basement. The downstairs was less crowded, and there wasn't a line. But the door opened and Parker led her group out of the room. They were headed upstairs, we were headed behind them.

It was a stale-mate as Parker careened to a halt. The rest of her group stopped with varying stages of hostility.

I gulped.

Parker stood and sneered at me, and her best friend Kate stepped to the side. The other two went to her other side, Jasmine and Natalie...I think?

Heather bristled next to me. "What are you looking at?"

Kate, who had a wiry body and snapping hazel eyes, skimmed her up and down. She had a similar sneer to her thin lips and brushed some of her dark brown hair back. While Parker was dressed in tight blue jeans, ripped at the knees, and a tight white top, her best friend was dressed in black. Her pants were a second skin and the top molded to her body. The other two had similar outfits, all tight, all slutty. Their bra straps were visible, except for Kate. She didn't seem to be wearing a bra. All of them had athletic bodies, with tight muscles, but I knew Heather could hold her own.

Kate advised against it. "Don't get involved, Jax."

She folded her arms. "You think that's ever stopped me before."

Natalie spoke up, flicking her long black hair over her shoulder at the same time, "Tate's back. Did you know that?"

Heather froze, her eyes went wide. Something that looked close to panic started to appear, but then she shook her head. Her own hostility showed now. "You're pissing me off. So what? Tate and I stopped being friends long ago, around the time she got friendly with you, Tommy P's."

"Tommy P's." Kate rolled her eyes. She folded her arms and stepped forward. She was the leader. "You seriously still call us that? We're not princesses anymore." Then her eyes slid to mine and hardened. "We're more like bullies now."

"Oh, jeez." Heather threw her hands up as curses spilled from her lips. "It's going to be like that?"

"Yeah," Kate snapped. Her eyes were heated. "So stay out of it."

Then an elbow was linked with mine, and she tugged me close. "No. I'm sick and tired of watching you guys do the same crap to other girls." Her chin hardened and she raised it a notch. "You've never gone after me so maybe it's my turn. Maybe if you're going after my friend, you're going to have to go after me too. And you might be surprised at how many friends I have at our school, friends that you don't even know about. How's that for fighting words?"

"Your funeral." Kate was cold as she raised an eyebrow, but then she stepped back. She commented under her breath as her friends circled around us, "Duly noted, Jax." Her eyes snapped to mine. "And thanks for the exile, bitch. You just made it worse."

Heather sucked in her breath as the four filed in a single line and went up the stairs. Once they were out of earshot, she whirled to me. "They were exiled?"

I nodded. That couldn't be good, I knew that much.

"Do you know what that means?"

I shook my head.

"They're out, Sam." Her hands gripped both of my arms and squeezed tight. "They're fully on the outs with the guys."

"What does that mean?"

"That means that they're not included with anything anymore. The guys are closing ranks and those girls," she jerked a thumb over her shoulder, "were the only girls they included in their group, but now they're on the outs. That means no talking to them, no sleeping with them, not even hanging out. The guys won't acknowledge them in the hallways or anywhere. Being exiled means that they're strangers to the guys. Oh. My. God. Mason did that?"

I gulped. That seemed harsh, excessively harsh. *But that's who Mason is...*

Heather started to jump up and down.

I'd never seen her so excited.

"You have no idea what this means, do you?"

I shook my head. "This was my life about five months ago."

"Yeah, but not for those four. This is awesome, Sam. Get excited. Your boy delivered a huge blow to them, and it's going to sting for a *long* time." A smile stretched from ear to ear over her face. "And you have no idea how many other girls hate those four in school.

Those four just got a lot of enemies that can finally push back. You have no idea!"

"You said that you have friends at school?"

Heather stopped bouncing. Her smile fell flat. "Yeah, I lied about that. I've got a few, but most of my friends go to Roussou."

"What's wrong?"

She glanced over her shoulder and bit her lip. "I'm still getting comfortable with this crowd. I'm used to being considered the enemy."

"You came here for me?"

She gave me a fleeting smile. "Yep, so you're stuck with me now. Let's go."

I gestured to the bathroom. "I really do need to go."

"Okay." But she kept looking around.

"What are you doing, Heather?"

"Looking for new friends." Her eyes snapped with a warning. "We're going to need them if we're going against the Tommy P's."

"I thought you said there were a lot of girls who could push back now?"

"Doesn't mean they're going to help us." She gestured towards the pool table. "I'm going to be over there. I know a few of those girls from the short time I was on the tennis team. Kate hates tennis, if I'm remembering right, and I know a few of those girls hated her back." She shooed me away. "Hurry up with the bathroom. There are a lot of people you need to meet."

She sauntered towards a group that looked perfect with smooth golden hair, tanned bodies, and faces that could've been in magazines. Each of them seemed cautious as Heather approached them, but it wasn't long until the group had circled her; listening intently.

Heather would have no problem making friends. I remembered Mason's words when he said Heather Jax wasn't a normal girl. I was glad she had befriended me. My gut was telling me I'd need all the friends I could get, and making friends was not a skill I had.

I turned around, and found myself face to face with someone else. I scowled. "What are you doing here?"

Jeff rolled his shoulders back and stuck his fingers in his hair. The ends were sticking up, but he spiked it higher. He flashed me a grin. "What do you think? Too high?"

I crossed my arms over my chest. "Jeff."

"Alright, alright." He stuck his hands in his pockets and his shoulders hunched together. He looked even smaller, and he was skinny enough. "So what's up with you and Jax?"

My eyes narrowed. "You know Heather?"

"Been to her place a few times."

There it was again, his same vague answers that I heard for three years. "Jeff," I warned. I didn't have time for his games. I needed to be making friends. No, I had to pee first.

"Okay, okay." He chuckled, "I come to you as a friend."

"You aren't anything else."

He frowned. "I know. You don't have to sound so happy about that."

"You cheated on me. For two years."

He lifted a shoulder in an easygoing shrug. "Bygones. I thought we made peace."

"I thought so too."

He studied me for a moment and then smirked, laughing some more. "Okay. I got it. No games, but seriously, how do you know Jax?"

"I work at Manny's." I frowned. "I thought you knew that."

"I didn't. Things make sense now."

I was growing tired of the conversation, but I knew something was wrong. He was stalling. "Are you going to tell me what you want or not? I just got served papers from the Tommy Princesses. Heather and I have to scramble so I don't get my ass handed to me at school."

"You?" His grin turned into a leer and he looked me up and down. "You can take 'em."

"There are four of them."

He shrugged again. "You could still take 'em. I heard about your rumble with Tate at that cabin party. You're tougher than you look. I think its cause you've got runners' legs. Might look stringy, but damn there are muscles there. If anything, you could just run in circles or run away. They won't catch you."

"Not helping," I growled before I started to move past him. He had wasted enough of my time.

"Okay, hey, hey. Stop. Please." He backtracked in front of me with his hands held in the air. I started another way, but he blocked me. "Please, Sam. I'm embarrassed about this and I don't know who else to talk to. You and me are different."

"I know. There is no 'you and me.'"

He scratched at his head. "No, I mean you're different than all the other girls. I know you and me weren't a good thing—"

My eyebrow arched.

He amended, "—and by that I mean to say that I wasn't good in a relationship. I'm still not good in a relationship."

"Wait." Wariness came over me now. "Are you still dating Jessica?"

His hand fell to his side with a thump. "Are you kidding? She's dating some wrestler from community college."

And from how he looked away, I knew there was more to it. I guessed, "And she's cheating on him with you?"

He looked down at the floor.

"Do you not learn, Jeff? My god." I wanted to wring his neck, but I needed to make myself clear. "Whatever you're going to ask of me, there will be no Jessica or Lydia attached at your hip. I mean it. You go back and forth with Jessica. I have no idea why, but I won't have her in my life again. I am done with both of them."

"I'm done with them too. I mean it. And that isn't what this is about. I promise."

I heard the insistency in his tone. I wanted to walk away from him, the guy deserved it after what he had done to me, but my feet didn't move. Then I realized what I heard, there was also desperation in him. And something that sounded close to…agony? When I looked again, I was seeing a different Jeff. He'd been a sarcastic badboy, but there was something new now. Vulnerability.

"What do you want?" I folded, but I was cursing at myself in my head.

A grin flared before he nodded, somber again. "Okay. So, we both know our history. I cheat on every girl I date. But I've met someone new."

I already knew where he was going with this. "And you don't want to do that to her?"

He nodded.

"You don't want to cheat on her?"

He nodded again, more eager.

"And you want to be the good guy she thinks you are?"

"Yeah! See you're perfect for this. It's like you know me."

I smacked him in the back of his head. "Because I do and you're not that guy. You cheat, that's what you do. Stop cheating and your problem is solved. Stop wasting my time. I have a mission."

"What mission?"

"I need friends. I have to make friends."

"I'm your friend."

"No, you're not. You're my ex boyfriend. We're not friends."

I started to leave again, but he darted in front. "Hear me out, please."

I growled at him.

"I will help you with your mission."

"You will?" Suspicion slammed against my chest. "How?"

"I know a lot of these girls. I cheated on you, a lot."

I growled at him again.

"You help me learn how to be a good boyfriend and I'll rally some girls to look out for you at your new school."

The suspicion lessened a little. "You heard about that, huh?"

"Everybody did. It's big news when Kade's girl won't be going to our school anymore. The Elite are crestfallen. They can't use you to get to them."

I frowned. "I thought they gave up on that long ago."

He shrugged. "I heard they were regrouping. Miranda's the leader again. She's preaching against any girl who sleeps with Logan Kade again."

I shook my head. "Will she never learn?"

"Who cares. Their funerals if they want to mess with the Kades again. Being burned by being a hypocritical bitch didn't teach her a lesson. Who's to stop her from getting burned again?" He winked at me with a devilish smirk.

"I didn't know you weren't such a fan of Miranda Stewart's?"

He glanced away as his shoulders tensed. "A lot's been going on you don't know about."

"Like what?"

"Look, will you help me learn how to not cheat? I'll get those girls to help you, promise. I'm good for that. I mean it."

"There will be no 'us' anymore. We're clear on that?"

Horror flared in his eyes before he shook his head, grimacing. "You think I want to get killed? No way in hell do I want to mess with either of those Kades." Then his face transformed. The same devilish look came back and he turned into the smooth Casanova I knew he could become. "I wouldn't mind meeting Logan Kade, though. I like to think of myself as an apprentice of his. We're cut from the same cloth."

"The same cloth?"

"Yeah." At my disbelief, he nodded again. "With the ladies. They love us."

"Logan had a serious girlfriend one time."

"He did?"

"You want to know how he handled that and his 'ladies'?"

He leaned forward. "I'm eager to learn. Yeah, how'd he handle having a relationship?"

"He didn't cheat on her." I grabbed his shirt and yanked him out of the way. Then I smacked him on the back of his head again. "Problem solved. Now go away."

As I pushed through the crowd, he called after me, "That doesn't help me, but fine. I'll hold up my side of the bargain, Sam. You'll see and then you'll help me! I know you will."

"Idiot," I mumbled under my breath.

CHAPTER TWENTY-SEVEN

"You did this!" she screamed at me. Her hands were raised, and she didn't look right. I gulped for breath. I couldn't breathe. My chest hurt, why did it hurt so much? But I couldn't tear my eyes away from her.

I whimpered, "Mom?"

She shook her head from side to side. She kept going, faster and faster, until she slid down the wall stopping in a huddle on the floor. She curled into a ball and rocked herself as her head kept shaking.

Oh god. I fell to my knees beside her. "Mom?" This wasn't right. I knew this wasn't right, but I didn't know what to do. "Please say something, mom."

Her hand twitched on her leg. Her head whipped up, and she hissed before she launched herself at me.

I jerked awake. My heart was pounding.

It was hot, too hot. I kicked at the covers so I could feel some cool air, and then I took deep breaths. I needed to calm down. My heart kept racing. It wouldn't stop. Easing to the edge of the bed, I pressed my forehead between my legs and gulped for more oxygen. My hands were clammy. My forehead was wet from sweat, the same sweat that I felt over the rest of my body.

Mason moaned next to me and I held still. I didn't want to wake him up. Slowly, inch by inch, I eased out of the bed but tripped as I reached for a robe on the couch. Catching myself before I fell all the way to the floor, I gritted my teeth and waited until my legs felt sturdier. I put on one of his sweatshirts and his sweatpants. Safe. I took another breath and felt my pulse slowing down. I felt better.

But I shook my head. I couldn't get her out of there. Flashes of my mother kept coming at me and I wanted to stop remembering that night. Even thinking about it made my heart start pounding again. I pressed a finger against my neck and felt my vein pulsating.

I was in a nightmare. She was always there now. Every time I closed my eyes, that night was there and I remembered the attack. I clenched my teeth together and clasped my eyes shut. I couldn't—I wouldn't. Not again.

Mason rolled over in bed. His hand started to reach for me, but he tucked it under his pillow. The sheet slipped down to his waist. His shoulders bulged as both of his arms were curled under his pillow. The movement set his shoulder blades out and his back tapered down to where the sheet had fallen, over his narrow waist.

I'd never get enough of him. I knew that, then and there, and a pang of guilt speared me.

He wasn't living with his dad because of me. I had come between them, and Mason would be gone after a semester. My stomach shook at that reminder so I focused on the year after. It'd be me and Logan, all alone.

It wasn't a viable option for Logan and me to live at Nate's for the next year. Mason wouldn't want that. I wouldn't even want that, so what then? And Helen? I knew she wouldn't accept this situation. I would bet money that she already had some plan concocted. She would want Logan to move back with her in L.A. or she would come here and he would live in her house.

Not me. I was alone. Every scenario ended with me being alone.

No mother. No father, neither of them. Something wet fell on my cheek and I brushed it away. I was so stupid. Why was I crying? But I was. I huddled back in the chair and lifted my legs. Pressing them against my chest, I wrapped my arms around them and drew in a shuddering breath.

I had to make the situation better.

I had to fix things.

My stomach dropped. I knew what I had to do.

I grabbed my phone and texted her. Then I waited with my heart pounding, but it wasn't long. I got the response within a minute and it was settled.

With lead in my gut, I got up and slipped on some shoes, and then I turned and headed out the door.

When I stepped into the Kade foyer, everything was dark and my heart skipped a beat. Maybe she wasn't there? A part of me didn't want her to be there, but I heard her move and my heart skipped over another beat.

There she was. She was in a chair at the table. The moonlight filtered in through the large windows behind her.

She spoke first, as if nothing happened. "Hello, Samantha."

I scowled, but hid it in the next breath. "Hello."

"No mother? No Analise? What have we come to?"

I readied myself. "So bright and cheery, it's like you've never done a thing to hurt me or my family."

She sucked in her breath. "It was my family too."

"No, mom. Your family is yourself, maybe James since he hasn't left you. But I doubt that'll last. You'll do something to push him away. You'll cheat on him, kill his baby, attack him even."

"You watch your words." Her tone was stone cold. "Right now."

"Fine."

"Fine."

A moment of silence passed between us, but there was so much I wanted to say.

"So you called me for this meeting," she prompted me.

My heart went flat. I couldn't say what I wanted to say, not to her. She wouldn't listen. She would defend. She would attack. She'd never listen so I sighed in surrender. "I want you to agree that you'll stay away from me."

"If?"

"What?"

She leaned forward. Her eyes sparkled in the moonlight, and I saw the rage in there again. It was contained now, for the moment. I wondered when it would come out again. Then she sighed from irritation. "You came to me. You want me to stay away from you. I'm guessing there's something that'll come after that. You want me to stay away from you if…if what? If you come back? If you move in with David? What's the if? What do you want, darling child of mine?"

"For one, never refer to me as that again. It'll be like we're not related. Do you understand?"

"Crystal."

I winced. A knife slipped inside of me with that one word, with the chilling tone of her voice. I tried to ignore the pain. I was the one who needed to act like we weren't family. I needed to forget her, forget that she had ever been my mother.

"Is that it?"

I could hear the rolling of her eyes. I gritted my teeth against it. "I think James is a good man."

"He is."

Her dark silhouette straightened in the chair. There was pride in her voice now.

I added, "Mason and Logan will not move back in with their father unless I come too. You know that and James knows that. And you know that James wants them here."

She murmured, softly, "He loves them very much."

My teeth gritted together. She didn't get to act like she cared. "Stop. Just stop. They're not your boys. They're not your family. You are lucky to have their father love you, but they will never accept you." I drew in a shuddering breath. "They'll tolerate you, if I ask them to. Or they'll make your life hell, and after Mason heard his mom, he wants to. He's waiting for the chance to make you pay. I know the only reason he hasn't is because he's been worried about me." I leaned forward and placed my elbows on the table. It was cold against my skin. Goosebumps slithered up and down my arms. "So I have a proposition for you."

I waited as she sat there. I waited for her reaction.

"What?" She lifted her shoulders, her tone snippy.

Anger exploded in me. I wanted to reach across the table and grab her. I wanted to slam her head down, and I wanted to keep doing it until she cared. But she never would. So I sat there, and I counted to ten for patience.

When I felt something resembling it, I waited another ten, and then started, "I will move back in if you agree that there is no relationship between us. We will live in the same home, but that's it. I'm no longer your daughter. You're no longer my mother. You have no say with me, whatsoever." I tried to ignore the pounding in my chest. "When I spend time with David, you will say nothing. You will do nothing."

Her mouth tightened.

I didn't care. "When and if I go to Boston to see Garrett, you will say nothing. You will do nothing. It's as if I'm not even your child. I will only be your future stepson's girlfriend, who lives here. That's it. And you won't say a word about this to James. If you do," a layer of tears rested over my eyes. They were ready to fall, but I kept going in a hoarse whisper, "if you say a word, I will allow Mason and Logan free reign on you. They can do anything to you that they want."

As she paled, a sick darkness started in me. It grew as I continued, "They won't just hurt you. They'll take him away from you."

Her eyes closed. Her arms started to tremble so she wrapped the ends of her nightgown around her. She seemed so tiny in that moment.

Again, I didn't care. I murmured, "You know what I'm saying is true. You have manipulated everyone in your life, and you have hurt everyone in your life. There's a trail of damage behind you, to me, to David, to Garrett, to whoever impregnated you." A wall of ice was forming around my heart. "You are manipulating James. You should leave him because you're hurting him."

"I'm not," she whispered.

"He lost his sons over you. Because of you, he threw them out."

Her hand jerked up and she flicked a tear away. "I didn't mean for him to lose them. I didn't, Sam. I just wanted respect—"

"You wanted control," I hissed as my hands curled around the edge of the table. I clung to it, holding myself back. I had to keep it together until I could leave. Then I would collapse, but until then, I fought for my own control. "You wanted Mason away from me because someone else would love me."

"No," she whimpered. Her head fell down.

I nodded, to myself. A deep sob hitched in my voice, "Someone else would be there for me, and I would leave you. That's what all of this was about. Wasn't it?"

I waited. She didn't answer.

"Wasn't it?" My voice rose.

She shook her head, but she whispered, "It all went so fast. I couldn't control it. It spiraled out, and I couldn't stop it." More tears fell, and she sobbed. "I couldn't handle it. What they did to me, what I saw them doing to you. They were taking you away from me. They were making me look like the bad guy, and then David and Garrett were there. They both wanted you in their lives, I couldn't handle it. I can't lose my only daughter—"

I almost stood, but clamped down on the chair. I willed myself to remain there. I needed to hear her submission.

She kept going, broken before me. "You're mine, Samantha!" Her eyes snapped open.

I saw her madness in them, but it didn't scare me anymore.

She spat out, "No one can take you away from me. No one can touch you—"

"I'm already gone."

She stopped as she gasped for breath.

"I'm gone. I don't care about you. You've killed every last inch of love I might've had for you. You tried to make things right before, but you couldn't even do that. You called Garrett and told him about me. You were trying to be a good mother to me. But you couldn't handle it, could you?"

"You're my baby. No one can have you." Her lip wobbled as more tears streamed down. "It was wrong to call Garrett. He shouldn't have ever known about you. And David…" She sighed and looked away. "He only stayed with me because of you. He left me once, did you know that?"

I nodded.

"Dad?" I pushed open their bedroom door.

The memory jarred me, but she didn't notice. Her eyes were downcast again. Her voice sounded distant to me. "What I did to you was wrong. What I did to your brother and sister was wrong, but I couldn't lose him. He knew that I had cheated. I couldn't keep the evidence."

My eyes went wide. That's what they were to her? Evidence?

"But I couldn't think about them—they weren't like how you were to me. I knew I was pregnant so I brought it up to David. We'd been together a lot more around that time, and we were always unprotected. He thought I was on birth control, but I stopped. I wasn't thinking right." Her voice lowered to a raspy sound. "I never knew he couldn't have kids. He never told me until that night. He said that I told him in the beginning I would never want any more children, that one was enough, so he never thought about it."

It was my worst nightmare come true.

"We fought that night. Later, I walked in on him packing a suitcase. I went crazy. I started throwing things. I threw his clothes everywhere. He couldn't go. He couldn't leave me." Her shoulders started to shake. She buried her head in her hands and more sobs came out. "I couldn't lose him, but he left anyway. He said that he hadn't signed up for that. I didn't know where he went. I kept calling and calling, but he never picked up. Then I found his phone, he had left his phone on the counter in the kitchen. I had nowhere to call, no one to help me. I thought it was the only thing I could do. No one wanted me. I couldn't lose David; I was still in love with him then."

I was frozen in my chair. I couldn't look away, but I couldn't keep hearing this. I didn't want to know, even though I already did know. It was the worst night of my life, unfolding before me again. I couldn't stop it. A part of me didn't want to; I needed to know everything so it made sense. Some of it had to make sense. Some of it had to be for some reason.

As she dissolved into tears, I ripped out, "And when you came back? What then?"

She sucked in her breath and lifted horrified eyes to me. They were bleak and empty. Her makeup was smudged around her. They formed black rings around her eyes and she shook her head. Her lip trembled again, but then she bit down on it. She sucked in her breath. Her chest tightened. Her shoulders lifted, and she kept shaking her head.

I closed my eyes.

She started again in a deep voice, "I didn't know what I was doing." No. That wasn't right. I shook my head, ready to tell her that when she added, "I was wrong that night. I killed my children inside of me and you were taking care of me. I was grieving, Sam, and I was keeping it a secret. I knew what they thought. They wanted me to go to counseling, but it wasn't my life that I wanted to end. It was theirs, but then you were there and they weren't. They said if I killed you, they'd come back."

I gulped and doubled over. Scorching pain ripped through me. It was as if she threw a pot of boiling water on me, drenching me. I couldn't breathe.

Her voice sounded strangled. "I went mad, Samantha. I knew it was wrong, but I kept hurting you. I forced myself to stop. I had to. I knew they wouldn't come back, and they told me that they'd leave me again if I didn't stop hitting you."

Oh god. She *heard* them? "You talked to them?"

Her face was closed off to me. She seemed void from all emotion. "I know they weren't real. I know I was imagining them standing there. But they comforted me. They still loved me, even though I killed them. That couldn't be imaginary, could it?"

"And that's why you stopped?"

She lifted a shoulder in a shrug. It was so easy for her. Hurting her child was something to shrug about. I couldn't believe her. Who was this woman? Then I asked, gutted, "Did you ever love me?"

She frowned. "Of course, honey."

"But—what?"

Then she looked away as her eyes grew vacant. The distant expression came over her and her voice softened. "I did two horrible things to both of my babies. I hurt them and I hurt you, but I learned from both mistakes. I will never have children again. James is my life now. I am dedicated to becoming a good wife to him, the best wife I could possibly be, and I know he misses his boys. I know I'm the reason they're not with him. It's why I responded to your text message. I knew you wanted a compromise."

She was insane. I had no other thoughts. This was my mother? This was a stranger.

She nodded, satisfied now. "I'll do as you say. You can move back in. I'll stay away. I will only focus on James and being his wife. I will stay away from you, and from Mason and Logan. You're right. They should be with their father. James feels the same. He wants his boys back. He knows he can't stop your relationship with Mason. You can all live here. That's fine with us."

Madness. That was all I could think as I gaped at this woman, but then I cleared my head. I still needed answers. "I remember being questioned by social services, but I was never taken from you." I never remembered being in the hospital. "Why not?"

Another shrug. Again. "You told them that some girls from school came to the house, and that I found you like that. I supported your story and David never knew. He suspected. I knew that, but I never hurt you again. I put it all behind me and we were fine for years after that."

"Until you started cheating on him. Again."

She nodded, but didn't respond. It wasn't worth commenting about.

I couldn't believe it. I couldn't believe her. "What about Garrett? What did you threaten him with?"

"Oh." A smile this time. For some reason, he got a smile while I seemed an after-thought to her. "I didn't say much, but I told him I would make you hate him. He didn't believe me, so I went and visited his ex-wife. I told her Garrett still loved her and he loved her when he was with me. I told her all about Helen and made her sound so evil that she'd never allow him to go back to her; therefore he wouldn't be allowed to see you. It worked." She grinned to herself and chuckled even. "I didn't think it would work, but I guess it did. He hasn't even called for you, Samantha."

A shiver ran down my spine as she said my name.

Before I could launch myself at her and do to her what she had done to me, I shoved back the chair. I couldn't feel my legs. I couldn't feel anything. I blinked and then turned away. I didn't remember leaving the house, but I stopped in the driveway. I had driven my car. James was standing beside it in his pajamas and a robe. He was frowning at my car with the morning paper in his hand. When he looked up, his frown deepened. The sun had started to rise, I wasn't sure the time, but I knew it was early.

"Mason and Logan will never move back without me." My own voice jarred me. It sounded haunted. "And Helen would make Logan leave, you know that."

His frown only deepened further.

"I fixed it. I'll move back in here with them."

His eyes grew bleak.

I kept going as my chest tightened, "I won't let them hurt her either."

He rasped out, "They won't do it."

"I'll make them do it."

Then he nodded and looked away. "I'm sorry, Samantha, I'm sorry for everything you've gone through."

I frowned. Why was he saying this to me?

"I love your mother very much and I want to help her. I can't help my family anymore, and I can't help my marriage anymore. It was my fault that Helen left me. It was my fault my family was torn apart. I won't let that happen again. I can help your mother. I really can, and I'm going to. I love her and I'm going to stay with her, no matter what."

He had no idea what he was getting himself into, but I kept my mouth shut. It was his life. It was his decision.

She'd make him miserable.

I didn't get in my car. I ran home instead.

CHAPTER TWENTY-EIGHT

"Your shift's over." Heather smacked a towel on my butt. When I turned around to glare, she gave me a crooked grin and wiggled her eyebrows. "Your dreamboat's here anyway."

Oh.

The fight in me subsided. I was ready to argue with her since it wasn't closing and I hadn't worked Friday, but when I looked over, all of that turned into a gushy mess. Mason had stepped through the door with a look of intent on his face. That made me pause. As he made his way through the tables to our back corner, I couldn't tear my eyes away. Confidence and power rippled from him. I couldn't fault the other girls who stopped and watched him as well. He was beautiful.

"Disgusting." Heather shook her head. "You're both disgusting."

"He's early. Did you call him?"

"I might've." She winked at me before she grabbed the next plate of food and put on the window, ready to be served. "But can you really blame me? It's your first day at FCP tomorrow. You're going to need all the rest you can muster when you're with that hunk-o-rama over there."

"Thanks, Heather."

She flashed me a blinding smile. "Just give me a heads up when you decide to tell them about our visitors the other night." She gave me a pointed look and I knew she was referencing the Broudou siblings.

She wanted me tell Mason now, better to get it over than deal with his anger about why he hadn't been told sooner. I had a different idea and I wanted to embark on one battle at a time. Convincing Mason and Logan to move back in with their father had been a big enough battle. It took me all weekend, and I still didn't have an answer. But as he stepped closer and caught my hand, he gave me a look as if to say, 'I hope you know what you're doing.' He shook his head. "Fine. We'll move back in."

"Really?" I started to launch myself at him.

He caught my arms and held me back. "But it's only because you're right about Logan."

I chuckled. I had called it. Helen called both of them the next day. She said they had two choices, live in Los Angeles with her or she would move back to Fallen Crest. Those were her two options and when I argued with Mason that Logan living with her our senior year would leave me without a home, he started to soften. I knew he was doing it for me.

"Thank you," I murmured as I tipped my head back for his lips.

He groaned, "You're going to be the death of me. I'm doing all this nice shit for you."

I pointed to my lips, still puckered and waiting.

With a soft chuckle, he touched his to mine and I was swept up. Squealing from surprise, he wrapped his arms around my waist and lifted me high. My legs swung up and I was thrown over his shoulder.

"Mason!"

He slapped my butt. "Logan's ordered the pizza. If we're not back in twenty minutes, he won't hear the end of it. He's got it timed within the minute."

Only Logan would time something like that. I wiggled to get free. "Come on. Let me go."

"Nope." He turned around. "Can you clock her out, Jax?"

We heard from the back, "Will do! Don't make babies."

Mason shuddered underneath me. I remembered the look on his face when I told him I was late for work and giggled. He slapped my butt again. "That wasn't funny. I aged an entire year that day."

Serves him right after this. "Come on, let me go. Please."

"Nope." And he didn't, not when he marched to his car and put me inside. He even strapped my seat belt on and off when we turned into the driveway to Nate's home. When he stopped the car and rounded to my side, I jumped out before he could grab me. I started to run for the door, but it didn't matter. Mason had me in two steps, and I was slung back over his shoulder.

"Mason! This is enough."

"Logan said to carry you home so I have to carry you home. He's very excited for something."

"For pizza?"

Mason shrugged underneath me. His arm tightened around my legs as he walked over the front patio. "I have no idea. You know him. The stupidest ideas are adventures to him."

"But—"

But then he shoved the door open and swung around. A chorus burst out, "SURPRISE!" And my mouth fell open as I lifted my head to gape at the crowd in the center area.

Logan was in front with his arms outstretched. "Happy birthday, Sam!"

Becky waved from behind him. "It's a week early, isn't it?"

"Oh my god!" I pounded Mason on the back. He chuckled as he flipped me back in his arms, and then lowered me to the ground. All the blood had rushed to my head so he kept me against his chest. His hands held me by my hips, but I could only look at the group they assembled.

Becky and Raz, who had a glazed look in his eyes.

Adam. He grinned and gave me a small wave. "Can you believe they even invited me?"

I grinned but looked around some more. I relaxed as I saw most of the Academy Elite hadn't been invited, but Mark had been. I tensed a bit, just a bit, at the reminder that he thought his mom was going to marry David sooner rather than later. But then I tensed even more. They could've gotten married by now. David and my mom had been divorced, for…I wasn't sure. I hadn't asked either of them about the divorce. I didn't want to know.

Mark nodded his head towards me. "Hiya, Sam. I asked to tag along. I hope that's okay with you."

"Sure…" It wasn't like we were family…or were we? Was David still family to me? I wasn't sure anymore.

Then Lily gave me an excited wave with a smile that stretched from ear to ear. "Surprise! I bet you thought you didn't have to deal with me, but nope. Here I am. It's my night off and I'm ready for some birthday cake."

"You're welcome to my piece." Then I leaned back and asked, "Did Logan get cake?"

Mason's hand tightened around my hips. His thumbs started to rub up and down. "Of course. A birthday party without cake is a crime to Logan."

"Oh."

He grinned down at me. "You don't like cake?"

I shrugged. "It's an acquired taste."

He chuckled, shaking his head. "Pretend to eat a piece for him. I think he made it from scratch."

"I'll eat two pieces."

"Happy birthday, Sam," Nate called out as he started over.

"Hell no! I get her first." Logan shot forward and plucked me from his brother. He threw me over his shoulder and turned back to the group. "Everyone gets to spank her except Mason. He does that all the time."

He bounded to the kitchen and I looked up in time to see Nate and Mason share a grin, both shaking their heads. As Nate lifted a hand to put on Mason's shoulder, Logan turned the corner. I couldn't see anymore, but he deposited me in a stool at the counter. A large white cake sat in front of me with eighteen candles on top. None of them had been lit, but then I peered closer.

"Logan!"

"What?" He'd been waiting for my reaction, brimming with excitement. "Don't you like it?"

Those candles didn't look right. "Tell me those are not joints." Please tell me they aren't.

He started laughing. As he continued, the laughing got louder and louder. Then Becky's boyfriend bounced to the cake and pulled them out. He wiped each clean and put them back in a baggie as he gave me a sheepish look. "He thought it'd be funny." He looked like he had more to say, but then he smiled and snuck back to Becky's side.

"I'm sorry," she murmured.

Logan was still laughing. "That would've been awesome."

"Too bad you haven't gotten tested for basketball season yet," Nate noted as he and Mason rounded to the other side of the counter.

A wistful sigh left Logan. "Tell me about it."

Nate flashed him a grin and for a moment, I didn't see the tension between the two anymore. What had changed? When I caught Mason's gaze, I made a mental note to ask him, but was distracted as he gave me a heated look, dark promises in his depths.

My eyes widened. A jolt of desire burst through me, and I clenched my legs together. It was my birthday party. A private party would have to wait a few hours. I licked my lips as I thought about it.

He smirked back at me, our gazes locked together.

Then Nate spoke up, "This is also a farewell party too, a small one. Since you three are moving back home."

Logan's smirk turned smug.

And I knew why the tension had been lifted between the two. Mason was now home, with Logan and me. Nate couldn't move in with us. Though, I bet he would've.

"Thanks for letting me stay here."

"Any time, Sam. I mean it."

His words sounded genuine so my smile turned genuine as well. Maybe the old fearsome foursome would come back with the move. I had missed it.

Lily moved next to me as Logan started to cut the cake. She gave me a small hug. "Heather and the rest of the staff are coming after closing."

"That's late. Are you sure they want to do that?"

She shrugged with a delighted spark. "I think Heather said they were going to close early. She said you're worth it."

I was taken aback. That was a lot of money since the diner was full every night now. The gesture spoke volumes to me and for a moment, I couldn't speak.

Then she started giggling beside me.

"What?"

She pointed at the cake. Logan hadn't cut the cake in small sections. He cut it into the exact amount of pieces needed. There were nine people there, so the cake was cut into nine large pieces. Six of the pieces were double in size and he delivered those to the guys. The last three were smaller, but still bigger than I wanted.

Lily groaned as she took hers. "I gained five pounds just looking at that thing."

"You gotta eat it!" Logan barked before he raised his hands again. "Okay, everyone! I have an important announcement to make." He grinned to himself. "Today is not Samantha's birthday." He pretended to wave off any boos. "I know, I know. This is a shock of a lifetime to you, but we'll get over it. We'll band together and we'll make do. Raz, where are the joints?"

"Logan!"

His grin doubled and two dimples appeared. "Okay, okay. In all seriousness, we did this a week early to shock Sam's panties off her. Which my big brother will be doing tonight." He lifted an eyebrow to Mason.

"Logan."

He continued, "But anyway, I'm doing the speech because I baked the cake, with all sorts of natural goodies." He pretended to scowl. "I wasn't allowed any of the fun stuff, but whatever. We'll get over it. Peace and prosperity, right Raz?"

"Right." A fist was thrust in the air.

Logan laughed to himself, but then a somber expression came over him. The jokes were done and he lifted his piece of cake to me. "Happy birthday, Samantha. I love you. You're going to be my stepsister and maybe my sister-in-law someday, but until those days come, you already know you're family. And I think I can speak for everyone in saying, you're going to get wasted tonight!"

He lifted his cake in the air. "Salute to Sam getting wasted!"

Everyone saluted. Then they tried their best to sing the birthday song to me, which was interspersed with Logan and Mark rapping "In Da Club" in the background.

I shook my head. My throat was thick with emotion and I turned away. I wouldn't start crying, not again.

Two arms came around me, both slender and soft. Becky was on my right and Lily on my left. They gave me a hug, squeezing me with soft smiles. "Happy birthday, Sam."

"Thanks, guys." I patted both of them on their hands and looked down. I really felt the tears now.

The doorbell rang at that moment.

Logan went to answer and came back with five boxes of pizza. They were put on the table and the lids were flipped open. Steam rose from each of them. Paper plates, napkins, and plastic silverware were already on the table and he gestured to the table. "Dig in, guys."

Nate called out, "We've got beer, some soda…I think, and other drinks in the bar outside."

The guys went first. After they trailed outside to grab a drink, the three girls followed with our own plates full of food. Everyone had taken a seat around the tables as Nate turned into the bartender. He made sure everyone had a beverage. Logan hopped around to make sure none of them ran empty.

It was easy.

I hadn't expected it to be easy, but stories were shared. The guys joked and no one was ready to bite someone's head off. The guys congregated around the bar with easygoing grins. Even when Becky sat beside me, I was glad that she was there. She'd been a good friend at a time when I needed her. I hoped she would still be a friend, maybe not the one I thought she had been, but one nonetheless. Lily surprised me the most. She had a crude sense of humor with one-liners delivered at the perfect time. The rest of the Manny's staff joined us two hours later. Anne settled next to Lily and cackled together as Heather shook her head with a small grin on her face.

When Mason folded me into bed later, I grinned up at him and whispered how much the party meant to me.

He slid in beside me and pulled me close to him. He tucked his head behind me and took a deep breath. His hand flattened under my breast and he held me there, tight to him. Then he whispered back to me, his lips a soft caress against my neck, "We just love you. All of us."

"Everything will be fine," I murmured, sleepily. "You. Me. Logan. Even Nate. All of us. And Heather."

His body trembled behind me and his arms pulled me even closer to him. "Everything will be fine."

"You promise?" I smiled as I felt him kiss my neck.

"I promise."

"Even the families?"

"Even the families." His arms bulged around me and he rocked me back and forth. "Go to sleep, Samantha. We have school tomorrow."

"I love you, Mason."

He pressed another kiss to my neck, then to my shoulder blade. "I love you too. Now go to sleep."

"..o..kay…" And I did.

9 781951 771010